Enthusiastic reviews for Lior Samson's novels –

The Rosen Singularity

"The plotting is ingenious and the characters come through strongly. "   — *Rebecca Goldstein, MacArthur Fellow, author*

"Vibrant and distinctive characters,... an exciting, pulse-pounding story."   — *Laurie Jenkins, book blogger*

The Millicent Factor

"A solid page turner. The author keeps the pace just right with action and chases ... and backroom dealings. "   — *RJ Beam, author*

Bashert (The Homeland Connection)

"Samson writes with a crisp elegance, like John Le Carré, and weaves his plot magically,"   — *James A. Anderson, author*

"[M]oving with the speed of light between interconnected events, three continents, and a group of unique and memorable characters."   - *Avraham Azrieli, author*

The Dome (The Homeland Connection)

"Suspenseful and timely, ... I cannot say enough good things about this novel."   — *Alan Caruba, critic, BookViews*

"An excellent read, and very highly recommended."   — *Midwest Book Review*

Web Games (The Homeland Connection)

"An outstanding tech thriller—better than Tom Clancy....one of the best [thrillers] I've read in 2011."   — *James A. Anderson, author*

"This extraordinary author has the ability to anticipate events. ... You will not put it down."   — *Alan Caruba, critic, BookViews*

Chipset (The Homeland Connection)

"[A] multi-dimensional thriller ... populated by flesh-and-blood characters."
— *Avraham Azrieli, author*

"Lior Samson hits another one out of the park. ... Few thriller writers can match Samson's ability to deliver a gripping story."
— *James A. Anderson, author*

Gasline (The Homeland Connection)

"Samson turns up the heat with a high-energy plot and ... a perfect mix of techno thrill and human conflict. ... a rip-roaring ride. Excellent!"
— *Avraham Azrieli, author*

"[A] great novel ... high concept, flesh-and-blood protagonist, and realistic action. ... [It] will raise your blood pressure and make you think."
— *Columbia Review of Books and Film*

Flight Track (The Homeland Connection)

"Well plotted ... compelling and entertaining. ... The characters are developed with dialog that provides insight ... kept me turning pages."
— *Harrison Jones, airline pilot, author*

"Stunning, compelling, thought-provoking. To the book's broad scope and expert pacing, add three-dimensional, engaging characters."
— *M. Thornburg*

The Four-Color Puzzle

"[A]n authentic thinking person's ideal mystery; an eloquent feast of words and an excellent story. ... [M]ay be the best [book] I have read this year."
— *Jeanie B. Clemmons, author*

"[A] fast-paced crime story that had me rooting for the hero while also feeling conflicted by his choices. The story challenges the reader."
— *Patricia O'Sullivan, author*

THE INTAGLIO IMPRINT

Also by Lior Samson, from Gesher Press

The Homeland Connection novels:

Bashert
The Dome
Web Games
Chipset
Gasline
Flight Track

The Rosen Singularity
The Millicent Factor

The Four-Color Puzzle
Avalanche Warning

Requisite Variety: Collected Short Fiction

Available from Amazon and other booksellers.

THE INTAGLIO IMPRINT

a novel by Lior Samson

GESHER PRESS

Gesher Press
Rowley, Massachusetts
Author site: www.liorsamson.com

Gesher Press and the bridge logo are trademarks of Gesher Press.

5 4 3 2 1

ISBN 978-0-9885275-9-1

Cover and book design: Larry Constantine
Set in Alegreya and Alegreya Sans
Cover photo: Larry Constantine

To Tovah, Devan, Heather, and Joy—with me for a time,
yet each so wonderfully not me

To be yourself in a world that is constantly trying to make you something else is the greatest accomplishment. – Ralph Waldo Emerson

Who knows who you are? ... A person is a novel: you don't know how it will end until the very last page. Otherwise it wouldn't be worth reading to the very end. – Yevgeny Zamyatin

Prologue

Paolo Carl Franzetti did not know who he was. Neither did we. Of course, we thought otherwise. I probably knew him as well as anyone did. I was there from the beginning, when he was born in 2009, even before that. I was his doctor while he was growing up and then, finally, something more. Still, I misunderstood him.

It was not reciprocal. By the time he was in adolescence, Paolo seemed to understand everyone around him, as individuals and as players in some larger and more intricate drama. He manifest a knack for deciphering even the most involved interpersonal relationships, for grasping the subtleties of the messiest situations. Except when it came to himself, that universal of exceptions, he understood. And we did not.

Of course, it all makes sense with the benefit of hindsight. That he asked me for my help in telling his story is less about our friendship than about how well he knows me: what I will say and not say, how I am put together, and how I will be propelled by the guilt I feel over my role in his deception.

In conversation, he let me off easy, but in writing I am expected to do penance. The assignment, though, is about redemption not revenge. He has no investment in punishment. It is for me alone that he hands me this yoke, knowing full well that I need the burden, that only by circumscribing my demons, transcribing them into words, can I excise them.

I am Leonard Royal Cahners, MD, PhD, Chief Medical Officer of the Fenix Foundation. Most everyone knows me as Roy, and I do now know who I am. For this I am, in no small measure, indebted to Paolo.

Traffic ahead was a red polka-dot carpet of blinking brake lights as Carla Franzetti approached the Weston toll plaza west of Boston. Vehicles without transponders for the decade-old Fast Lane jammed the toll-booths. Despite making good time on the car-clogged Turnpike from Logan airport, Carla had to pee again. Doofus was making it worse; the baby had chosen the occasion to start doing his stretching exercises against her bladder. Three more weeks of this, and then she was done. Three more weeks of waddling and sweating and getting up five times a night. Less than a month and she would have her body back, along with the money to get an apartment in Somerville and start rebuilding her life.

I should have known better than to follow Lando to Italy, she thought. The lying, slimy, selfish coward. But I got away. I found a way out, a way back.

Her back ached from the miserable all-day flight out of Rome's Fumicino airport. In her ethnic ledger, the magic that Italians could wield with wine and food was more than canceled out by their miserable mismanagement of trains and planes. But her boss had insisted she return to have the baby in the States. He even sprang for the airfare and provided the medical certificate to the airlines to allow her to fly this far along in her pregnancy. She could not believe her luck in landing such a dream job with the *Fondazione*. Why had they contacted her in the first place? Someone referred her. She had no idea who, but she was grateful—and to the committee that had accepted her.

With the traffic at a standstill, she checked herself in the rearview mirror. She had dark circles under her eyes from the fatigue of the flight, but her cheeks were rounded and rose-tinged. Her mother would note the former, and her father would comment on the latter. And she would try not to pick a fight with either of them when she arrived home.

Her parents didn't know she was coming, but they did know she was pregnant. They had not been happy at the news. They had warned her about Orlando, and they had been right. It was irritating for her to acknowledge now how often they had been right: about the men in her life, about her choice of entertainment management as a major in college, even about her taste in music. She had the hearing of a sixty-five-year-old, the foundation doctors had told her—too many years of punk metal screaming from stadium speakers or pounding in her earbuds. She thought she had flunked the physical because of that, but they accepted her anyway. They weren't interested in her ears. She was hired, and now she was back, the second-chance kid, as her mother always called her.

It was so goddamn hot in Boston, much hotter than she remembered. The stalled traffic swam in the heat shimmers radiating up from the asphalt. Carla reached toward the center-console to turn up the car's air conditioning, but with the seat pushed back to make room for Doofus, her arms were too short. Traffic ahead started moving a little faster as drivers with transponders shifted into the Fast Pass lanes. Carla undid her seatbelt as she approached the booth to pick up her toll ticket. She reached to bump the air conditioner up another notch, then leaned and stretched to tuck the ticket into her purse on the passenger seat while she accelerated out of the toll plaza in an attempt to make up for lost time.

○ ○ ○

Helen Bentley spotted Roy as soon as she pushed through the double doors at the trauma center. Dr. Cahners, a slim tower in whites with a stethoscope draped around his neck, looked out

3

over the heads of the others milling in the lobby, his anxiety casting out like a lighthouse beacon across the roiling tide of people. When he was anxious, he became critical and controlling, and it hardened his pale patrician face.

"I see you're dressed for the occasion." she said, approaching with an incongruous smile painted on her face, a lined face etched by the disdain and disapproval that it expressed even in repose. Friends and close associates knew her as a caring soul whose scowling face announced otherwise. "How's our girl?"

"Our girl is a vegetable, to use the crude colloquial term. And it's about time you got here, Helen. I hope you have the papers."

"Well, nice to see you, too, Roy. Of course I have the papers, but traffic was terrible, and I had to drive out to Newton first to pick them up at the office before coming all the way back in. Let's do this."

"It won't be all that easy. We can't just march in there now. The family has already arrived—her parents."

"How did you let ... how did that happen?"

"Next of kin, her ID, all standard playbook in these cases. And you only arrived just now. We wouldn't even know about it if I hadn't tried to call her cellphone after she was brought here. And you call me a worrier."

"You are, Roy. You take it all so seriously and personally."

"As if you don't."

"Seriously, yes, but it's never personal. This is just another problem to be dealt with, a contingency to be managed."

"Is that the takeaway from your MBA coursework? Just another problem, a contingency, as you call it. Well, this one happens to be a pregnant woman with massive head trauma being kept alive on a ventilator. Down the hall, a decade of work by hundreds of researchers hangs in the balance with her parents at her bedside, jockeying with the doctors over who is calling the shots. They don't yet know whether they want her kept on life support until the baby can be delivered by C-section." He bent low to be closer to her ear. "A messy court battle against them and the hospital to get custody is the last thing we need now. The publicity would kill us."

"Maybe there's another way." Her lips pursed and she pulsed air in a breathy half whistle. The frown lines that traversed her forehead deepened in concentration. If ever there were a candidate for Botox, it was Helen Bentley. "What if ... what if we let the Franzettis take over. We appeal to their Catholic roots, encourage them to become the loving grandparents raising their dead daughter's child. We always said we wanted the boy to be raised as normally as possible. We can hover in the wings and play supporting roles."

"And how does that work?"

"Well, let's see. As Carla's employers, we could provide benefits, the humanitarian thing—not the American way, more European—like a stipend to the Franzettis, free medical care, a trust fund for education, the whole package tied up with a pretty and plausible bow. 'Oh, Mr. and Mrs. Franzetti, we feel terrible for your loss and somehow almost responsible. Your daughter was traveling on business for us and ... This is just such a tragedy. We can't make it right, but maybe we can help make it easier—just a little, perhaps.' Something like that."

"It might work. But first let's find out more about what the parents intend. And then about the medical status of the baby."

"You take care of that, and I'll put the board of directors on standby, ready to convene quickly for an emergency decision on a critical change of plans."

Chapter 1

In the basement of the Institute for Business and Commerce History in Rome, a low-budget archival backwater at the periphery of academic research, Danbury Bradman leaned back, clasping his hands behind his head as he tilted the black-lacquered wooden library chair onto its back legs. He was on a deadline defined by the approaching centenary of the birth of his subject in 1926, and the work was proceeding at a turtle's pace.

Dust motes and the musty-toast aroma of old books hung in the air of the small reading room. He waited, squinting up at the bare fluorescents, poised to hear the faint fifty-cycle buzz overhead warp into a baritone voice in his head: his late father launching into another of the standard lectures. "Son, I would appreciate it if you put the chair back right. It was, as I am sure I have drawn to your attention on multiple occasions, designed to rest on all four legs, thereby distributing the load among the joints, preventing them from weakening and becoming loose over time." It was always the same lecture, nearly word-for-word. Marcus Bradman, who had been "Professor Bradman" even to his friends and "Sir" to his five children, almost invariably spoke from behind an invisible podium that separated him from his audience. He would tilt his head, peering over the top of his glasses as if he were just glancing up from consulting his notes.

The son, who was just plain Danny to everyone, had defined

his life as an intaglio to the bas relief of the father's unswerving example. Casual and warm, personal with colleagues and tradespeople alike, Danny prided himself in what he thought of as transparency but which was often more of a strained self-exposure with much the same discomfiting effect on others as had been his father's stuffy separation.

"*Scusi!*" The elegant archivist from upstairs entered the room carrying a handful of documents balanced atop a slim bound ledger. Danny guessed her to be about his age, but his hair was already a muddy gray while hers fell in ebony waves over her shoulders. The hair and dark eyes to match made him wonder if she might have some gypsy ancestry.

Danny's chair thudded back down, all four legs once more flat to the floor. "Sorry 'bout that, bad habit of mine. My father was always on my case not to tilt my chair back. I secretly vowed that when I was grown I would do it at every opportunity." He forced a laugh. "I suppose I'm a bit of a rebel, but mostly in small and harmless ways. Maybe pointless ways."

The woman gave him a "whatever" shrug and set the documents on the end of the long wooden table. "I have only these. I am afraid the, what do you say, the minutes, the notes of the incorporation meeting, they are not in the archives."

He studied her face, at once regal and untamed, as he considered what she had just told him. "But I emailed you just last week, and you said you had the originals."

"I did,"—she stiffened—"but they are not there now. The papers of *Fondazione Volo di Ritorno*, they have, it seems, flown away, but we can assume they will most probably be back. *E vero?*" She grinned at her own attempt at humor. Danny had requested material on the enigmatic Return-Flight Foundation, one of the dozens of obscure organizations he had been researching in recent months.

He scrunched his eyes closed and shook his head. "But documents do not just disappear, not documents as potentially important as those. Did you check the log or the register, whatever you call it? Surely you keep track of who looks at what."

"We do, Mr. Bradman, of course. Everything is recorded in a central database. I don't understand, myself. They were there when I checked after getting your message. No one has asked for them since, but they are not there now."

"Look, Francesca—it is Francesca, am I right?—I appreciate your help, but I need you to go back and check again. These"—he flicked a hand in the general direction of the documents on the table—"these are potentially helpful, but it is those original meeting notes that I really need."

It was all a longshot, a fishing expedition that had so far yielded little more than tantalizing tugs on the line and the occasional junk dredged from the bottom of a swamp of files and folders. He reached down the table for the bound book. Without a word, he opened the ledger to the first page and began reading as if he were alone in the room. He reached into his open briefcase and extracted a legal pad on which to take notes. After several pages of laboriously copying numbers and translating text, he finally looked up to see that the woman was gone.

There was nothing new in the records. He impatiently riffled through pages then stopped. A folded fragment of foolscap, torn edges darkened from age, was tucked in at the gutter of the ledger. He carefully unfolded the brittle paper and gasped.

Arturo Dermott's meticulous cursive—and his signature at the lower right with its expansive initials—were instantly recognizable. The language was not. It was definitely not Italian, not quite Spanish either, although some of the words seemed familiar. He recognized a reference to a doctor, a doctor with a

Spanish-like surname, but most of it eluded him. A translation might take research and time. Danny looked toward the open door, listening for footsteps. Silence. He gently refolded the paper and quickly slipped it into a zippered pocket in his briefcase.

A shadow. The archivist stood in the doorway, disappointment frosting her face. *"Mi dispiace molto,"* she said. "I am very sorry. I checked, but I cannot help you. And it is almost closing time. I regret to say that you must return these things."

"Can I get copies?"

She looked at the small stack on the table and pursed her lips. "It will take a little time, the ledger especially, and you will have to pay. Tomorrow. This one, the newspaper story,"—she tapped the top of the stack of papers—"it is a copy, a printout from microfilm. For you, I can let you take it now." She raised her eyebrows and smiled at him.

"Grazie, Francesca. *Sei molto simpatico.*"

"And thank you, Mr. Bradman. You are also very nice, I should say. If you come not too early in the morning, I will have everything copied for you. Perhaps you can ask the Foundation for copies of the missing documents."

"Believe me, I've tried. The Foundation is not very cooperative with the press."

"Oh, you are *giornalista*. I didn't know." Her face brightened. "Very interesting. *Quale giornale?*"

"Which paper? I write for the *Financial Tribune Europe*, and it's mostly not very interesting, at least not to me. I assume our readers are more excited than I by the stuff I crank out: corporate and executive profiles, gee-whiz stories about emerging industries, and deep dives into the future of the new Europe. But this story, this one is different; it's interesting ... and frustrating. I'm trying to find out exactly what happened to the

Dermott fortune—all of it. I've been digging for several months, trying to learn what I can about some rather obscure private foundations that were endowed by the Arturo Dermott estate, trying to make sense of it all. Return-Flight Foundation? What is that about, and why can I find almost nothing about it? It's not a registered charity or not-for-profit, but I can't locate tax records either. It's a subsidiary of a holding company jointly owned by a conglomerate and a closely held investment fund and ... and so on. There are layers on layers of corporations and off-shore accounts." He picked up the photocopied news story from the stack and slipped it into his briefcase. "Are you sure it's all right for me to take this? I can pay, of course."

"No, no. That will not be necessary now. But come back tomorrow, before lunchtime."

"I will. And maybe we can have lunch together afterwards."

She giggled. "I might like that, but not so much my husband." She gave him a wink.

"*Sono molto triste.*" He put on a crestfallen look. "*Domani.* Tomorrow, then. I'll be back for the copies." He watched her leave with the documents, savoring the rhythm of her hips as she started up the stairs. At the last second, she looked back at him and flashed a warm smile.

o o o

Outside, the weather had turned. A chill winter rain hurried the crowds toward their Fiats or their buses. Danny hugged the wall of the building as he ran for the car park. With his head down to keep rain drops off his glasses, he didn't see the two men rounding the corner. While one shouldered him against the side of the building, the other grabbed his briefcase with a quick jerk from behind. By the time he recovered and turned, they were already lost in the crowd boarding the buses.

Chapter 2

We did not have to pressure the Franzettis toward our position. Their faith forbade them from letting their daughter be taken off life support. Indeed, rather than let her go, they were prepared to live indefinitely with her in a chronic vegetative state. The hospital was a bigger problem, at least at first. The doctors could not agree about the timing of the cesarean. One faction wanted to wait until the first signs of labor, one lone voice argued for going in immediately, but the majority favored "watchful waiting," that sine qua non of postmodern medicine. We abetted the latter by facilitating a consult with her obstetrician in Rome, who arranged to share notes and records that were, of course, meticulous and comprehensive. Our computer models had become so refined that we could reliably predict the spontaneous onset of labor within a half day either way. Naturally, we did not go into the mathematics with the hospital staff, but we did convey confidence in our projections and provided detailed charts of the fetal development. They were pleasantly surprised at the advanced state of Italian medicine in prenatal care. If only they knew.

Two days ahead of the projected due date, the scheduled surgery took place. The Franzettis were spared lifelong agony when it turned out that the young woman had peripartum cardiomyopathy that had somehow gone undiagnosed before her trip to Boston. She went into v-fib and complete heart failure on the table before the surgeon could finish closing. It was a blessing, according to the Franzettis, a gift from the Lord who was ready to receive a faithful servant whose mission on earth was complete. To us, it looked more like a medical incident abetted by untimely inattention, but we were grateful nonetheless.

The baby was an Apgar 9 at the five-minute mark, as near perfect as anyone could ask, and all the subsequent tests confirmed our success. The extended stay on the neonatal ward—our idea—was rationalized by the possibility of sequelae from the traffic accident. Anoxia during the brief interval before the mother was resuscitated was a possibility, and trauma from the mother's impact with the vehicle could not be ruled out. We encouraged every conceivable test and co-signed for full financial responsibility. Compared to what had already been invested over the years, it was small change.

The baby was in perfect health when he was released from the hospital. The Franzettis christened him Paolo Carl after Antonio's father, with a middle name in honor of the baby's mother.

Giuseppina called from the kitchen. "The baby needs changing, Toni."

"How do you know?"

"By the way he's crying, silly. Can't you tell? Are you going deaf already? He's been crying like that forever."

"I'll let you change him. I never did quite get the hang of it." Antonio paged through his newspaper looking for the continuation of a front-page story.

"Then it's about time you did."

"You can do it, Seppina."

"I'm making dinner. I can't be in two places at once."

"He can wait."

"No, he can't. Go change him, Toni. Now."

Antonio folded his newspaper and tossed it onto the coffee table, then thought of his wife and reconsidered. He levered the recliner back upright and rose slowly from the chair that was his synthetic-leather throne in the gambrel-roofed colonial that was his castle. He refolded the newspaper and inserted it into the magazine rack beside Seppina's rocker in the opposite corner of the room. "There," he said to the air. As he stood listening, the crying from upstairs morphed into screeches. "I'm coming, I'm coming." He started toward the stairway only to be cut off by his wife pushing ahead.

"You can be such a baby, Toni," she said, taking the stairs two at a time. "A little poop, and suddenly you just can't manage."

"I'm not that good with babies. Remember with Carla?" He forced himself into a high-stepping double-time to keep up with her on the stairs. "Once they're out of diapers, that's different."

"Oh, I remember, all right. I remember." She turned toward the sewing room, which they had repainted yellow and turned into a nursery. "And what are you doing following me up here now? I can handle this even if you can't. Why don't you make yourself useful and go see if the lasagna is done."

"How do I tell?"

"Oh, for heaven's sake, Toni. What am I going to do with you? I'm almost fifty and all of a sudden I have two babies to take care of. Just go. Take it out of the oven; it's probably done anyway. If it's not, it'll be your fault we have pasteboard pasta for dinner. You'll still have to eat it."

As Toni left for the kitchen, she picked up Paolo to comfort him. "Whew, my you are a stinky boy. Let's get you cleaned up." She laid him on the changing table and fastened the Velcro safety strap; the flashing security light turned green and dimmed. "Everything's all so different now, my bouncing baby." She undid the tabs on his diaper, used the corner for an initial wipe of his bottom, and dropped it over the side. She tapped the pad on the diaper bin with her toe, it opened automatically, and the UV sanitizer turned on as it closed. She glanced over her shoulder at one of the two baby monitors in the room, more of the gadgets the Foundation had supplied. "If you're watching, Toni, this is how it's done. Even a man could do this."

The three sanitary wipes it took to clean up the baby followed the diaper into the bin, which was now blinking at her, a reminder that it was time to replenish the deodorizer. "Later," she told it. She spread Paolo with anti-rash ointment before fitting him with a new disposable. "You know, we didn't use these with Carla, but you can't even get cloth diapers now. I hear there are still a few diaper services, but we didn't have a lot of time to get ready for you. No we didn't, did we?" She picked him up and nuzzled his neck, setting him to giggling.

"What have we gotten ourselves into, Paolo Franzetti? Somehow I think it's a lot more than we bargained for."

She heard the front doorbell chime. Toni yelled up the stairs. "The doctor is here!"

She looked down at Paolo and grinned. "Well, my giggling boy, I can see you are much happier when you are not covered with stinky poo. Shall we go downstairs and meet the doctor? Yes?" He laughed. "Sometimes I think you already understand what I'm saying to you. You know that? Yes, I do, my beautiful boy. I do." He bounced excitedly in her arms as she carried him out into the hall and down the stairs.

o o o

Dr. Cahners closed up his bag. "All done. He's in perfect health, gaining weight, and right on schedule in everything. You two are doing a great job."

Toni leaned forward in his chair. "Can I ask you something, doc?"

"Go ahead. Anything."

"Do you do this with all your patients? I mean, like house calls, like every other week."

Cahners smiled. "Nearly all." It was the literal truth, since he took on only a handful of other patients—just enough for appearances and to stay in practice.

"Really?"

"Really. It's what these days they are calling concierge medicine. But you don't have to worry; it's all covered by your insurance."

"But I don't understand this insurance business either. I thought we had Blue Cross or something like that, because of the union and my early retirement."

"You do, you still do, but that insurance is subordinated to the special policy that you got after the accident."

"We can't pay for any extra insurance, you know."

"You don't have to, Mr. Franzetti. It's all paid for by the settlement."

"Call me Toni. Everybody does. I still don't get it though. Not that I'm complaining. The child care allowance really helps a lot, but ..."

"Good. We'll be taking care of little Paolo ... helping you take care of him, I mean. You can count on that. We can't make it right, but we can make it easier."

"Yeah, that's what the other doctor said, the lady doctor."

"Right." Cahners didn't correct him about Helen Bentley's professional credentials. "We know it won't be easy for you two to take on raising another child at ... at this point in your lives, but we're here to help. And we will be here whenever and as long as you need us. Okay? All you have to do is call the number I gave you. Anytime, night or day. Just call." He smiled at them, confident that they would manage, even more confident in what the Foundation and its resources made possible.

15

Chapter 3

Yet another jet on its final approach to Frankfurt airport passed low overhead, setting the office windows rattling. Danny shifted in his seat until the morning sun in his eyes was blocked by the black silhouette of a hawk pasted on the window to discourage songbird suicides.

Kurtis Trauben twisted his Mont Blanc ballpoint closed, then open again before drawing a line through something on his desk calendar, a dated affectation marking Trauben as an old-school editor, one who still used a red pencil to markup paper copy. "And the story? Am I going to see anything anytime soon?" Trauben spoke English with a French accent acquired from study in the Alsace. He preferred English when speaking with Danny, whose German remained awkward and heavily accented even after years as a correspondent in Frankfurt. "I am glad you had a good trip, but London is getting impatient."

"It's a complex story. I told you it could take months."

"And it did. Four, to be exact. With trips to Boston and Rio and Mexico City and Rome. And now you want to go to Valencia. Perhaps there is a story there, but perhaps someone else will have to dig it out. Write up what you have, Bradman." Trauben turned away in his swivel chair and started scrolling through a news feed.

Danny struggled to mask his frustration. "But it will end up little more than a fluff piece, a copycat profile for cucumber time. It—"

"Cucumber time? No, not a piece for the slow news season. It will be just the sort of thing for *FT Weekender* after you figure out an angle. We have a deadline. We are coming up on the centenary of Dermott's birth. Every publication on the planet will be doing a piece on him; we need to do ours. Push the economic impact of his inventions, map the multinational empire he built, highlight his reclusive, antisocial lifestyle. You can do it. Forget chasing mysteries that may not be all that mysterious."

"One more trip, Kurt. I'm convinced that the note I saw—"

"Which you lost."

"Which was stolen."

"After you stole it."

"Whatever! I'm now pretty sure it was written in Catalan. Dermott had a gift for languages, and he lived in Barcelona for a time. I have a contact in Valencia who recognized the name that I recalled from the note: a medical doctor. My friend thinks he can locate the doctor. And he's fluent in Catalan. One more trip, that's all I need, and I think I can blow this wide open."

"Look, Danny, this is a personality profile, a tribute piece not investigative reporting. And these"—he opened a manila folder on his desk and ran his finger down a printout—"these expenses." He flipped through several pages. "Enough to repaper the office. What are all these? This one: lunch in Rome, 142 euros, paid with the corporate credit card. What the ... ?"

"Francesca. The archivist. I was trying to ... ah, build a relationship with a source, to ..."

"I see. Well, on your own time and out of your own pocket from here on out. Understood? And write up the Dermott piece. Just write it."

"Right." He straightened his back. "*Jawohl, Herr Trauben.*"

"Don't go all Prussian on me, mister Danbury Bradman, unless you want me to decline to approve the whole lot of your expenses, not just this one overpriced lunch." He tapped out a paradiddle with his fingertips on the desk. "Okay, okay! Valencia. But this is the last time. One way or another, I want that story in my inbox by the end of next week."

o o o

Danny waited until he was back in his apartment to call Francesca at her office. "I'm headed for Valencia. Can you fly over and join me?"

"When?"

"This weekend, all week if you can get away."

"If only ... no, I simply can't. I ..."

"Just the weekend, then. Surely you can come up with some kind of story."

"You're the writer. You are better at stories than I am."

"Look, just tell your husband you have to fly to Valencia to authenticate something, some documents, historical documents from right after the war maybe, like about Fiat and the Fascists. Something like that."

"You are so into intrigue. I don't do that kind of work. It's corporate history, just that. But I have some ideas; I think I can convince Luca."

Danny felt a tingle of anticipation and a trickle of dread. This sort of deception was new to him, well outside his comfort zone. He had never had an affair with a married woman before. It was frightening, especially after he had learned that Luca was with the *Carabinieri*, Italy's national police force tied to its army. The fear, though, was also proving to fuel his ardor. "I can't wait," he told her. "I'll book a hotel and email you details—my flight, too."

"No, no email, no texting. Call me on my mobile; you have the number."

"You talk as if you've done this before."

"Would you want to know if I had?"

"Well ... no, I think not."

"So, then, I did not. But remember, I am Francesca Mara Zingari. I live up to my family name. We have the hot blood, we gypsies, and so, yes, I have thought about it before, an affair. My gypsy ancestors might not approve of you, but they would understand. What of your ancestors?"

"They would neither approve nor understand. They were German Jews, very strict ones."

"I thought you were English—your name—or American."

"The name was originally Breitmann. My grandfather, Salomo Breitmann, anglicized it when he emigrated with his family to England in 1938. It was Broadman at first, a literal translation, but when I was a boy my grandfather told me he had to drop the O because we were all too skinny for the name.

"He had a sense of humor, which was not, alas, inherited by my father, for whom life was about rules and order. My father might have made a good officer in the Wehrmacht were he not Jewish. No, that's unfair. My father dealt with fear by grasping for control, for command; my grandfather dealt with his fears by reaching for comedy. He literally died laughing, struggling with his last breath to get to the punchline of some multilingual pun that none of us could understand because he would squeeze out a few words and then start to laugh and lapse into yet another coughing fit."

"Now that is funny."

"My father didn't think so. At the funeral, he said that grandfather should not have tried to tell the joke, that he might have still been around if he had taken things more seriously."

"What was the joke? Do you remember?"

"Something about a Russian Jew, a *pushke*, and a poem by Pushkin and ... he never finished it, but he obviously thought it was hilarious."

"What is a *pushke?*"

"A little collection box for charity. It's a Yiddish word. My grandfather knew five languages. He was fluent in Yiddish and Russian, German and English, and could read Hebrew. He was very learned, very intellectual, as was my father. I'm merely intelligent."

"I don't understand the difference."

"I'll explain over paella in Valencia."

"Okay. I am persuaded. Oh, did you ever get your briefcase back?"

"I did. It was recovered from a trash bin not far from the bus stop. The thieves must have been expecting it to contain valuables or a laptop. They didn't realize until after they grabbed it that it was a cheap knockoff, faux alligator, not the real thing."

"Was anything missing?"

"Only my checkbook." He couldn't tell her about the pilfered note, which, oddly, was the only other thing missing. "I reported the theft to the bank and stopped payment on the checks. Otherwise I would not be able to afford to invite you to Valencia, my expensive gypsy."

"That remark will cost you. You'll find out just how expensive a gypsy girl can be."

"I can't wait. Ciao."

"Bye-bye." She disconnected.

Chapter 4

Paolo always connected well enough, but he was also a loner who had a habit of disappearing. We got through the vanishing-toddler phase with only one major scare—at a mall. Giuseppina recovered from her panic attack when he was located in the children's book section of a Barnes & Noble, paging his way through board-books from the pile he had assembled in a quiet corner.

When she asked him how he got there, to the store that was in a freestanding building apart from the mall itself, he said that he had followed the other children with their parents. What other children? The ones who looked like they loved books, he told her.

He was, as might be expected, remarkably self-sufficient and self-contained, which many adults read as evidence of maturity beyond his years. Children, on the other hand, seemed not to notice or care about his isolation. It was not that he didn't get along with other children, but his relationships were, from the earliest days, decidedly asymmetric. Others were drawn to him, despite his indifference to their overtures and intentions. He could at once be in the center of things and peripheral, as if he were observing the swirl around him, taking it all in with those dark eyes. Antonio once said it was as if the boy were always taking mental notes.

Later, Paolo would disappear even at home. They found him in the attic that first time. He was six.

"Now what on earth are you doing up here?" As Seppina reached the top of the switchback stairs from the pantry, she brushed imaginary dust from the front of her flower-print housedress. "Are you all right? We didn't know where you were. Isn't it too hot up here? I thought you were playing with your Legos. We've been looking all over for you." Hers was a rush of words, a torrent of relief and annoyance. She and Toni had been searching for an hour and were nearly at the point of calling the police. "Would you like some juice? You should have something to drink in this heat." She wanted to be angry at him, but the impulse was quickly overwhelmed by the Italian grandmother in her.

Paolo's pink tongue worked its way across his thick dark lips as he drew out a few more block letters and twirled his pencil to make a black dot after the last one. "I was just writing, Nonna Seppina." He looked over at her with serious brown eyes, his head haloed by the dusty beam of sunlight from the octagonal window at his back.

"What's all this?" she said.

"All this is my office."

He was kneeling before a storage trunk. The dulled brass of its reinforced corners peeked out from beneath Toni's old drafting board, a scratched and ink-stained makeshift desktop. The trunk dwarfed the six-year-old Paolo, who must have dragged it the length of the attic by its harness-leather handles to carefully position it where it would catch the light. In one corner of the drafting board, an empty jelly jar held a bouquet of sharpened pencils, to the side rested a stack of the lined note paper the boy preferred for everything from rough sketches of birds and trees to making paper airplanes.

"What are you writing, Paolo?"

He frowned in concentration as he drummed with his pencil on the edge of the drafting board. "A book."

"A book? Really?" Despite herself, Seppina could not help the tone of amused skepticism in her question. He had been this way, full of surprises, from the beginning. He was talking in complex sentences by thirteen months and had taught himself to read at four. She didn't know the full story of the strange and scary-smart boy that had come into their lives so late. She always assumed the father was Orlando, but Orlando had been no rocket scientist, and their daughter had never risen above "just bright enough." Even after six years, the precocious Paolo could still astonish his grandparents with his quick insight and inventiveness.

"Yes, a book," he said. "It's about a girl and a puppy, but I am stuck on the second chapter. I can't figure out her motorvation. It's perplexting. She ran away from home. But why?" He turned his dark face toward Seppina again and chewed at his lower lip in concentration.

"Well, maybe she—"

"I've got it! It's her father and his drinking." His tongue darted in and out as he returned to writing. Seppina looked over his shoulder at the sheet of paper covered in precise, tiny block letters, nearly as neat as if the page had emerged from the laser printer in the study downstairs

It was his way with everything: deliberate precision, a serious approach, even in eating, even in play. He did not laugh or screech when he rocketed down the high slide at the playground. If he landed too hard or scraped an elbow, he never cried out but would calmly go back and try again, angling his body a little differently or keeping his elbows tucked in more tightly.

"I'll leave you to it, then." Seppina told him. She started toward the stairs just as Toni poked his head into the attic.

"I see you found him. You'll leave him to what?" Toni, whose thick eyebrows were still black beneath his graying curls, smiled at the two of them. At fifty-seven, he looked like he could still put in a day at a construction site, and he favored the plaid work shirts that went with the image. Both he and his wife came from long-lived *paisano* stock. Their parents had led active lives well into their eighties, and despite their late start with Paolo, no one doubted the Franzettis would live to see him grown.

There could be no doubt that Paolo was not Toni's biological son. They were as unlike physically and in demeanor as any two males might be. Toni was ruddy-faced and barrel chested; Paolo was swarthy and fine-boned. On Sunday evenings, they would play chess, Toni grinning as he kept up a non-stop stream of banter, play-by-play commentary, and gentle instruction, while Paolo sat quietly, studying each move in silence before finally announcing "mate in four." At six, Paolo would still lose more often than he won, but Toni could already see the humiliation that lay not many years ahead.

As Toni picked his way through the stacked boxes in the attic, Seppina beamed over at him. "Paolo is writing a book. About a runaway girl and her puppy."

"A book. Now isn't that something. I always wanted to write a book when I retired. Now I'm retired, ahead of schedule, and I have no idea how to write a book."

"Like this, Nonno." Paolo set down his pencil. "You figure out what the story is about, you choose your people, you work out the plot, and then you start writing."

"Easy for you to say, kiddo." He laughed, a guffaw from deep in his chest. "I'll have to give that a try someday."

Seppina took his arm. "Let's leave our Hemingway hopeful to write in peace." She glanced back over her shoulder. "And I'll bring you some iced orange juice."

"Oh, that's all right, Nonna Seppina. I'm all set." Paolo held up an iced-tea glass filled with red liquid and beaded with condensation.

◦ ◦ ◦

Roy Cahners put the handset back in its cradle and turned to the rest of the team. "That was Toni with an update: there was no emergency. The Franzetti's found him in the attic. He's set up a sort of office up there so he can write in peace. Apparently he prefers pencil and paper to the tablet computer he got for Christmas. But we'll have to figure out how to help the Franzettis keep track of him as he becomes more mobile and independent."

"Becomes? What about that little incident at the Museum of Science two years ago?" Helen Bentley could always be counted on to dissent or to offer a counterexample.

"Normal. That's all, just normal." Chaim Danforth, their developmental psychologist, set down the Moleskine in which he had been making notes. Pronouncements were his favored conversational style, in keeping with the sartorial statement of his work attire that leaned toward sweater vests and tweed jackets with leather-patch elbows. If he could have gotten away with smoking a pipe at the office, he would have. "Toddlers and pre-schoolers can be counted on to lose themselves in a crowd. And the Franzettis found him at the museum—on their own—and without making some embarrassing announcement on the PA, like so many panicky parents would do these days."

"Well, they did call Roy." Helen tapped a finger on the corner of the conference table.

"But they are the ones who found him."

"But they did call."

Roy held up his hands calling for peace. "That's what we taught them to do: when in doubt, shout me out. I'm their link to us, the friendly physician always on-call and ready to help with a smile."

Chaim pointed with the corner of his notebook. "You know what I remember? How odd it was that all the other kids were fascinated by the exhibit, a Tesla coil or something, And there was Paolo, cross-legged on the floor, facing the other way, studying the crowd, fascinated by something he saw in their faces."

"It was a van de Graaff generator," Helen corrected.

"Tesla, van de Graaff, whatever. You're the engineer, Helen."

"I'm no engineer, not anymore. I gave that up after the Challenger disaster when I realized that the logical voice of engineering would always be drowned out by the pronouncements of politics and management. After a close friend at Morton-Thiokol attempted suicide, I decided to quit and get my MBA. I wanted to be one of the voices that gets heard. Ha! So I end up here, doing all the listening with the lot of you drowning me out."

Chaim gave her a closed-mouth smile. "Yeah, but you still think like an engineer, plodding and plotting your way through life."

"It's not plodding, just thinking without getting ahead of myself. It's step-by-step, without prejudgment, always open to whatever information the world next presents. The methodical mindset, my husband calls it, which he says with impatient annoyance whenever he thinks I'm too slow to concede an argument to him. Then again, there can be a hint of appreciative awe whenever I fix something around the house or come up with an unobvious solution for some problem Edgar is having in his own work at UMass-Boston. Engineers think differently, he says, except for Apple engineers, who think *different*—my husband's little dig about my stint working with Jonny Ives and crew in Silicon Valley. I lasted just short of a year."

"And you ended up here." Cahners made an expansive gesture taking in the conference room and the warren of cubicles outside the glass partition. He knew she hated the open-plan office suite enough to have the glass wall of her own office papered over with motivational posters.

"Yeah, here I am. We all gotta eat, and everyone rises to his or her own level of incompetence."

"How did you end up here, anyway." Chaim, a late addition to the team, had still not heard all the stories.

"I knew Arturo Dermott from a patent infringement dispute he had with Apple over a smartphone camera lens. He had a way of injecting himself into matters better left to his lawyers. He was a very hands-on engineer, a micro-manager who did everything himself. I guess I made an impression on him, because his will mentioned me by name. Then the Foundation hired me."

"Well, I guess if you're Arturo Dermott, always the smartest man in the room, it makes sense to call all the shots yourself."

"Maybe. An engineer would say it depends. You want the best people in each slot, especially if you have the billions to buy the best, as he did. That's why we have a team here. Speaking of teamwork, perhaps Roy could make a house call pretty soon."

"Sure, I could stop by to check on Antonio's cough."

"Good. You can get all the details of this latest hiccup from Giuseppina." Helen closed her laptop and started to leave. "What about an implanted GPS tracker for the boy? Hell, we've got the resources. Why not? We can have IT work up a proposal. And, Chaim, you team with Roy to prepare a risk-benefit analysis from the medical and psychological perspectives. We'll take the matter up at Monday's meeting."

Chapter 5

"I like the hotel. I like the bed." Francesca pulled the duvet up around herself in a show of delayed modesty. "Most of all I like the in-room massage service."

Danny bowed. "Yes, and what's more, we also offer concierge shopping with the duly famed *El Corte Inglés* right across the road. I was warned that you were an expensive gypsy girl, so I thought a large department store nearby would appeal."

"Oh, so I see you are not just a writer for the *Financial Tribune* but also of the same class as its readers. And with a bank balance to match?"

"Who me? I'm just a poor transplanted writer who couldn't get work in the UK. With my French even more limited than my German, my preferred choice, Paris, was out. So, I ended up in Frankfurt. Fortunately, I got the job in advance of the stupid Brexit vote."

"But you fly to Rome, to Valencia. You stay at nice hotels and take gypsy girls to expensive restaurants."

"Yes, well that last indulgence may be coming to an end. The rest of it is all underwritten by my expense account with the paper."

"Are you still chasing down the ghost of Arturo Dermott, Italy's one-man answer to Thomas Edison and Bill Gates?"

"Edison and Gates? The man had twice as many patents as Edison and was worth more than Gates—even before Gates started giving his money away. Besides, Dermott was also

American by way of his father. He exploited dual citizenship, being whichever best suited his interests of the moment. American, Italian, Italian-American: they were just labels to him, means to ends. But I'm less interested in the man than in the traces of his financial dealings. A lot of money has never been accounted for." He sat up to kiss her neck and take in the salty perfume of their lovemaking. "But, right now I'm even more interested in a certain Italian archivist who is helping me find the man's transnational footprints."

She playfully pushed him away. "And this Italian archivist is more interested in getting something to eat."

He stood and faced her. "Ah, but Peter down there is hungry for more Francesca. I won't even be able to get my pants on with him so ravenous."

She laughed, a rich alto laugh. "You are impossible. Come here."

○ ○ ○

By the time they had showered and dressed after the day's second round of lovemaking, it was getting dark and Francesca was famished. "If I don't get something to eat soon, I will shrivel like a raisin. My breasts will droop off, and—"

Danny couldn't help laughing. "Droop off. Right. Come then, let's catch a cab at the taxi rank and find this place that my friend recommended."

"I hope this place your friend recommended is not far, or you will have a cadaver for a companion."

○ ○ ○

The restaurant Danny had been directed to was a walk-down at the end of a cobbled alleyway too narrow for the taxi to enter. The building was fronted by a bright façade tiled in a mock Moorish pattern. Inside, the blue-green walls were decorated with fishing nets and glass floats interspersed with models of ships in bottles and fading photos of fishermen at work. As the waiter approached, Danny leaned toward Francesca, "Seafood or meat?"

"Do I have to choose? Can't I have both?"

"That would be what the locals call *preparación barroca*. It is considered a corruption, not authentic paella. The ancient original called for beans and meat, later amended to substitute seafood—in the shell. But mixing them in the baroque style, no."

"I am an archivist. The genuine and the historic, they are my life's work. However, I am a starving archivist. Just order some food before I faint."

"And you are an archivist given to hyperbole. But, it's an easy choice. Since both of us are from inland cities and now we are on the coast, we should make the most of the opportunity and order *paella con marisco*."

"I surrender. Just order it. And some wine."

They had nearly drained the bottle of Albariño when the paella arrived, a sizzling carpet of yellow-orange rice arrayed with prawns and shellfish. The rising steam tickled their nostrils with the scent of saffron.

"This is why we are here and not at the fancy place at the head of the street. This is the real thing."

"What was wrong with that other restaurant? It looked inviting."

"Inviting is for tourists. My friend said the paella there is an imposter. They use turmeric to make the rice look golden. They skimp on the saffron because it costs more. My friend told me that this little place at the end of the street is the best."

She spooned some of the paella onto her plate and speared a scallop along with some rice. There was a pause as she savored her first bite. "Mmm, *delizioso*! I think your friend was right. Does your friend have a name?"

"Bernat, Bernat Vilaró."

"And how do you know this Bernat?"

"We went to college together, Columbia, in New York. He comes from Spanish wealth and I come from English wannabes. My father wanted me to study at Cambridge or Oxford and become a surgeon or a barrister, so I studied literature and journalism in America—on scholarship: his ultimate humiliation."

"You do not like your father so much."

"I loved my father. I hated his fear and his inflexibility."

"What does he think of you now that you are ... a success?"

"Success would be writing for *The Guardian* or on-staff at *The Times*. Better still, it would mean the Bevins Prize for journalism. And he doesn't think anything of it ... or me. He died in my junior year at Columbia, a well-timed heart attack in the heart of finals week. I couldn't make it home to sit *shiva*. My mother and sisters have never forgiven me."

"Families can be so ... well, you know, *pazzo*."

"And you? Your family? Was it also crazy?"

"No. Yes. My father was an anti-corruption judge who was killed by the mafia when I was a little girl. I remember him, but it is a much redacted memory. I am the youngest of five girls and the only one without children. I was a disappointment to my father because I was not the long-awaited son and a disappointment to my mother because I was not interested in having babies—unlike her. Fortunately, my older sisters have given her grandchildren: nine, so far, and another coming."

"You're not interested in children?"

"I am very interested in children, especially my nieces and nephews. I said I am not interested in *having* children. It is one of the struggles with Luca. He very much wants a son. I think if I do not give him one soon, he will divorce me."

Danny held the wine bottle up to the light. "A few drops left. Shall we order another bottle."

"*Certamente!*"

○ ○ ○

Hoping to work off the aftereffects of dinner and dessert—and too much wine—they decided to walk back. As they approached the hotel, they were drawn to the lights along the City of Arts and Sciences across from it. The arc and cables of a bridge, *El Pont de l'Assut de l'Or*, formed a majestic 400-foot-high Celtic harp, white against the night sky above them. "Let's cross over the bridge and explore for a few minutes." Danny put his arm around her shoulders. "Are you warm enough?"

She nodded. "How can it be. All the cables are on one end and the tower, the spire, is curved, tilted, so graceful it seems impossible that it stands. How?"

"I don't know. I'm not an engineer. Something about the balance of forces." He took her hand and pulled her along at a brisk pace toward the center of the span where the cable stays were anchored. They strolled, staring up, following the thick tubes stretching into the night sky. On one side, the enormous tiled helmet of *L'Agora* cast blue-hued reflections from the spotlights around it; on the other, a chain of elegant modernist structures mirrored in reflecting pools stretched into the distance along the park that had once been a riverbed.

Back in the room after twenty minutes of exploration truncated by the night chill, Danny opened his laptop to check email as Francesca looked over his shoulder. "Well," he said, "another lead goes nowhere. This guy has the right name but is not the one I want to interview. At least he had the courtesy to reply to my email. A lot of the inquiries I send out disappear into a digital black hole."

"Why don't you just Google whatever you are looking for?"

"You don't understand. This is not the sort of stuff you find on the Web. That's why I had to come in person to your archives. The most important stuff was never digitized. You know about all this. For much of what I was looking for, the best you could deliver was microfilm or microfiche."

"There is not big funding for my sort of work."

"Right, which is why the real stuff I need, the hidden stuff, like that scrap of paper from Arturo Dermott I uncovered—it's not going to show up on the Web."

"What scrap of paper?"

"I ... I found a piece of paper tucked into a ledger book on my last visit."

She grabbed a pillow and hit him with it. "You didn't say anything about finding a piece of paper. What happened to it?" Danny sat in guilty silence. "You stole something from the archive? From me? You ..."

"I didn't steal it so much as borrow it. Obviously, no one knew it was there. It looked significant, even had Dermott's signature."

"With the centenary coming up, that could be valuable, important. And you just pocketed it and walked out."

"Well, I didn't exactly pocket it. It was in my briefcase."

"The one that was stolen?"

"Yes, the one that was stolen. And the paper was missing when I got the case back. Go figure."

"So, it's gone." She hit him again with the pillow.

"Look, if you are going to get violent, I'm done here. I'm going to brush my teeth and go to bed."

When he returned from the bathroom, Francesca was seated naked at the desk. "What are you doing with my computer?"

"Surfing. Don't worry, I didn't look at your stupid email." She kept typing, tapping, and scrolling her way through a chain of searches. Suddenly she lifted her hands from the keyboard. *"Si, lo sapevo!"* She pointed at the screen, gloating. "Yes! I knew it! Not on the Web, you say to me. And there it is, on eBay." The listing, which included a smartphone photo of the missing document, described an "authenticated signature of late billionaire Arturo Dermott" for only one-thousand euros "or best offer." Francesca puffed air from the corner of her mouth. "Authenticated? The cretins don't know the meaning of it. But now all you have to do is come up with a thousand euros."

Danny squinted at the screen and reached past her to position the cursor over the photo. He tapped, and it enlarged to fill the screen. "No, now all I need to do is save the image to show my friend Bernat tomorrow."

Chapter 6

The Franzettis, who had always wanted a son but who had been blessed with only a daughter, were delighted to be raising a grandson with whom they could be indulgent and generous thanks to the support of the Foundation. As good Italian-American Catholics, they were rather traditional in their views of gender and gender roles, leaning toward conventionally "masculine" toys for young Paolo: Tonka construction vehicles and plastic action figures, whiffle balls and kid-sized sports equipment. Paolo, however, had a mind of his own and found inventive ways to express his own emerging personality.

Both Chaim and I were conflicted about being parties to the politically incorrect pressure. Professionally and philosophically, we both inclined toward a modern, more gender-neutral view of children's toys. But we were constrained by the Foundation's mission, and, as time went on, became more aggressive in our attempts to draw out the latent talents we were certain lay dormant within Paolo.

He did like puzzles and challenging intellectual games, particularly the classics like Go or Chess, but left to his own, he preferred words. His creative writing—which had begun when he could scarcely read—continued non-stop, as if the act of creating information were more natural to him than the process of consuming it. As he grew, he jacked up his drafting-board desk with suitcases and pressed a crate into service as a chair. He wanted no more—no maple desk, no files, no computer or laser printer—though he could have had all of these and more. They were, he would say, "not efficient." He told the Franzettis many times, in the most serious inflection, "What I use are efficient for my uses."

Paolo, who was always punctual even if not always enthusiastic about dinner, was late. Six o'clock passed and he was still not at the table. Toni excused himself. "I'll go find him."

Assuming the boy was in his "office" and had lost track of time, Toni went straight to the attic expecting to find Paolo absorbed in his latest writing project. There, the stack of blank notebook paper was carefully straightened and aligned with the edge of the drafting board, the pencils were all restored to the jelly jar, and the attic was quiet.

Toni started a methodical top-down search of the old house: their bedroom, Paolo's, the sewing room, the living room, dining room, and front parlor. In the basement laundry, playing with his wooden construction blocks, was Paolo. He was not building with them. He had used a Sharpie to draw faces on the round columns and to turn an arch into a dog by adding outlined ears and a tail. He was acting out a story, quietly reciting lines of dialogue as he maneuvered the colored blocks along a meandering road made of torn strips of paper.

"Ah, here you are, Paolo. What are you doing down here in the dark?"

"It's nighttime in the story. I turned out the lights. Nonna Seppina doesn't like me spreading paper all over in the parlor."

"Your Nonna doesn't like picking up all the pieces of paper after you are asleep for the night."

"But I always pick them all up when I'm done."

"No you don't. You—"

"I do so. But sometimes it's bedtime before I'm done with a story. I should be able to leave them there until morning."

"But your Nonna likes to keep the house neat."

Paolo nodded vigorously. "She does. She's 'sessive compulsive."

"Where do you get such words?"

"I read. You should read more, too, Nonno Toni."

"Oh, you think so, my little bookworm." He swept Paolo up in his arms, then swung him onto his shoulders, almost whacking him against the exposed joists overhead. "Watch your head."

"How can I do that? I can watch your head, though."

"Sometimes you can be so ... so literal."

"Put me down."

"Why?"

"I want to go look up that word: literal."

"I can tell you what it means."

"No. I'd rather look it up in the dictionary. Then I know it's right, and I can know all the meanings."

"Don't dis your granddad, kiddo. Christmas is coming."

"Not until December."

"You're so right, kiddo. All the more reason to build brownie points with your grandparents. And let's not upset the lady of the house, who has dinner waiting for her overdue boys." Toni swung Paolo off his shoulders and set him on his feet at the bottom step.

"Ouch."

"What's wrong?"

"Your ring scratched me."

"This ring?" Toni twisted the ring from his right hand. "I'm sorry." He started to tuck it in the watch pocket of his jeans.

"Can I look at it?"

"Sure, here. It's an intaglio made of carnelian. Belonged to my grandfather."

Paolo held the ring up, tilting the dark-orange stone with its carving of a noble Roman in profile, catching the light from different angles. "It's backwards. It goes in instead of out, but if you hold it just right, it looks like it's not backwards."

"Yes, that's what intaglio means. If it were carved the other way around, frontwards as you might say, it would be called a cameo."

"I like it. I wish I had a ring like this."

"Someday you will, because this ring will be yours."

○ ○ ○

The Christmas after Paolo turned eight marked a cusp. Egged on by Dr. Cahners under a manufactured pretext, the Franzettis had been doing all they could to interest Paolo in the whole range of the subjects that had come to be known in modern America by the acronym STEM: science, technology, engineering, and math. Using funds from the generous child support provided by the endowment, they showered him with techy gifts: a large wooden-boxed classic Erector set they found on eBay, a new tablet computer with all the accessories, a fully functional digital microscope, a chemistry set, a scale model of the U.S.S. George H. W. Bush nuclear-powered aircraft carrier, and —just for good measure—physics simulation software and a ten-in-one set of computer "brain-training" games for the tablet.

"Thank you, Nonna Seppina. Thank you, Nonno Toni. This is wonderful." It was a litany recited after each gift was opened, repeated with all the manufactured enthusiasm an eight-year-old could muster. He examined the microscope with some interest but had trouble focusing it and couldn't get it to communicate with his tablet computer. He boxed it up again with great care.

He opened the Erector set and picked up a girder, flipped it over, and returned it to its place in the tray. An example of each of the varied parts was retrieved, examined, and returned to its proper slot or bin. "I'll have to read the directions later to figure out how to put this together."

"It's a construction set," Toni told him, trying to dampen the impatience in his voice. "You put it together however you want. You can make anything with that: a car, a derrick crane, a front-end loader, a—"

Seppina interrupted Toni by placing her hand on his arm. "Paolo knows. He'll figure it out. He's good at figuring things out."

At the end of an awkward Christmas morning, Paolo found one more small package tucked on the bottom shelf of the bookcase behind the tree. He opened it with some weary apprehension, as if he already had enough of gifts and gratitude for the day. Inside was a small blank book, clothbound in a bright highland plaid, with a ballpoint pen held in a sleeve at the spine.

"It's called a journal. Just a little something for your writing, to carry with you so you don't have to wait until you get back to the attic if you get some special thought."

Paolo gave his Nonna a big hug. For the rest of the day, the notebook was his constant companion. By bedtime the half-filled book was on his nightstand. He smiled up at Seppina as she tucked him in. "Thank you so much for the journal, Nonna Seppina. I hope I can get another one for my birthday."

"I have one set aside for you already." She wrinkled her nose. "You can have it when this one is filled."

Chapter 7

"And who is this beautiful creature?" Bernat's smile broadened as he gave Francesca a slow up-and-down before moving in for the continental kiss to the left and to the right. "She is gorgeous, Danny. And she has great taste in clothes."

"Courtesy of *El Corte Inglés*. This is Francesca. Francesca, this is Bernat. Don't let his leering fool you. He's as fey as the fairies."

"Ah, but even the fairies can be turned." He winked at her. "Or so I understand, never having myself succumbed completely to feminine charms. But, then, there might be a first for one such as you, Francesca."

"Keep it up, Bernat. I love it." She leaned in to repeat the kissing ritual. With her lips next to his left ear, she whispered something that brought a flush of pink to his cheeks.

"Oh my, Francesca," he said, mocking a girlish giggle.

Danny's eyebrows tented like mirrored accent marks. "What did you say to him?"

"We girls have our secrets, too. Right, Bernat?"

"Oh, indeed we do. And welcome to Valencia, both of you. Valencia is not my city but it is my home."

"And what is your city?" she asked.

"Why, Barcelona, of course, the someday capital of a free *Catalunya*." He snapped to attention then took a ballerina's bow. "But for now, we are here. Let me show you around my flat, starting with Pyotr here." He pointed to the wooden stand by the entrance, a headless torso of a muscular youth with an oversized erection angled skyward. "These are my companions"—he spread his arms and turned—"carved in exotic woods, appropriately, and one and all sculpted from life."

He crossed the room. "Next, this way, we have the balcony and its view of the city. It is not Barcelona, but we do have the architecture of Calatrava and Candela—so amazing. They are the greatest in Spain, in the world. Do you know our *Ciutat de les Arts i les Ciències*."

"Yes, we are staying at the Tryp hotel not two hundred meters from it. We can see the bridge from our window. "

"The bridge. Yes, so graceful. *El Pont de l'Assut de l'Or*, and next to it, the blue-tiled helmet, *L'Àgora*. We must see if you can go to a concert there while you are here."

"We're only here for the weekend—and Monday."

"Pity. A short holiday. What is it with you English?" He gave Danny a disapproving scowl. "But you, dark vision of beauty, are Italian, am I not right? Why are you in such haste to go back?"

"I have to ... I have work."

"I have work, too, but I never let it interfere with food or friends—or a fuck."

"Bernat is an artist and—"

"A sculptor and architect, please. Not on the scale of Calatrava or Candela, of course, but what you see around you in my flat, it is all my work."

Danny smirked. "So, you still haven't sold anything?"

"Oh, Danny." Bernat struck his chest with a fist palmed in the other hand. "How cruel you can be. I had forgotten about your swift thrust to the heart, an épée to the soul. But I have sold much—not as much as I have carved, it is true, but only last month I delivered a commission to the new Accor hotel."

"Class. If you are going to surrender your artistic integrity to a hotel chain, sell to the biggest in Europe. Considering that your art is mostly homoerotic, I am somewhat surprised they would take it."

"It was an abstract, symbolic: the stump of a mature oak wrapped in embrace by a growing fig tree. I called it *Connate*, a botanical reference I do not expect most viewers will understand. But you did not come to Valencia merely to discuss modern art or to insult an old friend."

"No, I came to seek the help of an old friend in finding someone."

"Ah, yes, the Dr. Manuel Fonseca y Morales you mentioned. I know of this man."

"How is that?"

"Because he was one of us, a flaming fruit, you might say, except he led two lives—the one, so staid and proper, the other ... so other. He worked in *obstetrícia i ginecologia*, a doctor for the women. How they adored him, with his specialty in helping them to have babies."

"Like in vitro fertilization, that sort of thing?"

"Yes, all that. He worked in Italy but retired here, where he was born. I met him at a party once."

"He is mentioned in this document I ... we found. Do you know where we can find him?"

"Of course, al *cementiri*. He is always there; call at any hour."

"So he is dead. What about the note we found. You can still read Catalan, right?"

"*Si, el català és la meva llengua materna*. You do not forget your mother tongue. Do you have this note?"

"We have a picture of it. I think it is readable. Here, let me bring it up on my laptop." He flipped open his MacBook Pro and tapped to open the saved image.

Bernat leaned close to the screen and studied the image of the text when it displayed, reading it aloud.

La carretera és massa llarga. Cal desviar-se a través dels esbarzers i aprendre dels plàtans. El Dr. Manuel Fonseca i Morales és el guia turístic. Ell hi estarà d'acord, perquè la seva carta és el nostre as a la màniga. Pot enfonsar el forat en un al novè green. Els coreans tenen bones relacions amb els afganesos, però els xinesos tenen millors laboratoris. Plantarem oliveres, però no en veure el fruit. Sempre he preferit els pitbulls, però els beagles són millors amb la lletra petita. Títol clar, ni més ni menys. La resposta és creu, espina, i zeta zeta zeta. Hauria hagut d'intentar això abans. Funciona.

"What does it say, Bernat?"

"It is nonsense. Or it is in a code."

"But what does it say?"

"Something like this: 'The highway is too long. We must detour through the undergrowth and understand the bananas. Dr. Manuel Fonseca y Morales is the tour guide. He will agree because his ace is our hole card. He can sink the hole-in-one on the ninth green. The Koreans have good relations with Afghans, but the Chinese have better labs. We will be planting olive trees whose fruit I will not see. I have always favored pit bulls, but beagles are better with fine print. Clear title, nothing less. The answer is cross, thorn, and zed zed zed. I should have tried this earlier. It works.' It reads like some drug-fueled free-association monologue."

"That could be it, like he was tripping. There were rumors that he had experimented heavily with hallucinogens in the late 1990s, not too long before he died. He was still working then, in his seventies, even though he already was one of the richest men on the planet."

"And what could a man who has everything want?"

"He did not have everything; he did not have a family. He died childless. Everything left in his estate went to a host of charities and foundations. That's what I'm looking into. The numbers don't add up. There's at least a billion or so unaccounted for. I—"

He was interrupted by a loud chime. Bernat stood. "And speaking of family, that will be my husband, Sherrod, and our son, Feliu, back from the zoo."

Chapter 8

Throughout elementary school, Paolo continued to write, always with measured precision in that legible block hand that he had adopted as a preschooler. Though it might take him weeks to finish a story, his fine mind deftly kept track of all the story threads and the details he strung upon them. He would finish one story and then begin another, rarely returning to anything once it was filed within the capacious cardboard box that sat always beside his makeshift desk.

From the age of nine, he was a regular in NaNoWriMo, the National Novel Writing Month, an annual fall frenzy of amateur authorship. His novels were never shared, though, but ended up instead, like the rest of his early oeuvre, in the same corrugated paper vault. He wrote to write, for himself it seemed, not to be read. But there, too, we misunderstood him and his perfectionism.

With far more determination than the average pre-adolescent, he also continued on his quest to decipher destiny, to discover himself. He did so in his writing and in his experiments with varied personas. He even tried his hand at sports, for which he had neither natural talent nor deep drive.

Paolo did have two great gifts that emerged early: his facility with words and his understanding of emotional relationships. He was never without friends, not merely casual ones, but fiercely loyal intimates who valued his friendship above all others. I do not believe that many of these early emotional attachments were reciprocal, but Paolo gave generously, nonetheless.

He gave each and all the same gift: insight. He was always the one to whom his young friends turned when they had trouble with parents or boyfriends or school. He rarely, if ever, gave advice. He would listen, then tell the seekers something about themselves. They left, armed with new self-knowledge, to solve their problems without him. He would often have gleaned something from the encounter that would become fuel for some future fiction of his.

Antonio once asked him about the many abandoned stories. Paolo was eleven, and they almost filled the storage box.

Toni could see his breath. "It's cold up here. How do you work with it so cold?" He walked over to Paolo's well-organized work-space just as Paolo straightened a stack of paper, fastened it with a paperclip, and dropped it into the open-topped box to one side.

"That's it? All done and it just ends up in a box?"

"They're just silly stories. Like this one." He riffled through the stack and slid out a thick sheaf of notepaper held together by a green binder clip. "It's a novella called 'Flight Track,' about a bird, an inadvertent stowaway on a space freighter. It's really quite childish. I was only a nine, just a kid when I wrote it." The summary judgement was delivered with no trace of irony. He returned the manuscript to the box. "I can really do much better now."

"Why don't you rewrite it, then, revise it in some way?"

"You don't understand. It's the thing as a whole. The theme, the plot, the narrative, the grammatical construction: they're all naïve. The gestalt is flawed." He paused and looked up at Toni, as if making sure Toni understood.

"I know what the word means, kiddo." Having grown used to the way Paolo would seem to underestimate the intelligence of the adults around him, Toni let it pass without saying more.

"Right. Well, it's better to start fresh on something else, to build something original, rather than to try to patch up something with the wrong design built on an old foundation." It was said with the simple factual detachment that his friends and the adults around him had come to expect. Only the fact that he was the shortest boy in his middle-school class kept them from thinking him to be much older. "Someday I will be able to do it, to write in the right way from the beginning, to change people. I just need to keep learning and trying."

"And speaking of learning, kiddo, I was talking with Dr. Cahners today while you were in school. He doesn't think the school should move you ahead a grade, but he's fine with you taking pre-calc and chemistry next year."

"What about the English classes I want to take, American Literature and Introduction to the Short Story?"

"He didn't say anything about those. I'll ask him. I think he really wants to see you keep with the science and math." Toni scratched at his left eyebrow. "Me, too. Your MCAS math scores have been so good. Ninety-ninth percentile."

"So were my language arts and reading comprehension scores."

"Well, yeah. I guess you're one smart kid. And it's time to wash your hands for supper."

"Nonno Toni, can I ask you something?"

"Sure. Anything, kiddo."

"Why do you think everybody pushes me into the STEM areas?"

Toni sucked air through his teeth. "What do you mean? I don't think anybody pushes you into anything."

"You know what I mean. They do, even you."

"We all just want you to be a success, to live up to your potential. I was going to be an engineer, you know, but I got into construction to support my family after my father was killed by a drunk driver. He wasn't supposed to be on the road—just out running an errand for a friend at work. The driver of the other pickup was a serial offender who kept getting let off from one 'dee-wee' after another. I was the oldest, at UMass-Lowell, about to start my senior year, but I never showed up for classes that year, just started with my uncle's construction company. You have chances that I didn't have. That's all."

"What about Dr. Cahners? Did he want to be an engineer, too?"

"I really don't know. Why don't you ask him next time you see him?"

"Yeah, next month. And he'll say something like you did, something about my potential, my innate abilities. And why am I seeing him next month, anyway? He makes home visits to check up on me. That's not normal. Other kids, the kids at school, they go to the doctor's once a year for a checkup or maybe when they're sick. Their doctors don't come to their houses four times a year."

"We got good medical coverage, that's all."

"Is it?" Paolo's eyes narrowed. "What's wrong with me? Why do they do the brain scans every year? Why is everybody so quick to call Dr. Cahners? I can hardly sneeze without Nonna Seppina reaching for the phone."

"Come now, it's not *that* bad."

"No, not quite, but it feels that way. What's wrong with me, Nonno Toni? Was I born with something messed up that you are not telling me about? Look, I'm going to be twelve. I can tell that everyone is in on something I don't know about. But I can take the truth."

"I bet you can."

"Tell me about my mother and father."

"You know the story." Toni's left eye began to twitch. "Your mother was our daughter, Carla. She was killed, in a car crash, just before you were born. She was on her way here. She ... she wasn't wearing a seatbelt and ..."

"What was she like?"

"Independent, single-minded, quick to jump from one lily pad to another, beautiful ... and brave. Knowing her, she would have been all fired up and ready to raise you on her own. She would have loved you so."

"You never say anything about my father."

"What can I say?"

"The truth."

"There's nothing much to say about your father. He left your mother. I met him only once, before the two of them ran off to chase some dream in Italy. He was a jerk, a handsome, charming, self-absorbed jerk. But that's not you. You're nothing like him. You don't even look like him, except that you look Italian. You're our grandson, that's what matters."

"What was my father's name?"

"Orlando."

"Orlando who?"

"I don't remember. Really. Russo, or something like that. There was only that one time. I didn't like him, and I could read heartbreak in the tealeaves right from the get-go. I tried to persuade Carla, but she was too starry-eyed and oppositional. Nothing we said mattered. It went in one ear and straight to the recycle bin."

Paolo laughed.

"What's funny, kiddo?"

"I was picturing this word balloon going into her ear and being dragged to a little trashcan icon."

"That is funny, kiddo. Now wash up for dinner."

"I will, Nonno Toni, in a minute. First, I want to start on this new story I just thought of."

○ ○ ○

"Scrape your boots and leave them by the door." Mud season, New England's annual interlude between winter and summer, had arrived early. Paolo shed his boots and crossed the kitchen to thrust the two-page form toward his grandmother. "What's this?" she said.

"Some form for the school, so I can play soccer."

"You want to play soccer now? Why now, all of a sudden?"

"It's spring. Soccer is a spring sport."

"But, I mean, I didn't know you were interested in sports."

"I didn't either, but I figure, you know, why not? I mean, how do I know what I'm good at if I don't try? Right?"

"Have you talked with Dr. Cahners about this?"

"No, why should I. I'm just trying stuff. Trying to figure it out. I mean, do you ever wonder who you are, like why you are here?"

"Sure, and I figure I'm here because of you."

"I didn't mean like that."

"None of us know why we were put here, Paolo, but we try to figure it out: who we are and what God intended for us to do."

"Well, I'm just starting with who I am. God will have to wait."

Her flash of disapproval melted quickly into a warm smile as she put out her arms. "It's you, my cheeky boy, who will have to wait. God has his own timetable."

Chapter 9

Sherrod sat next to Bernat on the sofa. "So, you are a reporter, Danny. And what are you reporting on?"

"I'm a journalist, yes, doing a story on Arturo Dermott for the centennial of his birth in 1926."

"Dermott. Is that the Dermott of Dermott Technologies, S.A.?"

"Yes, that Dermott. Also Dermott, Gmbh. and Telemedia Dermott and Dermott Industries Holding and the A. F. Dermott Foundation—the list goes on."

"I do not know much about the man. I read that he died some time ago."

"Yes, nearly twenty years ago. He was in his eighties and working eighty-hour weeks, as if he were some youngster still building a career."

"He was an engineer or something, right?"

"Engineer, inventor, entrepreneur. As an old man he styled himself a scientist—without the training and without ever doing much that resembled what I would call ordinary science. As I read it, he had no need for research. According to Abelman, his unauthorized biographer, Dermott would sometimes look at a thing, grasp it as a whole in less time than it would take an ordinary person to turn it over, then retire to his workshop. In a week or a year of work in near isolation, he would emerge from his retreat, bringing with him something new on the face of the planet. A gearless transmission, a lensless camera: whatever it was, it was almost invariably revolutionary—and very profitable. More than once his work brought ruin to established paradigms in physics or electronics or information science. Edison is always cited as the quintessential inventor, but Dermott had more than double the number of patents."

"Why don't we hear more about him, then?"

"He was a recluse, some would say a misanthrope. He avoided people and the spotlight as much as a billionaire many times over might manage. And he was very secretive. As a child, his special gift for the technical abetted his social isolation. Not only were his intellect and his mechanical abilities far above those of his peers, but his social skills were commensurately below. He seems to have been the consummate nerdy geek. People made no sense to him. Sense was found only in objects, and he failed miserably at almost every personal relationship he ever entered. That said, he was not without friends, but they must have been a special breed who could cherish and tolerate him despite his legendary insensitivity."

"Did he ever marry?"

"Twice. And according to the spate of supposedly tell-all memoirs after his death, there had been lovers—of both sexes. Women, older women especially, were drawn to him: some by his intellect, some by what may have seemed an aloof charm, others by their own needs to mother a sad, mad genius. Few stayed with him for long, and the marriages, both to much older women, were short, fruitless encounters made bitter by lengthy and costly divorces."

"Sounds like just the sort of guy to invite to a party. Not."

"I wouldn't know. He died before I graduated from college, so I never got to interview him. In fact, he gave only one interview in his lifetime, not long after he made his first billion. The reporter from the BBC savaged him. That was it for Arturo. Even the spokespersons for his many companies became known as Dermott's No-Comment Detail."

"And what exactly brings you here, to lovely Valencia in the not so lovely off-season?"

"Bernat is helping me translate a document. And I had hoped he could help me find this doctor, Manuel Fonseca y Morales, but he is dead, I hear."

"Ah, but his son is very much alive. A singer. He goes by the stage name Fernando Fernandez."

"How do you know this?"

"We were lovers ... before I met Bernat. He told me about when he was working in Italy, doing research, working under his father."

"But I thought Fonseca y Morales was also gay."

"Yes. And he had a son. So? I am gay and I have a son. There are many ways these days."

Chapter 10

To no one's surprise, Paolo did not find his true self on the soccer field. He stubbornly stuck it out through the season, but with the end of school, he returned to his fixation on writing. When Seppina insisted he get more fresh air, he would move to the screened-in gazebo in the back yard and continue writing. He was hardly an outdoorsman.

That summer before Paulo turned thirteen, we sent him to a summer science camp. He had been angling to go to a sleep-away camp for several years, but we were reluctant to let him out of our sight and fearful for what might happen to him. Many of his peers had spent part of their summers in Northern New England, either because their parents were wealthy enough to afford it or poor enough to qualify for financial aid.

The science camp struck us as a perfect compromise. It had fewer physical challenges than the typical outdoor adventure program, and it suited our agenda to steer him toward science and engineering. For four weeks, he would be surrounded by geeks, immersed in advanced STEM subjects, and lectured by professors from the nearby university that sponsored the camp and staffed it with regular students.

Sandwiched between coursework and laboratory experiments would be swimming and crafts and supervised nature hikes. Even the latter had a scientific twist, with an emphasis on identifying flora and fauna and collecting edible wild plants. The clever crafts component included laboratory glass blowing, computer art, and *knot tying coupled with studies in topology. It was perfect for our purposes.*

There was no way any of us could accompany him without blowing our cover, but we threw in a generous donation to the university and had a private chat with the headmaster of the camp about our concern for our shy and sheltered boy. The camp leaders reassured us that they would keep an extra close eye on him and would make sure nothing happened to him. Still, it was handwringing and nailbiting for us in the intervals between his irregular notes sent home by way of the official camp messaging portal on the Web.

The rest of the hikers were already around the curve in the woodland trail. Chrissy grabbed Paolo's hand from behind as it swung back and whispered sotto voce. "What do you say? Let's take the long way home."

"But they'll check. They'll notice we're gone."

"Der. I'm the sweep. They trust me to make sure nobody's left behind. By the time they figure it out when they stagger into camp, we'll be nearly around the mountain. We'll come in the backside and ask them what took them so long. I'll make up some story or other." She tugged. "Come on, follow me. Quick."

"I don't know. I ..."

"Come on. You're not afraid, are you?"

"No."

"Then let's go." She ducked under a low branch and pushed through several feet of scrub underbrush before emerging onto a weed-choked fire road. "See. All we do is follow this and we're fine." She took his hand again and gave it a squeeze.

Paolo liked the fact that Chrissy always seemed to know exactly what she wanted and had a way of getting it nearly every time. He knew she was interested in him—it was obvious from the way she looked at him and always managed to be on the same team when they played Techno Trivia or were volunteering for cleanup detail. The most obvious was the time at the swimming pool when, just as he reached the far wall, she dove off the high board and managed to come up beside him with her bikini top slipping. She squealed, took a panic breath, and dove under again as she pulled the strap back up over her shoulder, but he knew it was no accident. That night, he dreamed of that one brown nipple almost within reach and awoke with his pajama bottoms damp and sticky.

Of course, neither of them said anything about the encounter in the pool. He knew what was expected of him. It had never happened. Still, he would keep catching her following him with her eyes.

The unshaded fire road was baked by the afternoon sun. "Do you have any water left?" she asked.

"Sure." He unhooked a camp-issued orange water bottle from his belt and handed it to her.

"You can be rather stingy with words," she said, smiling. She took a swig of water, then tipped the bottle above her head and let it splash over her face and down the front of her tee-shirt. Her nipples stood out like dark pencil erasers through the wet fabric. Along with the other boys, Paolo had been pleased to notice the trend that arrived with the August heat wave. With no mothers to nag them, many of the girls had taken to going bra-less. He pretended to be suddenly interested in the surrounding trees but kept stealing glances toward her chest.

"It's so friggin' hot." She tugged at the neck of her shirt, pulling it away from her breasts. "Here, hold this." She handed the water bottle back to him, untucked her tee-shirt, and grabbed the hem. For a moment, Paolo thought she was going to take it off, but she twisted the cloth into two handles and tied them loosely just below her breasts.

"That's better." She noticed him watching. "What are you thinking?"

Paolo knew full well she would not want a straight answer. "Nothing."

"Nothing? Really? That's the best you can come up with?"

She was skating along the edge with him, and he knew it. Neither a lie nor the truth would be acceptable. "I was thinking, thinking ... how pretty you are." Pretty. That seemed the right word: not too open and not dishonest.

"You're pretty cute yourself." She took a step toward him and gave him a quick peck, just long enough to leave his lips tingling and his ears reddening. "Come on. You better come up with a few more words if you want to keep up with me. Or don't you like words?"

"Like words? I love words. Yes, love. Words are the music of the mind, the angels of the intellect, the bearers of meaning and intent between beings."

"Wow, did you just make that up?"

"No, not really. It's from a story I wrote. It was a long time ago, not very good, really."

"That was beautiful. You write stories? OMG. Could I read some of them? I absolutely love reading. I'm always reading. I read on my Kindle after lights-out here."

"Me, too. I mean reading. Especially science fiction. Classics. Philip K. Dick, Theodore Sturgeon, Ursula Le Guin, writers who really understood people. I love that. I have a Kindle, but I didn't think to use it after lights-out."

"Just turn the screen way down and get under your covers. Are you on a top bunk?" He nodded. "That's good. Harder for the counselors to spot what you're doing. Our cabin queen—what we call our counselor—she snores like a freight train. We could be screwing in one of the top bunks, and she wouldn't hear it."

Paolo tried unsuccessfully to hide his embarrassment. She smiled at him and shook her head. "You are kind of a goody-goody boy, aren't you."

"I guess." He couldn't think of what else to say. He knew what the old expression meant and knew that it fit him. "I'm sorry. I hope we can still be friends."

"I hope we can be more than friends, my Paolo, my Pauli boy. You know what they say, you never forget your first Pauli boy." He looked confused but she figured it was hopeless to try and explain the badly dated reference that she only knew because of her stepfather. She ran a finger down his cheek as it turned crimson. "Now, I want to show you something. Try and keep up." She started up the road at a trot, then suddenly veered off to the right through the trees. He caught up with her at the edge of a drop-off where part of the hillside had collapsed years earlier, stranding a struggling maple with its roots partially exposed on the edge of an earthen cliff. "Beautiful, huh?" She pulled him down beside her.

Paolo looked over the edge and down the ravine below, his heart pounding. "And ... you're beautiful, Chrissy." A Celtic drum boomed in his ears, the deafening thuds of his own heartbeat.

She wiggled over next to him and turned to put her arms around his neck. "And you are the sweetest, smartest boy here." She kissed him, then pulled back. "Here." She untied the bottom of her tee-shirt and took his hand.

Paolo wrestled with excitement that threatened to turn into panic as they kissed and touched. They both jumped at the cry of a crow. Paolo caught his breath. "I ... I never did this before."

"I knew that." She ran a fingertip over his lips. "Me neither. Believe that? I'm fourteen and never been felt up ... before."

"You're fourteen? I'm—"

"Thirteen, nearly. I know. You're in Alpha Group. So, I guess

I'm robbing the cradle. But I think you are way more mature than any of the boys in my group. And the Gamma boys can be so gross. You know what I mean? Anyway, we should be getting back." She stood, brushed herself off, and tucked her tee-shirt back into her hiking shorts. "You won't ... you won't say anything about this, will you? I mean ... to the other boys."

"Of course not. I'd never want to hurt you." He inched away from the edge. "If you give me your address I'll send you some of my stories at the end of the summer."

"I'd like that." She kissed him again, pressing herself against him. "Let's go back."

He was wondering whether that was possible, to go back, and what it would be like for the last week of the camp session, but he said nothing as he followed her, his eyes never leaving the ponytailed vision that marched ahead of him.

That night, he wrote a long entry in the latest incarnation of the bound notebooks that Nonna Seppina kept supplying whenever he needed another. And he read from his carefully dimmed Kindle while the others in his cabin snored and tossed and turned.

Chapter 11

Fernando Fernandez finished his folky jazz set at the wine bar and approached their table. He leaned his guitar against a painted pillar entwined with trompe l'oeil grapevines. "Sherrod told me to say hello." He pulled an empty chair from the adjacent table, spun it around, and sat down with his legs crossed at the ankles and his hands in his lap. "He said that you wanted to interview me."

"Well, talk with you—I wouldn't call it an interview." Danny set down his glass.

"Is this about the musical or about the arrest? You should know, the charges were dropped."

Danny snorted a quick laugh. "Neither. I'd like to know something about your work in Italy. And about your father."

"My father. Well, fuck that." Fernando uncrossed his legs and grabbed the edge of the table. "I don't talk about him, not anymore. I'm done with that, that whole business."

"And what business was that?"

"I think you heard me." He pushed himself and the chair back from the table.

"Okay, then have a drink with us. This is Francesca, my Italian friend."

She held out her hand across the table; he kissed it. "Charmed," he said. "From where in Italy?"

"Roma. And you? Where did you work in Italy?"

"Roma, mostly."

"Ah, yes, the Eternal City."

"Eternally corrupt, at least."

"How long were you there?"

"Long enough to learn that I didn't like the city, didn't like the people, and despised the work."

"Ah," she said, "I see. You were then perhaps working as one of the *netturbini?*"

"No, I was not a garbage collector, except maybe in the most metaphorical sense. I was a laboratory technician. Tissue cultures, analysis of biological specimens, that sort of thing. We did generate a lot of bio-hazard waste, true, but we simply flushed it into the sewer, since what we were doing was forbidden. It was my father's work, not mine. He was the doctor, the scientist; I was just another of the many people he used on the way to his goal. And when he reached it, he had no more use for any of us. Then he retired here."

"When was that?"

"2009, I think, maybe later. But I am talking too much, my lady. If the drink is still on offer, I'll take *Artadi, Viña El Pisón*, the 2023."

"Is it good?"

"The best Rioja in all of Spain."

"Then let's order a bottle. I adore Rioja."

Fernando laughed and leaned back in his chair and waved toward the bar. "José, my friends would like a bottle of the '23 *Viña El Pisón*."

"Sí, coming right away."

○ ○ ○

The second bottle was nearly empty, as were the uncollected tapas plates. Danny shook his head. "Wow, this is truly the most amazing Rioja I have ever had. Thanks for the recommendation. By the way, Fernando, do you also speak Catalan?"

"Valencian, yes: a dialect, except to the purists on either side of the divide."

"What would you make of this." He passed over a printed copy of the image off eBay.

Fernando studied it. "I would make it to be drunken nonsense. But it may be me who is the drunken one." He drained his glass. "No, wait. The signature. I know this one. It is Arturo Dermott."

"How do you know it?"

"I knew him. He was our boss. Also our benefactor. Boss and benefactor. On the project. He devised the stereo ... the stereo toxic ... no, the micro-manipulators that we used with the ... the cells ... the ... I forget the word. I ..." He slumped over with his head on the table, knocking over his empty wine glass. Danny grabbed for it, but only managed to push it over the edge. Francesca swept her arm around and caught it before it hit the floor. "Save!" she shouted, like an announcer at a soccer match.

"Good hands, there. Were you a goalkeeper?"

"I was. But it looks like we aren't going to learn any more from our singer friend tonight."

"I'll tell José at the bar and get the check. You try to make him comfortable."

Francesca tucked his guitar into a safer place against the wall and moved the last dishes to the other side of the table. Suddenly there was a shout from across the room.

"Oh my God! You gotta be kidding! No!"

When Danny returned, he was tucking his wallet back into his pants pocket. "What was that all about?" she asked.

"Do you know what he did? Our reluctant informant stiffed us for a five-hundred euro tab. The wine he ordered, it was over two-hundred euros a bottle."

Chapter 12

Paolo returned from that first summer camp a changed person. He remained indifferent toward math and science—despite straight As and standardized test scores in the top percentile—and continued to read voraciously and write with passionate dedication, but the focus of his passion had been redirected. Instead of short stories and novellas, he wrote letters: handwritten, filled with ardor and intellect, and delivered in envelopes with actual postage stamps and cancellations. He wrote to the Chrissy of his first summer romance and later to a succession of girls and girlfriends. They all loved it, this quaintly extended expression of attention and affection that contrasted so dramatically to the abrupt and misspelled texting of the other boys their age.

We had long anticipated when he would discover girls, but adolescence was proving to be less a challenge for Paolo than for us. Now there seemed no end to the queue of mostly older girls ready to hang on his every word and give their all to our quiet and once-hesitant boy.

Paolo carried epistolary romance to a new level. He would almost literally live in the attic for weeks on end, emerging for meals, school, and to run to the toilet two flights down, but otherwise spending his waking hours—and some of his sleeping hours—in his office. With climate change extending the August heat well into October, we paid to have an air conditioner installed. With Giuseppina more and more often finding him writing late into the night, then struggling to rise in the morning, she had Toni set up a cot for him, and we paid for renovations to put in a skylight angled to the east.

We could do even more, of course: build an addition to the house, convert the gazebo in the back to a freestanding apartment, even move the Franzettis to a bigger and better house, but we risked over-playing our hand and drawing too much attention to them—and to us.

This was the strategic ridgeline we walked: a freefall tumble down the sloping scree on one side should we fail to step in as needed or a precipitous plunge on the other should we play the remote control too tightly. We checked up on and came to know nearly all the girls who had joined his fan club and surreptitiously vetted them as best we could.

During that freshman year, he began, on rare occasion, to bring a girl home to meet his grandparents. More often, he would be invited for dinner or a weekend with some family at their cottage on Sebago Lake or in Connecticut, and we would hold our breaths. We had contingency measures at the ready should he ever "get serious" too early, or worse, get some girl pregnant. The latter, in a sense, would be more straightforward to deal with, and we were prepared to un-derwrite an abortion—an obvious necessity, needless to say—and to fund a substantial bribe if need be.

A second summer at science camp passed with only one passing romance. We were relieved, but we underestimated him, of course. We still didn't understand how he worked, but he largely knew what his parents and I were up to regarding his companions.

Paolo sat in the clinic office and played with the tiny volume bead on his Bluetooth earbuds. "You don't like Sosamma, do you, doc."

"What makes you think that?"

"I heard you talking with Nonna."

"You did? Well, I didn't say I didn't like Sosamma, but you do have to admit that her gothic pose—"

"Goth, not gothic. It's just a thing some kids go through. It's come back, you know, goth, the whole emo trip. Serious, all dark and serious. That's all it is. She's fun to be with, streams good music. We're going to an all-ages concert Friday night. Tessa Freedman is opening for Graphene Promises. I may not do the pose, as you put it, but I do hear the message. Some of their lyrics are, like, pretty deep."

"Don't you have SATs coming up?"

"Yeah, Saturday morning. No big deal. I'll ace them, like every other test. I think I have a knack for that kind of thing."

"Maybe, but I wouldn't encourage complacency. You need your sleep. And you need to save some of your hearing for when you grow up. Those rock concerts—"

"I can hear you just fine, doc. And I know what's going down. You check up on every girl you hear about. Nonna and Nonno copy down the return addresses on every letter I get, and I know the call log on my smartphone—the phone you gave me—is tracked."

"We're just looking out for you."

"I know, that's what you say, maybe even what you believe, but you can stop now. I don't need it. And you're not my parents. Neither are they. They're just my grandparents, and, truth, I'm beginning to doubt whether we're actually related. Where did I come from, anyway?"

"From your mother's tummy"—he winked—"like I told you last time you asked, when you were four."

"Ha ha. LOL, as they used to say. I just want you all to stop always looking over my shoulder. I'm not some stupid kid, you know."

"No, but the same cannot be said for some of those you hang out with."

"That's not fair. I—"

"What about Sosamma? She's still in middle school, she gets C's and D's, and her parents live on the top floor of a triple-decker in—"

"You're a racist, doc. You know that? And prejudiced. She's actually a year older because she lost more than a year when her family got out of Syria. She's plenty smart and could get better grades, but she still struggles with English and her teachers are prejudiced—like you. Besides, it's not all about just brains anyway."

"No, it's not." Cahners wanted to congratulate Paolo on the pushback, but he just smiled. "I think your grandparents are just concerned about what sort of a match you might make."

"Match? You gotta be kidding. I just turned fifteen, and—"

"And you're in high school and she's still in—"

"—and this is no Game of Thrones. I can pick my own friends. Sosamma is just a friend. Got it?"

"Got it. Anything else you want to talk about?"

"Yeah. When are you going to tell me the real story? And no bullshit or answering a question with a question. When?"

"What if there's no real story to be told?"

Paolo stood and leaned both palms on the desk between them. "There you go again. Screw this. I'll figure it out on my own. I can find out for sure whether the Franzettis are my real grandparents. I'll use one of those DNA services."

"You'll do what?"

"I can use, like, iGenTree.com. They have a DNA database and can find matches."

"You have to be twenty-one to—"

"Der. You think they check? I can put Seppina in, under a pseudonym, check for a mitochondrial match there."

"Just how reliable do you think those public testing laboratories are?"

"More reliable than what you tell me."

"You don't trust me?"

"No, I do trust you; I just don't believe you. I assume you have, like, no choice. There must be some confidentiality agreement connected with the adoption."

"That's what you think, that you're adopted? Well, you are. The Franzettis adopted you, their grandson. And, you would also know that before any records could be unsealed, if there were any, you'd have to be an adult."

"Three years, doc. Another three years and I can legally take you to court."

Dr. Cahners laughed quietly. "That won't be necessary, Paolo. You'll see."

Chapter 13

After seeing Francesca off on her evening return flight to Rome, Danny returned from the airport to find Bernat still in the extra bedroom that was now his studio, chipping away at a massive block of wood that was slowly becoming his latest soft-porn sculpture. "I need your help, Bernat."

"With what?"

"With digging into public records."

"I thought you were the journalist. That's your job, exposing crime and corruption buried in papers and files; mine is exposing the erotic beauty hidden in blocks of wood."

"Very poetic, Bernat, but I need your fluency in Spanish, Catalan, and Valencian. And your general brilliance."

"Oh, flattery. With me it works every time. Okay, we can set up in the living room. Let me grab my laptop from the bedroom."

o o o

Danny looked over at Bernat, finger on the touchpad of his laptop, scrolling through files. "It's like being back in college, roommates again, studying through the night for the test in the morning."

Bernat shook his head slowly. "No it's not. At Columbia, I had the hots for you so bad.'

"Really? No, you're kidding."

"Truth. I lived for those moments when you'd finish showering and casually let your towel drop before you pulled on clean boxers. I fantasized about you when you were out on a date while I stayed back to lie in bed and—"

"Okay, enough oversharing already. I get it. I didn't realize. If you'd rather not ... if it's too awkward, I mean, working with me, we don't have to ..."

"Relax. I got over you long ago. You were just one of many heartbreaks along my long road to Sherrod."

"You two are good? It works?"

"Best thing that ever happened to me—before Feliu came into my life."

"Whose son is he?"

"Ours."

"I meant who's the father?"

"Biologically? Who knows, we mixed our sperm. The donor egg was the contribution of this amazing pre-op transgender man we both know and love. He is so sweet, too. Pity he's one-hundred percent hetero."

"Wait a minute, let me get this straight. My brain is doing somersaults. This man, who was born female, goes for women. Wouldn't it be easier for her, I mean him, just to be a lesbian. It could have saved a lot on medical bills."

"But he's not a lesbian. He's just a regular heterosexual guy who was trapped in a female body, at least until he completes all the surgery. He's already got the beard and the biceps. Oh, he is gorgeous. If I weren't the faithful spouse, I would be tempted."

"I hope you don't get me wrong. I'm cool with it, just a little gob smacked by some of the emerging complexities of the modern gender spectrum. I mean, like, the fifty-plus gender options on Facebook. Is there a term for a woman who was a man but then changes her mind and decides she is a man after all?"

"Tragically mixed-up, maybe. I don't know. The very thought just makes me sad, not knowing who you are, thinking you have it figured out, then finding out you were wrong all along. Or is it *right* all along?"

"In a way, some of that applies to most of us: thinking we know who we are until we find out otherwise." Danny took a loud breath. "My own life has been one of perpetually discovering that I was wrong. Then I figure it out, then I realize I was mistaken. Isn't that life?"

"Maybe. Not for me. I knew I was a sculptor the first time I got my hands on modeling clay in preschool, and I figured out I was gay when I had my first boner at ten skinny dipping with my scout troop. This is what I am, a gay sculptor, and I have never doubted."

"I envy you that certainty. Well, I do know that I'm hetero, I know I like writing, although not so much what I have been writing in recent years. However, in some sense, I'm still trying to figure out what I'm going to do when I grow up."

"There's your mistake, my friend. Solve the problem the same way I did: don't grow up."

"Easy for you to say, old friend. You were born into money and married it as well. Sherrod keeps you very nicely."

"Catty. But true. Doesn't mean I don't love him with all my heart and all my hard-on. But who's to say it won't work out for you? Some wealthy widow could walk into your life tomorrow."

"Not very likely. Far worse, I think I may be falling for a married gypsy girl with black eyes and a quick mind and a quicker body. If she had her way, she would have mounted me in that café in Rome on our first lunch date. As is, I barely made it with my clothes still on by the time we stepped off the hotel elevator that afternoon."

"Yes, that side of her she made clear from the beginning."

"Speaking of from the beginning, what did she whisper to you that made you blush?"

"Whisper? Blush? Oh, that. Nothing really."

"Nothing? You turned red as a raspberry."

"Well, I shouldn't tell, now, should I, but ... she said something about the three of us. I told her you would never agree to a threesome." Bernat fiddled with his ear as his face flushed. "She is married, right? What about her husband."

"He's a federal policeman."

"Oh, you are screwed." He turned back to his screen and let out a yelp. "You should see this."

"What is it?"

"It's from an old local newspaper, no longer publishing, with a brief note on extradition proceedings against our deceased doctor and his son, wanted in Italy on charges of human trafficking, animal cruelty, unlawful medical procedures, distribution of illicit drugs. It's a litany of malfeasance, as they say.

"Your mastery of English is impressive. Where did you get that expression from."

"A course in criminal law at Columbia."

"Don't bullshit me. You never studied criminal law."

"Okay, I remembered it from an American television show."

"What ever happened to the extradition?"

"Apparently nothing, considering the doctor didn't die in an Italian jail and his son is a cabaret singer. Let me check for anything about this in Italy."

"You can do that?"

"Why do you think they called it the World Wide Web? And I can read Italian—mostly." He squinted in concentration for several minutes as Danny tried to act busy. "This is interesting."

"What did you find?"

"Nothing. That's what's interesting. There should be some hits: public records, news accounts, something. I mean, I'll keep digging, but this is odd, like things have been erased. You're more the technology guy than me. Can something be erased from the Web? Is that possible?"

"I suppose, possible in principle but extremely difficult in practice. You'd have to be the GCHQ with all their programming prodigies and supercomputers. Or be super-rich, like ..." His mouth hung open.

"Like Arturo Fabian Dermott." Bernat finished the sentence.

Chapter 14

Years ahead of the hundredth anniversary of Dermott's birth, we started planning, strategizing how we would handle the exposure. In the run-up, we learned, through the tendrils of a security force whose methods were a mystery, that a large number of publications were working on feature stories. We wanted to be ready to deal with the potential fallout. Most of the journalists were relying on public sources, previous writing, and the occasional odd interview here or there. A couple of cable channels were putting together specials that would end up as visual spectaculars focused mostly on the inventions and their industrial impact. A few reporters had already approached media relations at one or more of the stable of better-known Dermott corporations, unaware they were surveying a deceptive landscape: the archipelago of islands at the top of a massive undersea mountain range. None of them had dived far enough to reach us in the benthic depths. We were confident that their researches could take them only so far, and we were told by security teams in Rome and Macao that impediments were ready to put in place were any of them to burrow too deep.

That autumn, an extended heatwave would not let go. It hung on through the last weeks of October bringing with it complaints about government inaction on climate change along with out-of-season beach days followed by a sudden stream of uncharacteristic storms. Boston-area temperatures were soaring to new records, reaching the mid-eighties with thunderstorms on Halloween before dipping to something closer to a seasonal high in the low sixties the following week. Tropical storms that never became full-blown hurricanes still skittered up the coast without either intensifying or fully tapering off. Felled trees blocking roads or creasing car tops were becoming common sights in the aftermath of a string of windstorms.

While we made other plans that fall, life happened.

With the windows all open and the box fan humming, Seppina lay awake, anxiously listening to the howl and whistle of the gusts through the trees in front of the house. The street was lined with mature maples, now leafless, and the front lawn was guarded by two fir trees and a pin oak that stubbornly horded the last of its tanned-leather leaves. Tony, who slept soundly through even the worst thunderstorm, awoke at the crack and crash when the white pine in the back yard finally uprooted and toppled, full force, against the roof.

"What was that?" He sat up, blinking in the dark, heart racing.

"I don't know. Something crashed." Seppina scrunched up against him.

He patted her arm. "I'll go see if I can find out. Where's Paolo sleeping?"

"He may still be in his office; he was still writing when I got up for some warm milk."

"Oh, shi ..." He stopped himself. He knew Seppina didn't approve, but sometimes cursing just came out, and sometimes it even seemed justified. "You better go check his bedroom while I see what I can see." He put on his slippers, pulled on the plaid bathrobe that hung on the back of the closet door, and fished around for the flashlight he kept under the bed. "Sounded like it came from out back."

Toni went downstairs without turning on the light. Shuffling in the slippers that never quite fit, he swung the flashlight in a short arc to expose a wider path. In the kitchen, wind was whistling through the old cat door that predated their move into the house and that he had never gotten around to completely sealing off. He slid back the bolt and opened the door to the porch. A blast of damp air slapped him as he looked up to see the tree trunk now slicing through the porch roof. His flashlight beam tracked the trunk upward and his mind projected to where it would intersect the main roof. He swore again.

"Paolo!" He kept calling as he scrambled up the back stairs directly to the attic. "Paolo! Paolo, are you all right?" Just short of the landing, his right foot came out of the slipper, it went flying, and he went down hard, face first.

○ ○ ○

"Oh my God. Please no, God." She found Toni at the bottom of the back stairs with Paolo bent over him.

"I think he's okay, Nonna."

"But he's bleeding."

"Looks like scrapes from sliding down the stairs. I don't have my cellphone. Call Dr. Cahners, Nonna."

"Maybe we should call an ambulance."

"No. Call Dr. Cahners. Tell him what happened; he can call the ambulance if necessary. I'll take care of Nonno."

By the time Seppina came back to tell him that the doctor was on the way, Toni was coming to. Paolo had already bandaged a cut on his forehead and was using a gauze pad and rubbing alcohol to clean a bad scrape on his arm. Seppina pushed the handset toward Paolo. "It's Dr. Cahners. He wants to talk to you."

"I thought you said he was on his way."

"He is." She pressed the speaker button on the handset.

"Hi, Paolo, I want you to help me." It was a tinny version of Dr. Cahner's voice. "Can you give me Toni's vitals?"

"Sure. Hang on me a minute." He placed his fingers at Toni's neck as he kept an eye on his wrist watch, then took his hand away and kept watching. "Okay. His respiration is forty-four, heartrate seventy-six, BP unknown. Sorry, we don't have a cuff."

"That's okay. Is he awake?"

"More or less."

"Can you check his pupils?"

Paolo picked up the flashlight where Toni had dropped it. For each eye in turn, he gently held the eyelid up as he expertly flicked the beam in and out. "Pupils are even and responsive."

"Toni! This is Dr. Cahners. Can you hear me, Toni? Are you all right? Can you hear me?"

"Yeah, doc. But my ears are ringing and you sound funny, like over the phone."

They all laughed. "I am over the phone. Can you tell me if anything is broken? Can you move your arms and legs?"

"I can try. Oops, that hurts. That, too. And that hurts like hell. There. Legs and arms are still working, doc, but it kills when I try to move my right arm."

"That's the one that has rather severe laceration on the lateral forearm," Paolo added. "Might be a fracture."

"Okay, good job, Paolo. Keep him still. Put a pillow on each side of his head and a blanket over him. I'll be there in two minutes, three at the outside." The phone disconnected.

Toni lifted his head. "Where'd you learn all that stuff, kiddo? That was pretty impressive."

"At SciTech Camp this summer. We all learned first aid and basic emergency medical stuff."

"Maybe you ought to consider being a doctor."

"Maybe."

◦ ◦ ◦

Dr. Cahners had Toni admitted to the hospital for observation.

After the CAT scan of his head and x-rays of the arm came out negative, he was released in the morning. The storm had done widespread damage throughout Greater Boston. It took several days before a crew could come out to cut up and chip the fallen tree, then another week before the construction crew arrived to repair and re-shingle the porch roof. The repairs were all covered by the Franzettis' homeowners insurance, of course—yet another perk provided by the Foundation.

The day after Thanksgiving, Paolo came into the kitchen fiddling with the chinstrap of his bicycle helmet. "Can I go over to the Zecharya's, Nonna? Sosamma texted me, and I think she needs somebody to talk to."

"Okay, but be back before it gets dark. And watch out for fallen tree branches. Put that Velcro thingy around the bottom of your jeans."

"Nonna, please. I know all that."

"And remember to turn on your rear flasher."

"It's broad daylight, Nonna."

"Still a good idea."

○ ○ ○

When he arrived, Sosamma was sitting on the front stoop of her building staring at the pedestal birdbath to one side of the entrance. She was an unlikely goth, with naturally black hair and a Mediterranean complexion even darker than his. She didn't turn or say anything as Paolo leaned his bike against a tree, but as he approached, she suddenly crossed her arms, tucking her hands and wrists deep under her armpits. He sat beside her on the steps. "You okay?"

She shrugged.

"Wanna talk about it?" She shook her head. "Okay, let me guess. Del, again?"

"What makes you say that?"

"Just the way you look. You've been crying."

"What makes you say that?"

"Look in a mirror. You've got mascara streaks decorating your cheeks. I doubt you are trying to start a new makeup trend among your goth friends."

She wiped at her cheeks, only spreading the streaks into a messier pattern.

He gently grabbed her wrist and slipped the sleeve of her sweater farther back. "What's this? What have you been doing?" There were fresh gashes on the inside of her left forearm. "You think cutting yourself is going to make it better? Will that get Del back?"

"No." It was said so weakly that Paolo could barely hear. "But this kinda pain is … well, easier, simpler. It's sharp and quick and takes my mind off the rest of the pain in my life."

"A lot of pain in your life, huh. Besides Del, what else?"

"My father." She pulled her hair back to show a lump and a fresh scab in front of her ear. "My mother. Always on my case. 'Nice girls don't dress that way. Nice girls don't talk that way. Good Christian girls don't talk with boys they don't know.' And all the kids at school hate me. They call me Iraqi Wacky or Bin Laden's girlfriend. They think I'm Muslim."

"What about your friends?"

"What friends? Tina and Vanessa are the ones who've been slut-shaming me, telling everyone I sleep around, that I'm easy. That's all Del was interested in. He's, like, coming on to me, pushing. He goes, 'Everyone knows you spread for everyone else. Why won't you put out for me?' Stuff like that. "I told him I don't put out for nobody and not for him, then he slaps me and starts tearing at my clothes."

"And that's a reason to hurt yourself? Wouldn't it make more sense to let him be the one who's hurting?"

"What are you talking about. How?"

"You could dump him, you know. Or report him. You tell me he keeps acting like a jerk. You keep taking him back. What's that about?"

She looked up at him and started to cry. He pulled her over and hugged her.

"I'm ugly. I'm stupid. Who would ever want me?" She sobbed as he stroked her back. "And I can't figure this country out. I wish I were back in Aleppo."

"Right, Aleppo, where the last handful of Syrian Christians in the whole country are being killed off. Good idea. That way you could let somebody else do the cutting." He ran a finger across his throat.

She hit him playfully. "You! I'm serious."

"Of course you are. That's why you have to try so hard to keep from laughing."

"You do that with me, all the time, get me to see something in a way to laugh at it." She sniffled. "You think I should sleep with Del?"

"Not for me to say. Just be sure of what you want."

"I don't know what I want."

"Me neither. But I do know there are plenty of good guys around who would love to hang with you, take you out, show you a good time. Just that."

"Bullshit." She crossed her arms again. "Who? Tell me who."

"Look around you. Pay attention. You're scary to some of the boys. See who acts like they're scared of you."

"Then what?"

"Try to be a little less scary to them."

She smiled at him knowingly. "You're not afraid of me, are you. Are you Christian?"

"I've been raised Catholic."

"Clever words, a Paolo answer. Totally. The question is about what you believe in."

"Still trying to work that out. Look, I better be heading home. My grandmother expects me back before it gets dark." He gave her hand a squeeze before letting go. "No more hurting yourself. You get the urge to cut and you pick up your iPhone instead of a razor blade. You call, you hear?"

o o o

With Paolo still off on his bicycle, Toni wrestled the big aluminum extension ladder out of the garden shed and leaned it up against the newly restored gutter along the back-porch roof. In the rainstorm earlier in the week, a steady waterfall had flooded over the lip and leaked onto the porch, soaking a braided rug that was a favorite of Seppina's.

Toni slipped a garden trowel into his back pocket before climbing the ladder to see if he could clear whatever was blocking the gutter. At the top, he could see where, just out of reach, a clutch of pine needles was backed up against a discarded piece trimmed from a roofing tile. He grabbed the trowel from his hip pocket and reached to clear the blockage.

o o o

It was late afternoon, with the sun dipping behind the neighbor's wall of arbor vitae, when Seppina found him lying at the foot of the ladder, his neck broken.

Chapter 15

Danny and Fernando began their determined tour of Valencia's bars and cafés, drinking buddies of convenience on a bender that lasted to the end of the week, at least for Fernando. Danny managed to moderate his intake just enough to time his best questions for the window of weakest will just before Fernando passed out each night and to stay just sober enough to get the man into a taxi afterwards. The summary of what he learned was expressed by the summary in his notebook: "a handful of ambiguous paragraphs based on untrustworthy reports from an inebriated source." It had not helped that each time he wrote up his notes the following morning, the throb of his own hangover headache made it hard to sort out what had actually been said. It was clear only that Fernando had been roped into helping his father work on biomedical research of an unknown and probably unethical nature. His own role had been largely inconsequential but ultimately traumatic. On their last night of bingeing, Fernando confessed to being haunted by recurrent dreams of dead bodies: reddened, bloated, and disfigured. Before Danny could ask his follow-up question, Fernando had slumped to one side and passed out on the banquette.

Friday came and went with no copy sent off to Danny's editor in Frankfurt. He worked the weekend with Bernat at his side, the two of them running fresh searches and following unlikely leads prompted by the week's drunken discoveries. By the end, they had a list of potential fresh sources in Italy, Switzerland, and China, none of which looked very promising. Danny had no illusions about his prospects with his boss: a trip to China would definitely not be in the offing.

At the airport on Monday, Bernat gave him a palm-sized polished wood carving. "Thank you, Bernat, thank you. It ... it looks like ..."

"*L'Àgora*, the stadium here in Valencia."

"Ah, yes, now I see. Just that most of your carvings are, you know ..."

"This one, too. If you look at it from the right angle and with the right mindset, you will recognize it."

"I'm sure I will, my lecherous old friend. And thanks for the help this week."

"I was not much help, but I will keep my eyes open and my ears—what would you say, not open ... tuned? Maybe I will find something useful."

"Let me know if you do."

○ ○ ○

Kurt Trauben turned livid when Danny entered his office. He would have been yelling like an angry demonstrator had his deeply conditioned Teutonic discipline left him capable of raising his voice. Instead, his fingers beat an impatient tattoo on the edge of the desk as he spoke quietly in words that were italicized by clenched teeth and a deep glottal push. "You, you are strolling at the edge of a cliff. I should dismiss you right now. We do not miss deadlines, not in my bureau. You know that. You will walk down the hall, find an empty desk, and sit down to write. You will not move, even to go to the toilet, until you have finished the draft of your feature story. Is that clear?"

"Perfectly. But—"

"No. You have had more than enough time. How long does it take to crank out six thousand words of copy?"

"I can crank that out in a matter of hours. But I am still

researching a story, not cranking out copy. Besides, the special issue is still six months out. There is plenty of time."

"There is not plenty of time. The editorial calendar for the weekend edition is planned a year at a time. You have today. That's it. Then I am putting you on another assignment."

Danny spent the morning struggling to find a hook for the bullshit he would have to write. In the afternoon, he pounded away until he reached his quota of words. He gave the piece a quick read through to check for the most glaring typos before sending it off to Trauben. He was shutting down and packing up for the day when Trauben entered the office.

"What is this? What do you call this?" He slapped a paper-clipped printout down on the desk.

"I call it a piece of crap. That's what you asked for, that's what I delivered."

"I most certainly did not ask for this. I will not accept it. You are finished here, Bradman. As soon as London okays it, you will be redundant. You're fired, as they say in America. Don't even bother coming into the office again, and don't expect a letter of recommendation from me. I'll put Maxi on this assignment. She at least can write. And she takes editorial direction. She also does not insult her superiors. She does not run up excessive expenses. In sum, she is what you are not. Now get out before I am left no choice but to have security escort you out of the building."

Danny said nothing, knowing that anything he would want to say would only dig the latrine in which he was standing that much deeper. He shrugged, closed his laptop, and resumed packing up his briefcase. They had to give him six weeks' notice, he knew, and he had been ordered not to come into the office. He suddenly realized that he had been handed his manumission papers. For at least the next month and a half he was still officially on the staff of the *Financial Tribune* but free to do as he chose. You can do it, Danny boy, he told himself, you can do it. In truth, he had no choice. It was do or die for his career. One last push to break the story.

He elbowed past Trauben and strode down the hall. As he waited for the elevator, he started to grin. Trauben, in acting precipitously, had forgotten protocol. Danny still had all his notes on his laptop and a corporate credit card in his wallet. Unless they monitored the account online, Trauben wouldn't know what expenses had been charged until the next monthly report landed on his desk. Headquarters could cancel the card at any time, but until they did Danny could still cover expenses. He knew enough to get his plane tickets right away, just in case.

Chapter 16

To Paolo's ongoing embarrassment—and our consternation—he seemed to be almost totally lacking in mechanical ability. Despite his obvious intelligence, when it came to machinery, he was at a loss. As a small boy he even once argued that a propeller-driven aircraft shown in a picture book had its props mounted backwards. He knew that a fan blew air out the front, hence the propellers in the picture would blow the air the wrong way, pushing the plane backward. Toni tried to explain about airfoils and angle-of-attack, but Paolo was unconvinced. Only years later, when he encountered the equations of fluid flow in an AP physics course, did it finally make sense to him. The arithmetic sign of a variable in an equation was convincing where Toni's sketches and commonsense arguments were not.

Whereas Toni had always been handy with his hands and had an easy understanding of how things worked, Paolo was a klutz who bungled even the simplest of repairs. He could wreck a ballpoint pen in an attempt to change the cartridge. Growing up, he turned to Toni whenever something broke or stopped working. When the drive chain of his bicycle slipped off the gears on his way back from seeing Sosamma, he had no idea of how to fix it.

Seppina was sitting in Toni's chair, crying, when Paolo finally arrived home. "I'm sorry I'm late, Nonna. My bike broke and I had to walk it the last two miles. I'll have to get Nonno to fix it." Her sobs deepened, and he realized that she was certainly not crying because he was late for dinner. He put it together without her having to say anything. "It's Nonno, isn't it. What happened? Is he all right?"

She wiped her eyes with a wadded tissue and opened her mouth to speak but no words came out. Paolo slowly crossed the room and knelt in front of her, taking her hands in his. "Oh, Nonna. I am so sorry. I should have been here."

Her breath came in shudders as she struggled to speak. "You couldn't have done anything. They said it was quick, that he didn't suffer."

"What happened? Was it a heart attack?"

"No, a fall. He was on the ladder, trying to fix something on the porch roof."

"Oh, I knew it. I should have been here. It should have been me on the ladder."

"Oh, don't say that, Paolo. Don't say that. It wasn't your fault. Even if you had been here, it wouldn't have made any difference. God decides these things. He calls us when it's our time."

"I don't ..." Not wishing to add to her heartache, he left the sentence unfinished. "I am so sorry. I ..." He struggled to speak through choking tears, wanting to help in some way but feeling awkward and at a loss. "Can I do anything for you?"

"Just sit with me for a while." She got up from the chair. "Here, you take Toni's chair. You're the man of the house now. I'll sit in my rocker."

"Let's both sit on the sofa. That way we can hold each other." He stood, forcing himself to be the man he was expected to be. He took her hand and led her. "Okay?"

"Okay."

He hugged her as she shook with sobs and as he shook to control himself. Then they sat in silence until the fading light through the bay window left them in darkness. Over Paolo's protests, she insisted that she make dinner. Paolo steadied her on the way to the kitchen, then watched as she reheated leftover turkey-rice soup. "It's not much," she said.

"It's fine, Nonna, just fine. I love your soups."

○ ○ ○

Paolo's neck ached from looking up, but he could not take his eyes off the larger-than-life figure of a crucified Christ that dominated the front of the cathedral. It was hardly the first time he had been to church, of course, but it was his first funeral. Growing up, he had struck a bargain with the Franzettis, obediently attending mass and learning the catechism to complete his confirmation in exchange for the right to choose after that. He chose to opt out, as Toni had many years earlier. Sunday mornings became "guy time" for Paolo and Toni. While Seppina went to mass, they would read the paper and talk, often about politics and current events but also not infrequently about philosophy or ethics or faith.

Toni was a believer but not a practicing Catholic; Paolo was a non-believer but not a practicing atheist. His confession to Toni that he did not believe in God had been a turning point that somehow brought them closer. "Maybe it's more important that God still believes in you, kiddo. I still do. We're not going to give up on you."

As Paolo thought back to times with Toni, the funeral stretched on. In the pew next to him, Seppina noticed Paolo staring up at the crucifix, a lone tear rolling slowly down one cheek. She misread his thoughts and squeezed his hand. "They're together, yes. He's with our Lord and Savior now."

Paolo nodded to reassure her, but he was thinking of neither Antonio nor Jesus. The crucifix had reminded him of a favorite novel, *Masters of Solitude*, a science fiction story about death and life and the experience of nothingness that had helped shape his own views of life and faith. At one point, a group named The Coven were called to kill off the Kriss, a clan who worshipped a dead god in the form of a figure on a cross. He remembered talking with Toni about some of the ideas behind the book. "People invent gods, not because they fear death so much as because they fear nothingness," he had told Toni. "They fail to realize that there is nothing to fear in nothingness."

Seppina, sitting with him in the front pew at the funeral, leaned toward Paolo and whispered. "What did you say?"

"Nothing. I'm sorry. I was just remembering."

"I know you miss him. I do, too. I so miss him already, and I don't know what I will do without him." She straightened up and turned her attention back to the priest as Paolo started thinking about what he might do without Toni, without his grandfather to talk with about life and nothingness. He idly twisted the intaglio ring that he now wore.

○ ○ ○

"Can you check on him, Dr. Cahners?" Giuseppina sounded weary and anxious over the phone.

"What's up?"

"The school counselor called today to say Paolo's teachers are worried about him. She said he sits in class staring out the window or at the top of his desk. He doesn't ask questions, and when a teacher asks one of him, he shrugs and says he doesn't know the answer. It's just not like him. His homework and tests are still fine, but he barely speaks in class, and he shuffles like a zombie between classes. He's been late for class at least once a day for weeks."

"That sounds like he's depressed. What has he been like at home?"

"I don't know. I never see him. He stays holed up in the attic except to go to school."

"Okay, I'll drop by late this afternoon and look in on him. And how are you doing?"

"I'm keeping busy. There's still a lot of paperwork to deal with, and now there's only me to take care of things at home."

"Look, if you need housekeeping help, that, too, can be arranged."

"I don't want anyone else taking care of my house. Besides, staying busy keeps me from spending too much time feeling sorry for myself ... or thinking."

"Well, if you change your mind, let me know. I'll see you later today, after Paolo gets home from school. And remember, you can call me anytime you want to talk."

"I want to talk right now, but with my Toni, that's what I want."

"I understand. You two were together a lot of years."

"Forty-seven. Just last month, we were talking about our golden anniversary coming up in a few years. I ..." She started to cry. "I'm sorry, Dr. Cahners. It just keeps sneaking up on me and hitting me in the stomach, if you know what I mean. I better go and scrub the floor or something. I'll see you this afternoon."

o o o

Dr. Cahners climbed the steep back stairs to the attic. At the top, he knocked on the door that Toni had installed the previous summer to give Paolo more privacy. There was no answer. "Paolo, it's me, Dr. Cahners. Can I come in?" No answer. "I'm coming in." He opened the door and stepped in. "You okay?"

Paolo was seated at his desk. It had changed little since his childhood, but the writer sitting on the old kitchen chair now facing it was a young man with the sparse beginnings of a beard decorating his chin.

"I thought I'd check in on you, make sure you were all right. How's it going? How are you holding up?"

Paolo looked up from the blank sheet of paper in front of him. "I'm not suicidal."

"I didn't say you were."

"No, but that's why you came here: to find out if I was. I've been expecting you."

"Really?"

"I could see it on the faces of my teachers, especially Mr. Londquist. I have him for calculus. I knew that he at least would talk to Mrs. Klein in Guidance, and she would call my Nonna, who would, of course, call you. Here you are, just like clockwork."

"So now I'm a clock. That easy to read, huh?"

"Easier. Ever take apart a clock or study one of those see-through types, like the one Nonna keeps on the mantel? Very complicated."

"Do I seem that transparent to you?"

"Hardly. You're quite opaque, and you work hard to keep it that way. No, not transparent, but predictable."

"And what does our resident Nostradamus predict I'll do next?"

"You'll ask another question, as you just did."

"That's what you think? You think that all I do is ask questions?"

"It's not what I think, it's what I know. You're even worse than that shrink, Dr. Danforth, you sent me to last year."

"Okay, I give up. You have me pegged. So how are you doing? What are you doing?"

"I'm writing."

"Sure didn't look like it when I came in."

"That's because you don't understand what writing is. Most people don't. It's not putting words and sentences onto paper or into a computer. That's only one part, the mechanical part, the easy part. The hard part is the thinking, figuring out what to write, then what to write next, and next. I was writing when you came in, and I'll be doing it again when you leave. Unless you want to pull up a chair and watch me write. I don't imagine you'll find it all that interesting, though."

"Are you asking me to leave?"

"There you go again, doc. Always the questions."

"Fair enough. I'll leave you to your writing, then."

"Close the door on your way out."

"It's been a pleasure for me, too."

Paolo laughed. "Now that's good. You ought to try sarcasm more often."

"You think that was sarcasm?"

Paolo smiled and shook his head in disbelief. "Get out of here, doc, before I start throwing things in answer to your questions."

Cahners pantomimed making a note in the air. "Patient not suicidal but shows signs of becoming violent."

"You're well on the road to recovery, doc. I'll save you the embarrassment of a relapse by answering your next question before you have to ask it. What am I doing? I'm writing a novel, inspired by the work of Michael Novak. Do you know *The Experience of Nothingness*?"

"I do know the experience of nothingness. I've been there."

"I meant the book."

"I know that. And I meant the experience."

"And I know that. We had better interrupt our conversational recursion here to enable me to return to writing about my experience and for you to return to consoling the widow downstairs who is adrift in her nothingness."

"You know, you're all right, Paolo."

"I know. So are you, doc. Close the door on your way out."

Paolo waited until the doctor's footsteps faded before plunging once more into the black despair in which he had been swimming.

Chapter 17

Francesca sat on the edge of the bed, barefoot, buttoning her blouse. "Luca told me he thinks he can track down those records for you, the ones about the doctor."

"Luca? You told Luca? What the hell were you thinking?" Danny sat up in the bed and combed his fingers through his hair. "I'm a dead man. I'm a dead man."

"No you're not, silly. I just told Luca that we had a visitor at the Institute who was researching the Dermott empire and was interested in some old criminal case records. Besides, I'm not sure he would care all that much even if he knew what was happening between us. Last night he told me he wants a divorce."

"I'm sorry."

"Sorry?"

"I wasn't looking to break up your marriage."

"Neither was I. And you didn't. Luca and I were already on the path to separate lives. I knew about his affairs, and I could sense that the latest had the potential to go from passion to permanent. I told you, he wants children. Jovanna is much younger and built for babies, if you know what I mean. And she's blonde. Luca always liked blondes."

"Where does that leave you?"

"Not blonde, but still here. This is where I want to be: right here with you."

"I don't have a very good track record with relationships."

"I'm not interested in track records. I'm not betting on a race horse. I'm interested in Danbury Ephraim Bradman, who is interesting and handsome and makes me laugh. And who also happens to be an attentive and patient lover."

"Hang on there. You used my middle name. How do you know that? I never, ever, use it."

"What, you think only you can find things on the Web? It's not like you're invisible or something. You leave a trail of bits and tidbits behind you, just like everyone and everything else."

"Not everyone and not everything leaves a trail. Bernat and I ran up against a blank wall with trying to track down this Dr. Fonseca y Morales and his son. I mean we found them, but there's this mysterious indictment and a son who only talks when he's drunk and then says nothing of much use."

"Well, like I said, maybe Luca can help. He's already working on it. I'll let you know. Right now, I better get back to the Institute. Even in Italy, there are limits on how long we can take for lunch." She winked, then leaned over for another kiss. She pulled back after a breathless minute. "Oh, Danny, you do make it hard for me to leave you."

o o o

Luca was a buff, broad-shouldered giant looking down from the heights at Danny Bradman seated at the sidewalk café. "Ciao, Danny. I am Luca, Luca Volpone." He shook Danny's hand with force. "My wife, Francesca, thought I could help you."

"Thank you for meeting with me. Would you like a coffee?"

"I'm Italian. The answer is never no."

"I'll go get it at the bar. Espresso?"

"*Doppio, grazie.*"

Danny returned a few minutes later with two double espressos. "I hope I haven't put you to too much trouble."

"It was no trouble. I talked to some people and looked in

some file drawers. That is not trouble. Trouble is staying two steps ahead of the Mafiosi. Trouble is tracking terrorists from the Middle East and North Africa." He sipped his coffee. "The charges you are interested in, against Manuel and Fernando Fonseca and Arturo Dermott, they were dropped at the direction of a senior magistrate. Also, the extradition proceedings for the Spaniards. And against an American, years later, same charges, for some reason ending up in the same folder."

"Wait a minute. You are saying charges were also brought against Arturo Dermott? And an American?"

"Yes, Dermott was taken into custody but released within hours. The extradition papers on the American were delivered to the American Embassy but then withdrawn. Almost none of this is still in the computer databases but some of the paperwork was still there. There was a cover-up but not a terribly thorough one. Amateurs. Not the mafia, not any of the intelligence services, I don't think."

"Clearly, you're no amateur. What about the American, you remember the name?"

"Yes, of course. His name was Orlando Rossi, a musician. According to the files, he toured here with a local heavy metal rock group for part of a summer before going to work for Dermott. He overstayed his visa, then went home, at least as far as we know."

"And home? Did the records show where that was?"

"He entered the country on a flight from Boston; I assume he went back there, but I didn't find anything on that. I didn't look. I thought you were interested in the doctor."

Danny finished his coffee. "Yes. I can't thank you enough. This could be most helpful. Thank you."

He reached out his hand. Luca took it with what started as a handshake before turning into a vise grip. "Remember always,

Signor Bradman, where you are and who you are dealing with. This is not your England where men might turn quietly away when confronted by betrayal. I do hope this information proves useful to you and that you will take it with you when you leave Italy. And I do hope that will be soon. Understood?"

Expecting to hear bones cracking in his hand at any moment, Danny fought to ignore the pain. He wanted to object but knew better. "Understood."

"*Molto bene.* We never spoke, understand? Not of either of these matters. Never." He released Danny's hand. "I would say *arrivederci*, but that would not be fitting since I will not be seeing you again." He stood. "*Buona fortuna, Signor Bradman.* Good luck."

Danny flexed his aching hand as he watched the man thread the throng of pedestrians and disappear down the boulevard.

○ ○ ○

"But you just got here." In the subdued lighting of the restaurant, the candle flame glinted in Francesca's dark eyes. "Now you're leaving already."

"I have to go while I can still travel at the newspaper's expense. And while my bones are still unbroken."

"What?"

"Let's just say that I've been warned not to push my luck."

"Warned? What about? Who warned you?"

Danny ignored the questions. "I fly to Boston in two days. And I am very busy, so I probably won't have a chance to see you again before I go. I'm sorry."

"When do you come back?"

"I don't. I mean, I don't know. After I wrap up this story, I'm going to have to look for work. I have no idea how long that might take or where I could end up."

"You could end up here, in Rome. Your Italian is not too bad, and it is getting better."

"I don't think so."

"Oh, it is, it is."

"I don't mean about speaking Italian, I mean about working here."

"What is wrong?" She tilted her head as her gaze roamed over his face in search of a clue. "Oh, no, not that. You really are leaving. You are ending it, aren't you. And I thought you were different, not like Luca, not like others. But you are already tired of me, and you are moving on."

"That's not it. Not—"

"Shut up. I don't want to hear lies. Your timing could not be more perfect, you know. Luca and I went to a judge yesterday, to apply for the *separazione formale*. With the current law, we will be divorced after just six months of separation. Luca has left me and now you are leaving me."

"I am not leaving you. I am ..."

She waited for him to finish, but when the seconds dragged on, she folded her napkin and rose from the table. "You are so right, Danny. You are not leaving, I am." She spun around and headed for the door just as the waiter arrived with their pasta courses.

Chapter 18

After the funeral, Paolo retreated to his attic with growing fre-
quency and for longer stretches. Although I would not have termed
him clinically depressed, his many good friends worried, however,
and his school counselor kept getting concerned notes from both
students and teachers. The school year was in its final term before
Paolo emerged from his funk and came down from his lofty retreat.

It had been a difficult time for all of us and especially for Seppina.
Just when she needed Paolo as someone to take up the slack around
the house and, even more importantly, to be the vessel to accept the
overflow of her love and nurturing, he was withdrawn into a world
of his own. I visited him frequently and kept a close watch on him,
and Seppina reached out to him as often as he would accept. That
winter and spring, he would allow us into his retreat, at least for
brief visits, but not into his world. I did worry about suicide. He had
identified so closely with Toni, and this was one of the things I was
paid to be concerned about.

When finally, as the end of school approached, Paolo seemed to
snap out of it, he returned to seeing friends and even joined the
science club. I asked him what had happened. He told me only that
he had finished his first novel. What about, I asked him. Life, he
told me.

True to form, he filed the manuscript away in his discard box and
said nothing more of it to any of us. I could read the title page as it
rested on the top of the deep stack of his writings: The Nothing
Matters. It was vintage Paolo wordplay. He noticed me reading the

title upside down. I wanted to ask him about it, and I was certain he knew that, but neither of us said anything.

As a clinician, I listened and watched for the suicidal impulses that so often can attend an apparent recovery as people rise out of depression. If there was a silver lining to the tragedy of losing Toni, it was that Paolo had largely isolated himself from the media and the family was too distraught and distracted to note the early wave of stories about Arturo Dermott.

Paolo plopped his backpack on the kitchen chair next to the door and headed directly for the refrigerator to rummage for a snack. "I won. I got it. I'm a finalist."

Seppina looked up from the carrots she was slicing. "There's still some potato salad if you're hungry. And what did you win?"

"The one-act play competition. I'm a finalist. They're going to do my play, like, with real actors."

"Who's 'they' and what play?"

"MassPlayFest, the student competition, and my play, like I said."

"That sounds wonderful. I didn't know you were writing plays."

"Well, yeah. I've been writing plays for years. But this is different. Miss Prentiss—she teaches AP Euro—she's also the drama coach, and she said I write well and maybe should write something and try. So I did. That's it."

"When did you find time for that with your school work and all. Every night you finish dinner in six minutes flat and tell me you have so much homework, and then you disappear."

"I do. I do have a lot of homework, but it's not really hard. It just takes time. Anyway, I wrote the play at school, during study period. Miss Prentiss read it and made some suggestions and ... yeah."

"When is this supposed to happen, this play festival?"

"Two weeks. Not really enough time for rehearsal, but the actors are pros."

"Will I get to see this play? Where is it?"

"UMass-Lowell. Sure, you can see it. I'm hoping Dr. Cahners can come, too. It's, like, a whole festival: ten plays, all day Saturday. At the end, they announce the top awards."

"That sounds wonderful. I don't remember seeing you quite so excited before."

"I think this is who I am, Nonna. I've been trying to figure that out all my life. Who am I? This is me."

"All your life, huh?" She scraped the carrots from the cutting board into a saucepan. "Well, there's plenty of time yet to figure that one out. Right now it's plays, next year maybe it's robotics. Who knows what next? Computer programming?"

Paolo shook his head in sad disbelief as he swung his backpack over one shoulder. "I'm headed up, Nonna. I have a lot of homework and a test to study for."

"What's wrong now? One minute you're excited and the next you go all mopey on me."

"What's wrong? You tell me, Nonna. Everyone seems to have some agenda for me; no one is interested in my agenda."

"I don't have an agenda for you. I just want you to be happy, to live a good life. I'm glad you like writing plays. Writing plays is just fine, but it's not like a real life. Look, sit down for a minute." She waited while he set his backpack on the floor and slumped into a kitchen chair. "You have a gift, Paolo, a wonderful mind that can do wonderful things. You're brilliant. You could be anything. You could be a scientist, an engineer, anything. You'll figure it out: what God intended for you, why He put you here, why He loaned you into our hands to raise you for the special purpose He has for you."

Paolo sat in silence, nodding obediently, considering his words. "Your faith works for you, Nonna."

"Yes, it does. Without it, I could never have survived losing Toni. Your grandfather was my life; now you're my life. It's all part of God's plan. We can't begin to know what His plan is."

"Yeah, probably true. Except it always seems like everyone else knows it better than I do. Everyone else acts like they know me better than I know myself."

"Who is this 'everyone'?"

"You, Dr. Cahners, my guidance counselor, that shrink. Everyone. Even Vera, in a way."

"Vera?"

"Miss Prentiss, Vera Prentiss. Sometimes it feels like she really understands me; sometimes it feels like she has her own agenda."

"I don't remember meeting her before, not at any of the parent-teacher meetings."

"She's new. Started in the middle of the year when Mr. Schmidt had his heart attack. You'll meet her at MassPlayFest.

◦ ◦ ◦

The crowd settled down slowly as the mistress of ceremonies finally took the stage and tapped on the microphone. "Hello, everyone. Can you hear me? Excellent. I'm Jennifer McCormack, President of the Commonwealth Academy of Theater Arts, and on the behalf of CATA and on behalf of drama teachers and coaches throughout the Bay State, I want to welcome you all to MassPlayFest: the Fourteenth Annual Young Playwrights Competition. Let me just say that you are in for a treat today as professional actors from around the region present the work of some exceptionally talented young writers."

The auditorium at the Lowell campus of the University of Massachusetts was crowded by the friends, families, and teachers of the featured student playwrights, but it was nowhere near filled to capacity. On the first sunny day after a week of spring rains, only an audience with a vested interest could be expected to sit through six hours of back-to-back one-act plays by high-school students.

Paolo's entry was scheduled right after lunch. The morning slate of five plays ranged over the full theatrical spectrum from naïve attempts at high drama to laugh-laden vignettes by young playwrights with a future writing for streamed sitcoms. By the lunch break, the audience was clearly getting restless. Polite applause followed the last entry for the morning: a two-person play about LGBTQ issues and the anxiety over coming out while still in high school.

As the audience stood and started milling around, Paolo took Seppina's hand. "Come on, Nonna, there are some people I want you to meet." He edged his way through the crowd, guiding her toward a knot of students and teachers chatting at the foot of the steps leading to the stage. As they approached, a young woman with fluorescent pink lipstick and a rainbow feather-boa wound around her neck threw open her arms and called out, "Paolo, Paolo, over here." She greeted him with a hug and a continental air-kiss on the cheek. "Are you psyched for this? I am. And who is this?"

"This is my grandmother."

The woman took Seppina by the shoulders and repeated the air-kiss ritual. "I am so glad to finally meet you. I'm Vera, Vera Prentiss. Your grandson is just so amazing, isn't he?" She sent a wink and a smile toward Paolo. "And you must be so proud of him, Mrs. Franzetti." She reached out and put her arm around Paolo's waist to reel him in to her side.

"I am, yes." Seppina looked anxiously toward Paolo, as if unsure what was expected of her.

Paolo stepped into the awkward silence. "So, Nonna, now you've met my drama coach. And you already know Sosamma." He reached a free arm toward Sosamma, who squirmed and looked down at her shoes while she nodded. "And this is Jake, and over there is Denise from AP Euro, and Mr. Londquist, my calc teacher, and hanging back like he always does, is Harold, the Herald of Nothingham, as we call him." The boy named Harold rolled his eyes as he stood, hands in pockets, chewing away on something. Nods and handshakes crisscrossed the circle.

Vera put her hand up to call for attention. "Hey, everybody. We should get some lunch. There's the caf across the way for anyone who is ready to brave the gantlet for college cafeteria food, or you can follow me to a funky pizza place down the block that I hear is good. But we will have to hustle to get back in time for the world premiere of 'Your Peeps, My Peeps' by the up-and-coming playwright Paolo Franzetti."

Paolo held his hands in front of his face in feigned embarrassment. "Take your time, people. No hurry. It's just a student play."

Vera took his arm. "Yeah, right. Just wait until it's performed off-Broadway. Okay, who's for pizza, follow me." She waved an arm toward the opposite exit and started in the lead. They were almost to the door when someone called from behind.

"Paolo, wait up." It was Dr. Cahners, standing in one of the middle rows talking with a man and a woman. The three of them sidled out to the aisle and made their way against traffic down to the front of the auditorium.

Paolo looked pleased. "Dr. Cahners, I wasn't sure if you could make it."

"I wouldn't miss it for the world, Paolo. We just got here a little late, missed the first play."

"Hi, I'm Vera Prentiss, Paolo's drama teacher. Frankly, you didn't miss much. I'm not sure how that first play got into the finals."

Cahners took her hand. "And I'm Roy Cahners, Paolo's doctor, and these are my colleagues, Helen Bentley and Dr. Chaim Danforth." A wave of perfunctory greetings rippled through the group. "I didn't know you were taking drama this term, Paolo."

"I'm not. Vera ... Ms. Prentiss has been coaching me one-on-one, helping with writing. She's the one who suggested I try for the one-act play competition."

"Well, isn't that something. You know, Ms. Prentiss, I hope you don't take this wrong, but I have to confess that if you hadn't introduced yourself, I might have taken you for one of the students."

"I will take that as a compliment, Dr. Cahners, even if slightly sexist, but I've been teaching almost seven years."

"Please do take it as a compliment with apologies from an old-school doctor who's been doctoring almost forty years."

"Compliment accepted and apology accepted. Now, would you like to join us for wood-fired pizza?"

"Thank you, but no. I've already agreed to a working lunch with my colleagues here. You go ahead. We'll catch up again for the big premier at 1:30."

○ ○ ○

The CATA president took the stage ten minutes late with a smile hastily pasted on as she crossed to the microphone at center stage. "Welcome back, everyone. Did you enjoy your lunch?" The chorus of "Yes!" and "Sure!" was lacking in conviction and intermixed with some quiet groans. "Well, are you ready for some more great plays? What's that? Come on, I can't hear you. Are you ready?" The audience, hoping not to have to respond a third time, gave it their all with an enthusiastic unison shout of "Yes!"

"Well, then, let's start off the afternoon with 'Your Peeps, My Peeps,' a one-act play from the youngest finalist in this year's competition, Paolo Franzetti—did I say that right?—of Peabody Academy." She clapped with her hands held high to cue the audience applause.

The play started with a group of five young people milling around, three boys and two girls talking in a kind of waiting-for-Godot scenario. Their conversation varied over a spectrum of contemporary teen angst, but gradually began to focus on a sixth, unnamed, member of their circle, someone for whom there was clearly a deep but largely unspoken affection. The dialogue was pitch-perfect, authentic, and pointed, particularly when it came to the social dynamics of high-school and relationships with parents. As the play unfolded, the discussion turned darker and more heated, with suppressed tension threatening to erupt at any moment. The audience inhaled almost in unison as one of the boys, without warning, grabbed another boy by the shirt. A shoving match seemed on the verge of becoming a fist fight when one of the girls shouted, "She's here!" The five actors turned to stage left and froze as a casket was wheeled on-stage. The lights were killed.

The only sound in the auditorium was that of the curtains closing, then nothing for several seconds before an explosion of applause as the houselights came up and the five actors emerged for their bows.

On the aisle in the center section, two seats away from the playwright, a black-haired girl with heavy eye makeup and a long-sleeved tee-shirt that covered the scars on her arms was weeping with head bowed. Paolo reached across in front of Seppina and touched the girl's arm. "For you, Sosamma."

Chapter 19

Danny had avoided Francesca and steeled himself to keep ignoring her calls until his flight. Waiting in line to go through security at the airport, he turned around at the sound of raised voices behind him. An argument in Italian between two passengers in line was escalating into shoves and shouts. Danny watched in amazement as a pair of well-armed airport security guards approached the two squabbling men. Suddenly a heavy hand grabbed his arm and a baritone voice near his ear told him, in Italian, to be quiet and come along. He twisted and looked up into the face of Luca Volpone, with another, equally tall *Carabinieri* behind him, both of them armed and in uniform.

"What the ... ? What are you doing. I have a flight to catch. I'm an American. I—"

"*Silenzio!*" Luca jerked him out of the line and spun him around. Quietly, between clenched teeth, he added. "Be quiet and do as you are told and you will be all right. Keep protesting and we all will be in trouble."

The two national police flanked Danny and escorted him across the departures hall toward a door marked for authorized personnel. Luca's partner punched a code into a key pad at the side. When the lock clicked, he held the door as Luca pushed Danny ahead into a long corridor without doors or windows. He backed Danny against the opposite wall as his partner closed the door behind them and stood with his hand resting on his holstered sidearm.

Luca brought his face close to Danny's. "Well, Signor Brad-man, I should have said *arrivederci* after all. Or maybe simply *ciao*. We do meet again."

"What the hell is going on?"

"Nothing is going on, we hope. You are being afforded a special escort, that is all. You want to leave the country, and we want you to leave. We just prefer to see that you actually get on the plane."

"Why would I not get on the plane?"

"*No lo so*. Who knows? Perhaps you might encounter an un-fortunate accident in the airport." He looked to his companion, said something in Italian, and they both laughed.

"I don't understand."

"No, you don't. And neither did I until I started to hear warn-ing bells. I didn't realize how intricate were the, shall we say, alarms connected to the material I researched for you. It seems there are important people who do not like police—or anyone—poking into certain matters. We are both in possible danger now—you more than me. I am a police officer in an elite unit. I have dodged bullets before. You, I don't know about."

"What are you going to do with me?"

"Why, escort you to your plane, as I said, and make sure you are comfortably aboard, on your way to Boston, Mr. Panos." He handed Danny an Alitalia ticket wallet. "Here. Enjoy your flight. You have been upgraded."

The business-class ticket was made out for Cyril Panos. "But I'm not ..."

"For now, you are. Most unfortunately, Danbury Bradman failed to show up for his flight. We will escort you through secur-ity and to the gate, so there will be no problem with identifi-cation papers. We are pleased that you travel light. Checked bags would have been so much more complicated."

"Why? Why are you doing this?"

"Because if certain people think you are still here while you are actually elsewhere, there will be time for us to figure this out and paint over some slips of the brush. Don't flatter yourself to think this was all about you. I have myself and my wife to think of first. If everyone looks for you, they do not look for us."

"I really don't understand. I assume now that you staged the argument in the departures hall as a distraction. But somebody is after me? What's it all about?"

"You are a journalist, I am a policeman. Which of us is the better at investigating such questions? Who will figure it out first? We shall see. *Buon viaggio*, Signor Panos. We will see you to your plane, but please let us do all the talking."

o o o

"I could get used to this," Danny said, as the flight attendant poured him another glass of a beautifully dark Montepulciano D'Abruzzo. He waited until she finished clearing his tray before he reached for his laptop. The weird meet-up with Luca had confirmed he was onto something, and his discoveries the night before had daubed in the details. What had begun as another sweeping search was turning into an orchestrated scavenger hunt with Massachusetts his next stop. The old news item from a small community newspaper had been tough to dig out. "Malden Musician Orlando Rossi Returns from Italian Tour." It was more than a decade-and-a-half old, but it confirmed that Rossi had, indeed, returned home. A search of online phone and address listings soon located a man by that name living in East Boston not too far from the airport.

Danny had sweated through every minute of the nearly ninety-minute delay at the gate in Rome. "Typical," the businessman across the aisle remarked each time the captain or purser announced another delay. Danny had pretended to be reading the in-flight magazine, expecting at any moment to see airport security marching down the aisle to pull him off. Whatever Luca and his colleague had done, though, they had done it well. The flight finally left the gate and Danny let out a deep sigh when the fully loaded Airbus 330 rotated and rose from the runway, heading into the afternoon sun.

Chapter 20

Paolo's first play did not win the competition, although it was singled out for honorable mention. His drama coach explained that the judges usually saved the top awards for seniors and almost never gave them to first-timers. They figured there was always next year for the newcomers. She invited all the students to celebrate over dinner, but everyone except for Paolo had other plans or was being picked up by parents. She promised Seppina to bring Paolo home early, and the two of them marched off arm-in-arm.

The play was confirmation of two things that we already knew about Paolo but had not yet abstracted into a single clear formulation. The first of these was his long-noted grasp of human relationships and social connection. The second, so evident at the one-act play competition, was his willingness and ability to stage an elaborate scenario as an intervention. With perfect hindsight, it was clear to us that the entire sequence of events—his entry into the competition, the play itself, and his guest list—was in service of a single purpose. The unnamed Godot of the play was his friend Sosamma. He had written the play for her, as a kind of love letter in an attempt to derail her from the downward track she was on.

Going over my clinical notes, I was reminded of talks with Paolo about Sosamma that were, almost word-for-word, drafts of lines from the play. It was a sort of condensed contemporary version of the Ghost of Christmas Yet to Come, a foreshadowing conveyed to change the future. I thought at the time of the graveside scene in which Ebenezer Scrooge asks whether these were the shadows of *things that will be or that only might be. I spoke of this with Paolo one afternoon and he said that the future is always changing.*

How true, how very true.

"I really do not want to go again this summer." Paolo speared the last sliver of strip steak, flicked a few grains of salt at it from the salt cellar, and stared at it on his fork. "I'll work, I'll get a job, whatever—just not science camp."

"Why not? You had fun at science camp. You met some nice kids. Remember that girl, that …"

"I remember Chrissy, even if you don't."

"It gets harder to remember some things at my age. And I never met her, but I remember you wrote to her a lot."

"We don't write anymore, Nonna. She's got a boyfriend and is headed to California to take summer courses at Cal Tech. She finished high school a year ahead of schedule and got early admission in comp sci. At this rate, she'll be graduating from college when I'm a freshman somewhere."

"See? Now that's the way to do it. You already have advanced placement credit for calculus and European history. You could really apply yourself and also finish high school early. MIT is just around the corner, so to speak. They're the best in the world in science and engineering. I bet they'd accept you in a second."

Paolo clenched his jaw as he placed his knife and fork together at a diagonal across his dinner plate and neatly folded his napkin. "Right, science and engineering, the best. Look, I have finals to study for, Nonna." He picked up his plate and started toward the kitchen. "I'll do the dishes later, before I go to bed."

"That's okay. I can clean up. Your school work comes first."

"I am so glad to hear that, because I would like to sign up for a summer course."

"Okay. At the University?"

"No, I want to sign up for the Proscenium in the Park program. I want to try acting. I figure that the experience of just being a bit player in an ensemble will teach me something about the whole theatrical thing, something that will help me write better plays."

"Have you talked with Dr. Cahners about this yet?"

""No, and I don't see why I should. *You* are my grandmother, not Dr. Cahners. I really don't understand why it is that he is so involved in our family and why he seems to call the shots on so many matters."

"Talk to him. Will you do that anyway?"

"Yeah, sure. After the end of school."

○ ○ ○

Paolo waited until the classroom was cleared before walking up to the desk where Vera Prentiss was grading papers. "I have something for you."

"You do? What?"

"It's another play." He laid the blue presentation folder on her desk and turned it to face her.

"Wow. Thank you so much." She flipped open the folder and read the title page: "Stepping Off-Stage: A Play in Two Acts for Two Actors."

"It's dedicated to you."

"Oh, that is sweet. Thank you."

"And guess what. I'm going to be acting this summer, the Proscenium in the Park program: Shakespeare, Miller, and what's-her-face."

Vera stood and came around the desk. "Fantastic! Good for you." She put out her arms for a hug. Paolo pulled in close and slowly ran his hands down her back. She pulled back but he held on. "Whoa. It's a little hot in here. Don't you think it's getting a little hot in here?" She leaned back to look him in the eye. Her smile became a straight slash and her eyes narrowed. "I'm serious, Paolo."

"I'm serious, too."

"No, you are not." She gently prised his arms away. "You're a student and I'm your teacher. There are rules."

"I'm not a student here, not at the moment. I just finished my last final. I'm on summer break. I could be anyone. And you are not my teacher, not anymore, because I finished AP Euro and aced the exam."

"You may be a darn smart debater and maybe more than a little precocious, but you are still just a kid. I am sorry to have to say that. I don't want to bruise your budding male ego, but to this woman in her late twenties, you are just a kid—a very nice kid, a very smart kid, but just a kid."

He pulled back but didn't stop smiling at her. "Your words are said with such conviction, but in your eyes I read no confidence."

"How poetic, Paolo." She lowered her voice to a whisper. "But this has got to stop. Do you hear me? I like you, I really do. I think you have amazing talent and you will do amazing things with your life, but this is going nowhere. You have misread me, misunderstood my enthusiasm. I'm a teacher. I'm happy when a student succeeds. I'm happy for you—as a teacher for a student. That's it."

"Then why is your voice shaking?"

"Because ... because I don't want to lose my job. Because I don't prey on vulnerable kids. Because ..."

He kissed her. "I don't want you to lose your job either. I'll go."

She watched him leave the room without turning back, then finally exhaled.

Chapter 21

Danny tried to act relaxed as he handed his passport to the Customs and Border Protection agent at Boston's Logan Airport. What was going to happen now? Would some computer algorithm compare his passport number and name to the passenger manifest of his flight. He knew those lists were sent ahead to the US authorities, which could then confirm that Danbury Bradman had never boarded the flight, yet now he was arriving in Boston. The agent held up the passport to compare with Danny's face, then kept glancing back and forth between his computer and the passport. "Can I please see your boarding pass from this flight, Mr. Bradman?"

Now I'm screwed, Danny thought. He fumbled around in his pockets. "I don't know exactly what I did with it, I ..." Then he remembered, he had already checked in when Luca and his pal had pulled him from the security line. He still had the unused boarding pass for economy class. What had he done with it? He had been holding his passport along with the boarding pass while waiting in line for the security check. He would have put them together into the breast pocket of his sports jacket. He reached in and felt the stiff paper. "Oh, yes, here it is." With his heart still pounding, Danny handed it to the agent, who squinted at it and said "Uh!" then handed it back.

"What brings you to Boston, Mr. Bradman?"

"I'm a journalist with the *Financial Tribune*. I'm here on a story. I can show you my press credentials if ..."

"That won't be necessary. How long will you be in the country?"

"Two weeks."

"Okay." He stamped and initialed Danny's entry form and slipped it into a tray, then stamped his passport and marked his customs declaration form before handing them back. "Good luck. Enjoy your stay." He raised his hand to signal the next person in line. "Next."

Danny took a deep breath and let it out slowly as he stepped onto the escalator down to baggage claim. He walked straight through to the green "Nothing to Declare" line and waited behind a long queue of arriving passengers who gestured and argued in disparate languages as if there were nobody else in line. Yet another wait at the rental counter convinced him to change his plans. He had intended to go directly from the airport to the address in East Boston, but it was clear he had not been realistic about either Alitalia or US Customs and Border Protection. A projected 6:45pm arrival time had turned into almost nine before he was finally pulling out of the lot in his rental car. First stop would be a hotel, a shower, and a night of jet-lagged tossing and turning.

○ ○ ○

The address in East Boston turned out to be a vacant lot resembling a fresh archeological dig, with the outline of where a house had, until recently, stood. Next door, a run-down gray-shingled triple decker was now in midstream of being dismantled. Danny got out of his car and joined the elderly couple who stood watching a wrecking crew gradually reduce the wood-frame house to stacks of building materials and piles of rubble. "What's this all about," he asked.

"Someone with too much money putting up a house nobody can afford." The man spoke without turning to face Danny, as if the comment was directed toward the house or its owner. "They buy two lots and put up one monster house."

"Really? Here? I mean, in this neighborhood ..."

The woman faced him with a grim smile. "The old neighborhood is a Cheshire cat. Know what I mean? Soon there will be nothing but a smile, then nothing."

"That's a pity."

"You from England or someplace?"

"Yes. Amazing you could guess that." He let his broad grin signal his teasing intent.

"It's your accent. You sound like that guy on television." She did not pick up on his tease.

"No, he sounds like me."

"What brings you here? You on vacation?"

"No, I'm not on holidays. I'm looking for someone. Rossi, Orlando Rossi. I thought he lived here."

The man at last looked away from the wrecking crew. "Naw. The Rossis are long gone. They were the first to sell, before the Figlios."

"You don't happen to know where they moved to, do you? I'm looking for Orlando Rossi."

"You'll have to stand in line."

"Why is that?"

"You're the third person this week to ask about him."

"Really. So, can you tell me where I might find him?"

"County jail if they caught him. South America if they didn't."

"Are you saying Mr. Rossi was wanted by the police?"

"Well, yeah. The police wanted him for questioning. The other guy was some foreigner with a funny accent. He claimed Orlando owed him money. Funny. The Rossis were so quiet when they lived here. Didn't much talk with nobody. We never saw much of them. Now they're gone, and suddenly they're as popular as peanuts."

"You say they sold the house."

"Yeah. I don't rightly blame them. It was a good offer. Even I might be tempted, you know what I mean. But I do hate to see the area go all upscale just because there's all that money coming in from the casino and the bio labs and all that."

The trio watching the demolition crew was joined by a boy of about twelve or thirteen who arrived on roller blades and did a smart toes-up stop next to Danny. "You lookin' for the Rossis?"

"Yeah. You know where I can find them?"

"Der." The boy held out his left hand palm up.

"Ah, I see, a shakedown. Do you take euros? All I have is twenties in American money."

"Twenty is just fine." He raised his open palm.

The woman looked away as the man curled his lip in disapproval. "Don't pay the little shyster."

Danny fished a twenty from his wallet and slapped it into the boy's hand. "I need to find Orlando."

"You need to? Then maybe another twenty and I'll tell you."

Without warning, the man's hand shot out, grabbed the boy's wrist, and twisted it behind him. "Tell the man or give him his money back. Or I'll tell the Pelletiers who broke the windows in their garden shed."

"Okay, okay. They moved up to Chelsea, some dump over a storefront on Spruce, I think."

With an extra twist and a shove, the old man let go of the boy. "Get lost, Darian."

"Fuck you!" the boy shouted as he skated off.

○ ○ ○

Danny found a coffee shop with Wi-Fi and settled in to do some research. Eventually he located a record of a year-old sale of "retail space with two-bedroom apartment" on Spruce Street in Chelsea. The buyer was listed as Roma Properties Development LLC with an East Boston address that Danny recognized as the very spot he had just visited. He called the telephone number but got only a voicemail announcement. He disconnected without leaving a message. Before he could put the phone down, a ringtone started; he answered reflexively after the first notes and without checking the caller ID.

"Oh, Danny, finally I reach you. I've been calling and calling, but you never answer and you never return my calls."

"Francesca?"

"Where are you, Danny? We need to talk."

"I'm …" He hesitated to say. Perhaps it was better nobody knew where he was. "I'm on assignment. It doesn't matter."

"It matters to me. Can you meet me at the café? You know the one."

"No, I can't. And I don't think you should call me."

"I know, but we really have to talk. Something has happened. I know what Luca told you. Now he's in the hospital."

"What happened?"

"He and his partner were ambushed. He told me it was a setup. I'm scared. I'm scared for you, too."

Danny's mind was racing, sifting through options and scenarios. "Look, I don't have time to explain, but you need to get out of Rome. Cover your tracks as best you can. Don't fly. Take the train to Germany. Get to the Tribune office in Frankfurt and talk with a man named Kurtis Trauben. Tell him about me and all this. I'll reach you through him." Danny took a breath. "Listen, be careful. And … I love you."

"Oh, Danny, Danny. I love you too."

"Hang up now. Don't call me. Wait until you hear from me."

Danny sat staring at the phone and wondering whether he

was overreacting. Maybe it had become too easy for him to imagine intrigue and to get caught up in conspiracies of his own misconceptions. Maybe too many years of covering boring financial stories had primed him to blow things out of proportion. No, he thought, this one was real. He had walked into a minefield, and now buried ordnance was exploding all around him.

He scrolled through his contact list and tapped the entry for his Frankfurt Bureau Chief. Kurt answered on the third ring.

"*Hallo, hier spricht Trauben.*"

"Kurt, it's Bradman."

"Where the hell are you? And what's going on?"

"I want you to hold that story on Dermott. I have some rather dramatic developments."

"The story has been moved up. *The Guardian* jumped the gun and also a couple of newsmagazines: *Das Bild* here and *Time* in the US. We already will come off looking like slow ponies late out of the gate."

"Then let's do a story that will blow them all out of the water."

"What, that PR piece you wrote? Even after Maxi rewrote it, it's still as limp as *spätzle*."

"No, not that, the real story. I'm sending someone to meet you. She should arrive from Rome in the next few days. Listen to her, then give me a call." He hung up.

○ ○ ○

Danny found the boarded up storefront with the apartment above on the first try. He parked across the street and walked around the corner to the residence entrance. When he pressed the intercom button, a female voice answered. "Yeah?"

"I'm looking for Orlando Rossi."

"Who are you?"

"Danny Bradman. I'm here from Rome. I—"

"Rome, huh? Does he know you're coming."

"No, I wanted to surprise him."

"Okay, I guess. He should be back before too long. You're a friend, right? I suppose you can come on up and wait for him here." The door lock buzzed, and Danny pushed his way into an empty stairwell that smelled of stale cigarette smoke.

Chapter 22

The electricity between Paolo and his teacher should have been obvious at the one-act play competition. He had been following her every word and move with his tongue hanging out, and she was not exactly discouraging his attention. Her behavior bordered on unprofessional, but we chalked it up to some combination of her inexperience and the festive occasion. In addition, Vera Prentiss was an artsy sort, flashy and unconventional in dress and demeanor, a twenty-first century edition of an Isadora Duncan. Somehow we took that as a reassuring explanation.

Paolo's interest in the theater intensified over the summer. We allowed him to do the acting program with the naïve confidence that it was a passing fancy. We were surprised, however, when he announced midsummer that he wanted to switch from Peabody Academy to another prep school that had a better theater arts program. We said we would consider it, but that the decision would depend on the quality of the academic programs at the new school. With that, we sealed our fate and clinched the decision. As we checked into the school, it became clear to us that Paolo had already done his homework and lined up his ducks in a neat row. We had been set up.

St. Xavier Preparatory School had strong programs in math and science and a well-deserved reputation for rigorous academics across the board. In the previous five years, dozens of graduates had gone on to top-ranked schools, including several to MIT and a couple each to Stanford and Cal Tech. It was also an all-boys school, which we regarded as a bonus in light of Paolo's emerging and sometimes problematic interest in the opposite sex. The fact that it was a Catholic school, put Seppina squarely in Paolo's camp. In short, we could not construct a persuasive argument against the move. Paolo applied for admission and, to no one's surprise, was immediately accepted. At the start of the school year, Paolo made the switch from Peabody Academy to St. Xavier Prep.

It was a year of many changes. Paolo turned sixteen, got his learner's permit, took driver's ed through the school, and passed the driving test on his first try. He absented himself as often as ever, but retreats to the attic were now often replaced with borrowing the car for trips to other venues, not all of them known to us at the time.

Paolo leaned against the archway into the living room and swung the keychain in front of him like a censer at high mass. "Can I use the car tonight, Nonna?"

"What for? Where are you going?" Seppina frowned. "It's a school night."

"Yeah. I want to study with Spike."

"Spike? Who's that? What kind of a name is Spike?"

"Greek or something. Spikolonus I think. Everyone calls him Spike. I don't even remember his actual first name. Todd, maybe. Can I go?"

"Okay. Back before midnight or I call the cops." She waved an index finger toward him.

"Right, like you'd actually do that, Nonna."

"I would. Now give your Nonna a kiss. And drive safely."

Paolo gave his grandmother a peck on the cheek. "Don't worry. I'll be careful."

○ ○ ○

The little house in Amesbury looked deserted when he arrived. Despite his research, he was not even certain he had the right address. The town was nearly to the New Hampshire border, and it seemed an unlikely locale. The house itself was tiny and dark. The only reassuring thing was out front, where a green VW Electric Beetle with flower decals was parked in the weedy driveway. It seemed to fit.

He walked slowly up the path and stood on the brick front steps, still uncertain whether he could actually go through with his plan. The rush he felt was new to him, a mixture of hesitance and eagerness, something he had read about but never experienced. He pressed the button beside the door. Nothing. He pressed again and waited. Nothing. One more time, he told himself. One more time, and then you can leave. He pressed and held the button.

The door opened the moment he released the button. "The doorbell doesn't work." The woman was holding back a small wrinkle-skinned dog that was panting and pawing the air, struggling to reach the screen door. "Easy, Mooshu, it's just somebody at the door." She looked up from the dog. "I thought I heard somebody drive up. I was just on my way out to get ... Oh my God! What the ..."

"Hi, Vera."

"What the ... ? What are you doing here, Paolo? How ... ?"

"I just wanted to say hi, get some acting tips from you, maybe get some suggestions on my new play."

"Oh, no. You can't ... I mean, I can't."

"If you want me to go away now, I will. If you want me to stay away, I won't."

She held tight to the dog's collar as she opened the door and looked up and down the street. "I guess you can come in. For a minute. But how did you find me?"

"The Internet. Easy."

The dog panted as it tried to jump at Paolo. "She'll calm

down in a minute. She's not used to visitors."

"At least she doesn't bark."

"She's a Shar-Pei; they're quiet. And she's pretty well trained. Mostly. Go ahead and have a seat while I take care of Mooshu."

Paolo took a seat on the couch opposite a bricked up fireplace and sat with his hands folded until she returned without the dog.

"So, Paolo, what have you been up to? How's school going this year?"

"It's going. St. Xavier is a good school. My drama teacher is not as good as you, but he's okay. I'm learning a lot."

"That's good. You know, I really was looking forward to having you in class this year."

"I know. That's why I left."

Her eyes widened. "I don't understand. I thought you ... liked me."

"I did. I do. That's why."

"Oh ... okay, now I think I get it. Look, Paolo, maybe it's better if you did leave."

"I brought you another script, a screenplay." He pulled a rolled up sheaf of paper from his pocket. "I'd like to get your feedback and help on it."

"What about your drama teacher at Saint X?"

"Mr. Nivens is more of an acting coach, not so much into writing. And he's not you. Please take a look at it." He handed her the screenplay. "Go ahead. Read it."

"Now?"

"Why not?"

"Okay." She unrolled the script and rerolled it backwards in an effort to flatten it. "So, 'The Fourth Wall.' Do I detect a recurrent theme here? 'Stepping Off-Stage' and now 'The Fourth Wall'?"

"Go ahead and read it."

She sat down in the overstuffed chair next to the fireplace and started paging through the screenplay. "This reads like a rewrite of your play from last spring. You still ..."

"Have a thing for you? Yes, you could say that. And you?"

"Oh, Paolo, I don't know what to say. I told you once before, there are rules."

"But I'm not at Peabody Academy anymore, I'm at St. Xavier Prep. And I'm sixteen. In 2013, the Massachusetts Supreme Judicial Court ruled to reaffirm that the age-of-consent legitimized—"

"Oh, so now you're a lawyer?"

"No, just in love with the most amazing woman."

"Don't say that. Please don't ..." She bit her lip. "This isn't right."

"Then tell me to go." He stood up, a look of resignation on his face.

"Okay. Go." Paolo didn't blink, but a tear started welling up. "Oh, Paolo, my sweet Paolo. I am so sorry." She held out her arms. "Come here." She held him to comfort him.

Minutes passed and neither of them moved. He could feel her breasts against his chest, two bright and burning spots. His head rested against hers; heartbeats thundered in counterpoint in his ear. "I want—"

"Shhh. Be quiet. Just be quiet."

Chapter 23

Francesca hesitated before knocking on the Institute Director's door. He was casual with staff, but his unwritten rule was that a closed door meant not to disturb him. "*Scuzi*. May I come in?"

"I suppose. What do you want?"

"I am sorry to interrupt, Emilio, but I would like to take the rest of the week off." She stood before his cluttered desk with her hands clasped behind her. "My husband is in the hospital, and I need to take care of him. Perhaps you heard about the two *Caribinieri*?"

"I did. That was your husband? Oh, I am so sorry. Yes, of course, take the time. I hope he recovers quickly."

"Yes, I hope so, too. If it's all right, I'd like to leave right away." He nodded, and she left, closing the door behind her.

She had spent the evening before planning her moves, hoping to make up for her ignorance. As she crossed the front hall on the way to her cubical, she picked up the guest register from the table by the entrance and held it at her side, partially hidden by her full skirt. At her desk, she used a modeling knife to cut out a page, being careful not to leave any visible residue at the binding. To make the gap in dates and times less obvious, she filled in a few blank lines at the bottom of the verso page with concocted entries and carefully altered a few adjacent ones. She then turned to the online databases.

She knew there were automatic overnight backups created somewhere offsite, but she had few ideas about how she might trick the system. Using the page cut from the guest book as a guide, she started deleting retrieval requests. She searched for and deleted all the records documenting Danny's research, then used her administrative account to reset the system date and time, forcing a backup cycle. While the system churned and spewed its stream of records to some invisible destination, she paged back through her desk calendar to make sure there were no incriminating notes. Finally, she logged back in as administrator and restored the reference time and date. She wasn't sure whether her crude and hasty hack would work, but it was the best she could think of and it might help. She considered herself lucky that she worked for an underfunded organization that used outdated software without the kind of safeguards a better endowed facility might have.

She jumped at the voice behind her: "What's this? You're still here?"

"You startled me, Emilio. I ... I was just making sure everything was complete and up-to-date before I left. You know me."

"Yes, I do—always thorough. That's what makes you so good as a librarian. But please, go look after your husband. The archives will take care of themselves for a few days without you."

○ ○ ○

On the way to the train station, Francesca detoured to stop at the hospital. At first she was told that no visitors were allowed, but the nurse relented when she pleaded as the distraught wife. In the intensive care unit, she was shown to a bed where her husband lay unconscious, surrounded by cables and beeping, clicking medical machinery. An oxygen mask covered his nose and mouth, and a surgical dressing covered much of the rest of his face. Francesca bent to lay a gentle kiss in the exposed space above his left eye. "*Mi amore*, I will return."

○ ○ ○

Danny stared at the wall of the apartment as Mrs. Rossi busied herself in the kitchen. He jumped at the sound of a key in the lock. The door to the stairwell banged open, and through it came a short, red-faced man in cargo pants and a blaze-orange Carhartt construction shirt with a coffee stain at seven o'clock. He stopped to twist the deadbolt closed before turning to notice Danny. "Who are you?"

"My name is Danny Bradman." He rose from the chair. "Are you Orlando Rossi?"

"What do you want?"

"Are you Orlando, the musician?"

The man guffawed. "No, I'm Orlando the developer, Roma Properties Development. Orlando the musician died of malnutrition a decade ago." He laughed some more.

"But you are Orlando Rossi, right? You toured with a punk band in Italy."

"Punk? Hell no. Heavy metal. We ... Wait a sec. How the hell you know this? Italy was a one shot when I was not much more than a kid. Did Guido send you? Huh? Tell him I'm not interested. I been there, done that, know what I mean?"

"I don't know Guido. I just flew from Rome. I work for the *Financial Tribune.*"

"And this financial rag from wherever is interested in long-dead rock bands and decrepit ex-guitarists?"

"Well, not exactly."

"Then what, exactly? Hey, you want a beer? I got Miller's and Bud Lite. Name your poison." He passed Danny without offering his hand. When he returned from the kitchen, he had two cans of beer cradled in his left hand. He paused to wipe his right hand on his pants leg before extending it to Danny. "Welcome to America, home of the freeloaders and the brazen. In case you don't know the difference, I ain't no freeloader. Sit. Here." He handed Danny a Bud.

Danny tried to open it without spraying all over but ended up having to awkwardly slurp cascading foam from the side of the can. "Sorry."

"Just beer. Don't worry. You met my wife? Hey, Suze. Come in 'ere. Meet Danny. He's from—where you say you're from?"

"England. But I flew in from Rome."

"Ah, here she is. Suze, this here is Danny."

"Yeah, I know."

"How you two know each other, anyway?"

"He showed up at the door not five minutes ago, dummy."

"Oh, I thought, like, you meant you knew him. He's here to talk about heavy metal."

"Well, not really. I'm a reporter, working on a story about the late Arturo Dermott, and—"

"Gimme the beer. And get outta here." He stepped toward Danny. "Get out before I break something."

His wife looked on wide-eyed. "Whatsa matter you, Lando? You losing it? Let the man drink his beer."

"He's from ... he's ... Look, I don't wanna talk about it. It was long time ago, 'fore we met."

"Maybe you don't wanna talk about it, but maybe I do," she said. "I'd like to hear about this old stuff. You never talk. It's like you was born the day before you met me. I don't know nothin' about you back then."

"Maybe it's better that way." They looked at each other in silence.

Danny took the break in the argument as a chance to probe provocatively. "What's the big deal? The charges were dropped, extradition withdrawn. Right, Orlando?"

Suze looked at Orlando and narrowed her eyes. "You were in trouble, weren't you. In Italy. That's why you never talk about it."

"Yeah, and I still don't want to talk about it. I put together a life here. I've played it straight. I work hard, keep my nose clean, and we get by. Once we remodel the downstairs and rent it, we'll be good. That old stuff? It's done, over, nothing to see here, so let's move on, people."

Danny gestured with his can of beer. "Then why did you suddenly move? Why have the police been looking to bring you in for questioning?"

Orlando's face whitened and a tremor started in the hand holding his beer. He backed into the barstool in the corner and plopped down. "You really done it now. You done it good, mister newspaper man."

"What have I done? Tell me about it. Set me straight."

"What the hell, it's going to blow anyway. Somehow I knew it would catch up with me someday."

His wife stood beside him and put her hand on his shoulder. "Look, whatever it is, we can face it together." He patted her hand. "You didn't kill nobody, did you?" she asked.

"No, Suze, I didn't kill nobody. Least I don't think so. But I did do some things I wasn't proud of, and I got myself in trouble with them Italians. I ..."

Danny reached for his reporter's notebook. "Please continue."

"You can't use my name. Ya hear? No names."

"Okay. So, tell me. What happened in Italy."

"Well, me and my girlfriend went to Italy to work with this band she heard of through some friends from school. She had just graduated, some certificate in music management. Who would've believed you could go to college for something like that. She was going to manage the group, and I was going to fill in for the rhythm guitar. He, like, got food poisoning or something. Anyway, the tour tanked. They didn't like my style and I didn't like theirs. I mean, it was like heavy metal watered down with fizzy-pop folk shit. No wonder they were playing to empty halls.

He took a sip of beer. "So there we were, in Italy, no work and no money. We're back in Rome panhandling, sleeping under bridges, and this guy comes up to me one day and says he knows a guy who's hiring and would I like to work as a recruiter. Recruiter? Turns out it's this fancy-dancy medical place that does research. They need guinea pigs, girls only, like between eighteen and twenty-something. They pay really well, and for me there's a finder's fee. My cut is good money, so we're all of a sudden living okay. And I get paid in cash.

"I'm bringing in these girls I meet—always have been a real charmer with the ladies—and they're all happy with the money. I mean, like, not so much Italian girls, mostly kids from Africa, Morocco, Greece, ya know, immigrants and like. For every one I find that passes the physical and all, I get a wad of euros.

"Then I get this idea. I know the girls are getting lots more than me: money upfront and a big bonus when they finish the experiment. I'm chill with what's going on, seems like an okay place. There's doctors and such from around the world: China, Brazil, Spain, all over. I know at this point my girl doesn't exactly trust me no more. She didn't know what I was into to get the bread, but she wanted no part of it." He took a sip of his beer. "So I tell them about my girl, tell them to call her, like she's been referred or something. They call her, she gets accepted, and then has to spend time at this research hospital. We don't like being apart, so I get this idea to go visit, sneak in and see her.

"That's when the shit hit the ceiling fan. I get spotted and suddenly I got these guards tearing after me down the halls. I mean, they have these AK-47s, and I'm thinking, what kind of research hospital is this? I find this emergency exit and push through into an alleyway. I'm running, turn the corner, and there's this guy in a white coat carrying this big clear plastic bag. I push past him, and I see what's in it: body parts. It looked like chopped up body parts, and I don't mean chicken parts, neither.

"Next day, the police come knocking at the apartment we was subletting. I grabbed my stash from the recruiting and hightail it out the back. I make my way back home the long way around, by way of Austria and Switzerland. Took three months." He took a big swig of beer and looked at the floor.

"Your girlfriend, the one you abandoned at the hospital, what was her name?"

"I said no names."

"Just for my notes. I won't use it in my story."

"I feel so guilty about that, but I was real scared. Still, like, I seen other girls back from the research all just fine. I figured she'd be okay, too."

"Do you remember her name?"

"Course I do. How could I forget Carla? Carla Franzetti."

Chapter 24

We knew Paolo was in some kind of intense new relationship, but, short of tracking him, which had its own risks, we couldn't seem to be able to find out where he was going or who the girl was. In his talks with me, which were becoming more irregular and infrequent over time, I would try to probe without being too intrusive. Not surprisingly, Paolo always knew exactly what I was doing and would deflect my every oblique thrust with a deft verbal parry. It became a kind of game between us. I would dig for tidbits of information, and he'd supply disinformation. I would leave sentences unfinished and wait for him to fill in the blanks as if we were doing ad hoc Mad-Libs. I would drop the names of girls from his past or new friends made through play productions and watch for a reaction. He would either deadpan through it all or give me an ersatz response that would send me off chasing the wrong scent.

I once told him that his acting skills had grown impressive. He grinned and said it was the result of good one-on-one coaching. That one sailed right past me. I guess I thought it was another decoy.

We might have remained in the dark were it not for the next Young Playwrights Competition. In accepting the first prize, Paolo thanked his acting coach at the Prep, his grandmother, and, finishing with a flourish, his first drama teacher, who, he told the audience, remained his most important inspiration. His look past the footlights was like a laser pointer into the front row. As he passed Vera on his way back to his seat, there was a knowing exchange of glances and a hand-squeeze so quick that anyone not watching closely might have missed it.

I face-palmed as Paolo slipped back in among his friends. It should have been so obvious. At the Foundation there was a collective sigh of relief. Chaim was disapproving, as could be expected of a closet Freudian, but the rest of us figured that at least it was unlikely we would be facing an unwanted pregnancy. I wavered over whether to let on to Paolo that we knew or to keep mum. True to form, Paolo gazumped me at his next physical.

Paolo buttoned his shirt and rolled the right sleeve back down. "So, what's the verdict, doc? Am I on death's door yet?"

"Hardly, although the brain scans show signs of adolescent hubris and post-pubertal petulance."

"Har, har, har. So tell me, doc, when did you figure it out?"

"Figure what out?"

"*Cherchez la femme.*"

"I should look for the woman?"

"You already found her. You already know who my girlfriend is."

"Really? What makes you think that?"

"It's so obvious. You stopped playing the feint-and-jab word games about girls. That could only mean you had it figured out."

"Or that I no longer cared."

"That'll be the day."

"You think I care about your love life?"

"Yeah. And so ... ?"

"So?"

"So, aren't you going to say anything?"

"What do you want me to say?"

"Cut the pre-shrunk shrink game, doc, and answer the question with a statement."

"Okay. I can certainly understand what you see in Vera. And, it goes without saying, what she sees in you. But she's too old for you. Maybe you're too young for her, which is actually a different matter that also bears exploration. She's intelligent, attractive, and no doubt exciting to be with. I wouldn't have pegged her as your type, but there's no accounting for taste—or animal attraction, for that matter. There, how's that? You got a whole series of statements."

Paolo clapped. "Bravo. But you still don't approve."

"Is that what you want, my approval?"

"You're at it again, doc. Okay, let's say I do want your approval, just for the sake of argument. Then what?"

"Then the answer is yes, I don't approve, but then I know you well enough to be sure that you don't give a shit."

"She's good for me, you know. And I give her—I know this may sound weird—but I give her a sea anchor, a stabilizing force against wind and wave."

"No, it doesn't sound weird. I believe it, especially expressed in such poetic language. You are quite the writer. This relationship is probably good for both of you, even if the greater society would sooner see her stoned and you institutionalized than accept it. How old is she anyway? Twenty-nine? It can't last. She'll be getting on in years and you'll still be growing into honest adulthood. She'll start sagging just as you're at your peak of prowess."

"You think that matters to us? It's a lot more than physical. We've even talked about marriage. And children."

Cahners leaned back in his chair and nodded gravely. "Time will tell, my boy, time will tell. In the meantime, you have classes to take and she has classes to teach. A lot of twists and turns may lie in the road ahead. Have fun, but don't lose sight of where you are going."

"Wherever that is, which everybody else seems to know. What about you, doc? You never talk about any family—except my family."

"I'm your doctor."

"You don't get off that easy. Tell me about your family."

"I'm it. I'm an only child and an orphan."

"No, I'm serious. I want to hear."

"And I'm serious and am happy to tell. That's the truth. My parents were killed in a freak accident while I was away at college: an avalanche on a ski slope where no one thought there could be avalanches. Suddenly, I was on my own. I was settling their estate between graduation and the start of med school. They left me enough to get by on, plus I was on a Tundsted Grant, so I managed."

"No brothers and sisters?"

"Nope. Like you, just another spoiled only child." He winked.

"And Mrs. Cahners?"

"Nope. Never married."

"Not even in love?"

"In love, yes, but that's the easy bit. Love is harder than being in love, and marriage is harder still. It didn't work out."

"What happened?"

"Alicia chose another man, and I chose medicine, not in that order, however. Alicia preferred an exclusive relationship, a noncompete agreement that I couldn't give her at the time. Medicine can be a demanding mistress, but also a comforting companion. I'm contented with permanent bachelorhood. My family is right here."

○ ○ ○

Paolo knew better than to be open with Seppina about his relationship with Vera. It could only anger and confuse her. Still, he kept yearning for acceptance and something like normalcy.

Inspired by their shared interest in the theater, he and Vera had found a way to date more or less openly. Paolo called it cosplay, a term he picked up from a couple of school pals, super-hero fans who had recently attended Boston Comic Con in costume. He gave his scraggly beard free rein and subtly darkened it. He would dress up in a sports jacket and polo shirt, and Vera would fix her hair in a ponytail and dress down in clothes that looked as if they might have been borrowed from one of the high-school girls at Peabody Academy. Then they would head north into New Hampshire where they could pretend to be just another young couple in love and were less likely to be spotted by someone who knew them.

Seppina kept asking when he was going to bring his girl home to meet her. Paolo pretended to be playing the field and told her there was no steady girl to bring home. On the other hand, he talked up his teachers, particularly Mr. Niven. "Do you think it would ever be all right to have Mr. Niven over for dinner sometime? He's wicked funny and real nice."

"Well, I suppose ... but it's hardly the usual thing. I mean, there might even be rules against it. The school might not think that would be ... appropriate."

"Why, Nonna? What would be wrong with that?" He was playing a game, but it was too subtle for his grandmother.

"Well, it could look like favoritism between the teacher and his student."

"Yeah, right. I can see how someone could see it that way. Like, because he's still my teacher." He paused for emphasis. "Yeah, of course."

○ ○ ○

Returning from a trip to one of the local malls, Paolo bounced into the kitchen and sat down. "So, Nonna, you'll never guess who I ran into at the Apple Store."

"Who?"

"I don't know if you remember this teacher, from way back, when I was still at the Academy. Ms. Prentiss? Remember her? I didn't recognize her at first, it's been so long. I was surprised she remembered me."

"Ms. Prentiss? Which one was she? English literature?"

"No, European history. Anyway, she's down this way for a teacher's workshop or something today and tomorrow, and I suggested she stop by before she heads back home. She lives like, Vermont or New Hampshire or something. She's tied up with late sessions tonight, but I thought maybe we could have her over for dinner tomorrow, after the workshop is over. What do you say?"

"Well, I suppose ..."

"She's really nice. I mean, I don't really know her all that well—I only had her for that one course—but I think it could be fun to have an ex-teacher over. And I hate for her to be getting home late and have to cook dinner and all."

"What about her husband? Is she married?"

"I don't know for sure, never thought to ask. We can find out tomorrow. I told her 6:30. But I can cancel. I told her I had to check with you to confirm."

"Well, it hardly would be right to uninvite her now. Sure, she can come to dinner. I'll do my special meatloaf."

Paolo kissed her cheek before heading for the stairs. "That's great, Nonna. I'll let her know."

○ ○ ○

Dinner finished with a fresh-baked peach pie that Seppina flanked by spherical scoops of her homemade raspberry granita. "Humble meatloaf but elegant dessert," she said as she placed the plates."

"The meatloaf was anything but humble, Mrs. Fanzetti."

"You're very kind, Ms. Prentiss. In Italian we say *molto simpatico*. And there's no Mr. Prentiss?"

"There is. My father, Ronald Prentiss, down in Florida. But, no, I'm not married ... yet." Under the table, Vera felt Paolo's hand on hers.

"A smart, pretty young woman like you?" She recognized Paolo's look from across the table as her cue to back off, but she ignored it. "Why? I think you'd be what we used to call a catch."

Paolo stared at his pie and squirmed, but Vera smiled warmly at Seppina. "I probably am a catch, as you call it. Eventually, yes, I expect to marry and have children, but it has to be with the right person and you never know when the right person will arrive or who they will be."

"Well, don't take too long. You don't want to waste your best years." Seppina took a bite of pie. "It's a little runny, isn't it."

"I think your pie is perfect, Mrs. Franzetti. Uh, did you marry young?"

"Young enough. My Toni moved here from Connecticut, we saw each other at the nine o'clock Sunday mass, went out for coffee after, and he asked me to marry him three weeks later. I had just turned twenty. He swept me off my feet." She bit her lip and looked away.

"You had a daughter, am I right?"

"Yes. Carla, Paolo's mother. I guess we were not good Catholics, as they used to say, not that we didn't try, but I had three miscarriages before Carla and then the doctors told us that was all. And then we lost Carla, and then I lost my Toni, and ... I'm sorry. It still is ... Please excuse me. I'll be right back." She pushed back from the table with her head turned away and headed for the kitchen, closing the door behind her.

"I'm sorry. I didn't mean to upset her. I just want to get to know her."

"I know that." He gave her hand a squeeze under the table. "I think she knows that, too. Give her some space and she'll be all right."

o o o

Seppina apologized as she returned from the kitchen carrying a tray set with a coffee service. The conversation turned from family to theater. "Have you had a chance to see much theater, Mrs. Franzetti?"

"Oh, yes. You wouldn't know it to look at him, but my Toni was quite the intellectual. Paolo can tell you what a whiz he was at chess. Right? And we used to go to quite a few plays. We saw Peter Sellars' version of 'Orlando' at the A.R.T. and the premier of David Mamet's 'Oleanna' in Cambridge. But My Toni and me, we liked music even better than plays. We used to go to the symphony open rehearsals, which were much less expensive than the concerts but just as much fun. And you'd get to see how it was all put together, how they polished a piece or subtly changed it. Of course, after Paolo came along, we could afford the regular tickets but we never had the time anymore. Isn't that just how life seems to work? Now I have the time *and* the money, but no one to go to the symphony with me."

"I'd gladly go with you, Mrs. Franzetti, anytime."

"Aren't you the sweet one. I didn't think young people cared for that sort of music anymore. It's all rock and rap and new-metal and ... you know."

"I love symphonic music, especially the big romantics—Wagner, Berlioz, Schubert, all of them. And the greats of the last century, like Stravinsky, Prokofiev, and the three Bs: Bloch, Bartok and Bernstein."

"That's some collection there. I can't say we ever thought much of Stravinsky—too strident—and I always thought of Leonard Bernstein in terms of 'West Side Story' and the like."

"I'll have to take you to hear Bernstein's *Chichester Psalms* sometime. Gorgeous. It'll bring tears to your eyes."

"It doesn't take much to do that these days. I guess you could tell that."

"That's all okay, Mrs. Franzetti. I'm a three-tissue movie goer myself, as Paolo can confirm."

Paolo held his breath at her slip, but Seppina ignored it. "Please call me Seppina, dear." She reached across the table and laid her hand on Vera's."

"And you call me Vera, please. I'm serious about the symphony. It's time to get you back into good music. And I think Paolo could benefit from broadening his musical tastes. We can drag him along, whether he likes it or not."

Chapter 25

Danny spent several hours glued to his laptop, searching public databases for traces of Carla Franzetti. He decided to start with the simplifying assumption that she had returned to the US after her stint as a lab rat for the unknown and probably unlawful medical study. When no one by that name turned up in current records in any state, he turned to the historic record. She might have married and changed her name, but nothing popped up in his search of marriage licenses or wedding announcements. He eventually hit pay dirt with a birth certificate and a death certificate, both in Massachusetts, for a Carla Josephina Franzetti. She had been twenty-four when she died during surgery following a traffic accident. A search of news archives for that period recovered an earlier report of the accident that contained a small detail confirming that it was the right Carla Franzetti, most likely fresh off a return flight from Rome: "Police said that the car driven by the victim, not named pending notification of next of kin, had just been rented less than an hour earlier at Logan airport. The woman was taken by helicopter to Boston Trauma Center where she is reported to be in very critical condition. The driver of the truck with which she collided, a Mark Denfield of Troy, New York, was unhurt. No charges were filed."

That was that; the trail ended in a cul-de-sac. He idly tapped the down arrow key, staring but not watching as the results page from his search of Massachusetts birth records scrolled by. Suddenly, something caught his attention: a date. He flipped to the tab displaying the death certificate for Carla Franzetti. It was the same date! He switched back, called up the birth certificate, and let out a shout: "Eureka!" Heads turned in the Starbucks. Danny grimaced and shrugged. "Sorry."

There it was, in front of him, the breakthrough that had eluded him. On the very day that Carla Franzetti had died, a baby was born in the same hospital: a boy, Paolo Carl Franzetti. The woman had been pregnant. Orlando Rossi had a son.

○ ○ ○

Danny was trying to keep his voice under control. "Did you talk with her, Kurt? Did she tell you about what happened." He pressed the cellphone tighter against his ear.

"I talked with her. *Sie ist ein Zigeuner, ein Wahrsagerin.*"

"She may be a gypsy, part gypsy anyway, but she's no for-tuneteller."

"Then she is sick in the head, a conspiracy-theory crazy. She talks nonsense."

"I am telling you, there are records connecting this man here in Chelsea with Dermott and the medical research facility out-side Rome and the two from Spain who were charged. The wo-man here who died was carrying a child after she returned from participating in some experiments at that place. This guy, Rossi, was a procurer for the clinic that Dermott was involved with."

"But Dermott was dead by this time, if the timeline you outlined is correct."

"Yes, but it was the same clinic, and the records had been filed together, so someone thought they were related."

"So you think. Do you have these records?"

"The records here, yes. I can get printouts of everything. And I'll keep digging. The ones in Italy, well, I have a contact there who might get access, but he's unconscious in the hospital after being shot."

"Inconvenient. Or maybe convenient. More conspiracy theories, no doubt."

"It's not theory. Something stinks about this whole thing. You have to hold the story until I can wrap this up."

"Can't. It goes to press for next weekend."

"Then take my name off the byline."

"Gladly. Besides, you don't work here anymore."

"For four more weeks, I do. Technically."

"Three-and-a-half, technically. And as soon as we're off the phone, I am going to call London and tell them to kill your credit card immediately. I don't know what idiot failed to do that the day you were given notice, but from here on out you can pursue your quixotic quest at your own expense."

"*Vielen dank.*"

"*Bitte.* You're welcome. It's the least I can do for my star reporter."

"Fuck you, too, Trauben."

"Likewise." A faint and distorted sound was just audible: fingers rattling a syncopated rhythm on a desktop. "Good luck, Bradman." Click.

○ ○ ○

Danny called Francesca's cellphone again. No answer. She had made it to Frankfurt, this he now knew, but he could not get through to her. He was feeling as if he were on an amusement park ride, with the scenery whirling in a blur first this way, then that. He was simultaneously elated and depressed, anxious and calmly determined.

His phone played its tinny version of a vintage Stadio track, an Italian-rock ringtone that Fancesca had passed to him. It was her.

"Francesca, at last. Are you okay?"

"Yes, I'm okay. I just got back to my hotel from talking with your mister Trauben. He should maybe be called *Herr Saure Trauben*.

"Sour grapes. Very good. So you know some German?"

"A little. *Ein bischen*. I'm sorry I didn't get your calls. They kept dropping before I could answer or going directly to voice-mail, and I couldn't figure out how to pick up messages from here, and I wasn't sure whether I should call. You said wait until I hear from you. I'm sorry."

"I'm sorry, too. I'm sorry you had to worry. I talked with Kurt, *Saure Trauben*, but got nowhere with him."

"He is a stubborn and closed-minded man."

"He is. Look, I want you to come here as soon as you can. I bought you an open ticket from Frankfurt to Boston on Luft-hansa, very expensive, but I put it on Herr Trauben's tab, which I won't be able to do again. You can collect it from Lufthansa at the airport. When can you leave?"

"I can't. I have to go back to Rome."

"Why?"

"Luca died. I have to go back to bury him."

"Oh, I am sorry. That must be ..."

"It was already over, but I still ..."

"Look, I hate to say this, but I think returning to Rome is not a good idea. It could be dangerous. I think these people, whoever they are, have infiltrated the *Carabinieri* and who knows what other parts of the police and government."

"I have to go. I'll be careful."

"Please don't go."

"I must. I love you, Danny."

"I love you, too, Francesca. Please be careful, cover your tracks if you can."

"It is hard to hang up. I have missed your voice. Not just your voice."

"I know. *Buon viaggio.*"

Danny stared at the silent phone for several minutes before planning his next move.

Chapter 26

We knew there was a reporter for the Financial Tribune Europe pursuing a story about Dermott. We even knew the man's name. I don't pretend to understand how our security people do it, but they have ways of knowing whenever anyone taps into certain databases or makes particular searches online. They are not really our security; they worked for a subsidiary of one part of the European empire that Dermott had established. I think they were based in Italy, but the details had never been made clear to me. It was all on what governments call a "need to know" basis, and up to that point it had been deemed that I had no need to know.

They, the security people, may or may not have thought they were right on the reporter's heels, but it later became clear that they did not yet realize he was in the United States nor how close he was to us. I don't know what we would have done had we known, and I hesitate to imagine what the security people would have done had they known.

Seppina looked out the sidelight beside the front door. The patterned glass distorted the image of the man standing there, but she didn't think she would recognize him in any case. She opened the door a few inches. "Yes?"

"Are you Mrs. Franzetti? Giuseppina Franzetti?"

"Yes. What are you selling?"

"I'm not selling anything. I—"

"They all say that."

Danny laughed. "I guess they do, but I'm not a salesman. I'm a reporter, Danny Bradman, with the *Financial Tribune*. Here's my card."

She took the card and held it at arm's length, squinting to read it. "I don't have my reading glasses with me. What exactly is this *Financial Tribune*?"

"We are based in London and are one of the world's foremost publishers of international business and financial news. I work for the Frankfurt bureau, in Germany."

"My, very impressive. And what could you want with me?"

"May I come in and talk with you a few minutes? I just have a few questions. Would you mind?"

"Mr ... ."—she checked the card— "Mr. Bradman, I don't know anything about international finance. I'm just a house-wife, and that's what I've been all my life. I don't understand what this is about."

"It's about your daughter, Carla Josephina."

Seppina's lip quivered. "My daughter's been dead over six-teen years, Mr. Bradman. What business could you possibly have asking questions about her? I think you better go." She started to edge the door closed.

"I understand, believe me I do. I truly do not want to trouble you. I know about your daughter's death, and I am so sorry. It must have been terrible for you. She was so young." Seppina said nothing as she stared off into the distance. "I believe she had a son before she died. Paolo Carl. Is that right?"

"Our grandson. I've been raising him alone ever since my husband passed away, God rest his soul. I really don't think there is anything for me to talk about with you, and you can't talk with Paolo. He's just a boy, in high school, and he has enough to handle without having some foreign reporter barging in and asking questions."

"I understand you wanting to protect him, and I would need your permission to interview him in any case, but maybe you could help me. I'm wondering about his father. I—"

"Now stop right there, Mr. Bradman. You just crossed the line."

"I'm sorry. What did I say wrong?"

"There are some things that are meant to be left alone. Who Paolo is has nothing to do with who his father was. We are all born in sin, Mr. Bradman, not just this baby or that. God gave us a way to wash away our sins, and it's up to each of us to find our way back to God and his Grace. Are you Catholic, Mr. Bradman?"

"No, I'm not a Roman Catholic."

"If you were, you'd understand, and if you were, you would know enough not to ask a question like that. Now leave us alone, leave Paolo alone." She closed the door in his face and watched through the sidelight until he turned and walked back to his car.

○ ○ ○

Paolo found Seppina in the kitchen, washing the floor, something he had come to recognize as a favored activity whenever she was stressed about one thing or another. "What's this?" He held up the business card he had picked up from the table by the front door.

"Oh, that. Nothing." She dipped her sponge mop into the bucket again, worked the lever to squeeze out the excess water, and returned to working it back and forth over a smudge only she could see.

"This is some nothing. I mean, the guy is a reporter from Germany. Wow. What did he want?"

"He was looking for somebody. I can't remember who. He had the wrong address." She stopped mopping and reached for the card. "I'll throw it away."

"I can do that."

"No you can't. I don't want you tracking over my clean floor. It's still damp."

"No prob. I'll chuck it in the wastebasket in the living room."

"No. Then I'll just have to fish it out and put it in the trash."

Paolo opened his mouth, then thought better and closed it without saying anything. It was clear that the visit had not been about nothing, and the card was important. He handed it to her. "I'm going up to study. I'll be down for dinner."

He paused at the bottom of the stairs to retrieve his ever-present blank book from the mesh pocket on the outside of his backpack. He flipped to a fresh page and wrote down the name and telephone number from the card before he forgot them.

○ ○ ○

During the especially busy couple of days that followed, Paolo forgot about the business card. He was about to make some notes about an idea for another one-act play when he saw the entry he had made: Danbury Bradman, Senior Correspondent, Financial Tribune. "What the heck. What do I have to lose?"

He tapped in the number but got an intercept saying that the number was invalid or not in service. Funny. Then he realized he had forgotten to enter the international access code first. He was not even sure whether his account would allow international calls, but he tapped a plus sign, then 49, the country code for Germany, and the phone number. Cool, he thought, it's ringing. He waited. It kept ringing and ringing without an answer. Finally he shrugged and disconnected the call.

He wrote down his ideas for the new play but kept thinking about the call. Silly me, I forgot about the time difference. It would be the middle of the night in Germany. No, that shouldn't matter because the man was in the US and the number had been clearly marked on his card as his mobile phone. Maybe I misremembered the number and wrote it down wrong.

Paolo took the backstairs down to check the kitchen trash bin. It was empty and lined with a fresh plastic bag. Too late. Ah, well, so much for that little mystery, he thought. Unless.

Paolo trotted back up the stairs to see if he could track down the man online.

Chapter 27

Danny didn't recognize the calling number, but it was local. "Danny Bradman here."

"Hah! I found you. I knew I could."

"Who is this?"

"You talked with my grandmother a couple of days ago. Mrs. Franzetti."

Danny's heart started pounding. "Paolo? Is this Paolo Franzetti?"

"Yeah. What did you want with my grandmother?"

"Did she tell you to call me?"

"You remind me of my doctor. Do reporters also answer questions with questions?"

"Did she give you permission to talk with me?"

"No. Do I need her permission?"

"We really should play it straight. Look, can we meet, can I come over and talk with you, for a few minutes anyway?"

There was a long pause. "I don't know. Can you tell me what this is about? What you want to know?"

"It's about your parents."

"My mom died when I was born—actually before I was born, which probably sounds weird, but that's the true story. I don't know who my father was. My Nonna doesn't talk about it. She's kinda old-fashioned about those sort of things—out-of-wedlock, as they used to call it. Look, maybe I should check with Nonna. Don't call me, I'll call you if it's okay with her."

"Wait, I—" The call cut off.

○ ○ ○

Danny spotted the *Trib* among the overseas newspapers at the crowded international newsstand in the middle of Harvard Square. With its tinted paper, a trademarked pale yellow-green, it was not hard to pick out among the other foreign newspapers. Danny picked up the last copy of the weekend edition and found the feature story on Arturo Dermott. The byline listed Maxi Hauptmann, with reporting by Dan Bradman. "The bastard just had to do it."

"Hey, mister, you want the paper or not? You can't read it unless you buy it."

"Sorry. Yes, I want it." He fished a bill from his pocket. "Here, keep the change."

"You pay over at the counter. Just take your turn."

Danny started reading the story as he waited in line to pay.

Dermott. The name is part of the corporate identity of some twenty-six companies scattered over much of the globe. At least another dozen lacking that recognizable hallmark are known to be part of the empire of enterprises left behind by the late Arturo Fabian Dermott, the Italian-American inventor and entrepreneur who was born a hundred years ago next month. It is rumored that many more companies are part of the financial web woven by the world's most famous businessman that nobody knew.

His net worth in 2007, not long before he died, was estimated by Financial Tribune Europe at €85 billion ($114.8 billion in today's dollars), but only a handful of his companies were publically traded, so the full extent and worth of his holdings is speculative. In his last years, Dermott donated large sums to numerous not-for-profit foundations involved in scientific research, including many originally established by him.

Dermott, though famous, was a recluse about whom surprisingly little is known. The only child of an Italian nurse and an American civil engineer, he was born in an Italy between wars. He was sent to America to live with his maternal grandparents at the age of eleven after the Italian Fascist government under Benito Mussolini barred Jews from public schools. (His mother was Jewish but not observant.) He never saw his parents again.

A scientific prodigy, he filed his first patent application in 1943 at the age of seventeen. The device, a special microphone that could capture clear speech in environments with very high noise levels, was deemed to be of strategic value for the war effort, and the patent was not actually issued until several years after the end of World War II. Dermott went on to be awarded well over two-thousand patents, more than twice the lifetime record of Thomas Edison.

Arguably the best known of his inventions is the Dermott Flexi-panfocal Lens, a miniature zoom lens without moving mechanical parts now widely used in smartphones and pocket cameras, but his inventions range widely, including devices used in construction, aerospace, communications, optics, and even, late in his life, bio-technology. The fully-automated trait-specific gene-editing technique he devised is the secret weapon behind the so-called New Agron Revolution that has, in recent years, given the world a cornucopia of faster-growing, disease-resistant fruits and vegetables that are also more nutritious. His final patent, awarded not long before his death in 2008, was for an elaborate scheme to create artificial mammalian egg cells for in vitro fertilization and implantation. It is not known whether the technique ever found application.

Maxi had done a decent job with her rewrite, and, to his surprise, she had included material from his own notes about trying to track down what had happened with all of Dermott's wealth.

"So close. I'm so close, but you just couldn't wait, could you, Kurt."

"What did you say, mister? Here's your change." The man at the cash register held out a mix of coins and bills.

"Oh, I'm sorry I was—"

"Talking to yourself. Do it all the time myself. Here."

"No, keep it." Danny walked away, head down, finishing the story as he headed for the underground parking garage diagonally across the street. He was getting angry. There was still a story to tell, but it was not this one. He chided himself for his caution. Why should he stop with just a phone call to the boy? He had an address and a name. What was stopping him? He was a reporter, and it was time to start acting like one.

He fished out his parking stub.

○ ○ ○

Danny parked well down the street where he could keep an eye on the house without being too conspicuous. There was no car in the drive. He did not want another rejection by the grandmother; he wanted a talk with the boy. There was no way to tell who might be home and who was not until somebody arrived or left. It could be a long afternoon.

Danny whiled away the time by reading the *FT Weekender* cover-to-cover, including a report on the impact of the growing regional drought on the future prospects of Catalonia. In his absorption, he almost missed the car rounding the corner from the other direction. When it slowed and signaled to turn into the drive, the blinker caught his attention. Danny reached for the cheap binoculars he had picked up at the mall across from his hotel. He leaned back in the seat in an effort to be less conspicuous as he tried to bring into focus the Volkswagen Electric that was stopping in the driveway. It looked like there were two people in the car. The driver was getting out. "Okay, turn around so I can get a look at you. Let's see what Orlando's teenage son looks like." The young man started walking away, toward the front porch. The passenger was getting out: a woman. The grandmother? No, too young. She was saying something to the boy as she walked around to the driver's side. At the front door, he turned back toward her. Danny twiddled with the focus knob, trying to get a better view of the boy's face. He did not look like any son of Orlando Rossi, but his face was somehow familiar. "Oh my God," Danny whispered. "This is impossible."

He was startled by the shadow and the sharp tap on the driver-side window. He lowered the window and looked up at a uniformed policewoman. "Is there a problem, officer?"

"Can I see your license and registration?"

Danny fumbled for the papers. "It's a rental. Here's the rental agreement. And here is my UK driver's license. I'm visiting for a couple of weeks. If you want, I can get my passport out for you."

The officer bent to get a better look into the car. She gestured toward the binoculars on the passenger seat. "You looking for something or are you a birdwatcher or what?"

"No, I'm a reporter." Danny realized the situation looked pretty sketchy. "I can show you my press credentials."

"What are you doing here, Mr. Bradman, in this neighborhood? We got a complaint call that said you've been sitting here for hours. What have you been doing all that time?"

"Not much. Actually I was reading the paper, *FT Weekender*. I write for it."

"That so? Well, this is a residential neighborhood. You can't just decide to park here to read the paper. You need a resident parking sticker to park on the street. Didn't you see the signs?"

"No, ma'am, I didn't. I'm sorry. I didn't know one needed a permit. I'm from England. I've only been here a few days."

"Yeah, well, I should cite you anyway. Next time, read the signs. Here's your license and the rental agreement. I suggest you don't come back to this neighborhood. People around here can be a little suspicious of strangers, and they don't take to nosy reporters either. Got it?"

"I do understand, officer. I'll be on my way."

○ ○ ○

Danny drove straight back to his hotel. He checked his watch and added six hours. The Frankfurt office would still answer, but Trauben would probably have gone home already. He could call Trauben's mobile number or he could text him. In for a penny, in for a pound, he thought. He called and waited through five rings.

"What do you want?" Trauben sounded like he had downed a few beers since leaving work.

"You'll never guess who I saw today."

"The ghost of Arturo Fuckin' Dermott, I suppose."

"Close."

"I'm not in the mood for guessing games tonight, Bradman. I got reamed today by London over your expenses and my, quote, inept handling of Mr. Bradman's abrupt departure, un-quote. Just tell me what the hell you're talking about, and let me get back to drinking my dinner."

"I saw Arturo Dermott's son."

"What the hell are you talking about? The man died childless. Everybody knows that—documented fact."

"Well everybody is wrong, then. I saw his son, spitting image of the old man. Now are you going to let me finish this story?"

"You've been fired, remember. Two weeks left, that's it, and then you are not only physically but fiscally gone. Dead. I will not mourn your abrupt departure, which has not been abrupt enough for me or for my boss."

"My love to you, also, Kurtis. Enjoy your dinner."

He hung up and immediately dialed Francesca. An intercept message said the caller could not be reached. He left a voicemail asking her to call back as soon as she could.

He was just stepping out of the shower when his phone rang. He scrambled to reach it in time.

"Bradman here."

"It's Orlando. They're after me."

"Who's after you?"

"The Italians. They're trying to expedite me or something."

"I think you mean extradite, that they're trying to get you to Italy for prosecution, right?"

"Right. They came around asking questions. Really scared Suze. Ya gotta help me."

"I don't know what I can do for you. If extradition proceedings are started, you'll need a lawyer."

"Thanks a lot. Thanks for nothing. You're the one that led them to me."

"Pardon? What makes you think that?"

"Because they mentioned you when they were talking with Suze."

Chapter 28

We breathed another collective sigh of relief after the FT Weekender story hit the newsstands. It was mildly provocative, but it was not the exposé we feared, nor did it seem to us there was much chance that the wrong people would read it and put two and two together.

Of course, we didn't know it at the time, but Paolo and Vera had settled into a routine of thinly disguised dates that ranged from public park concerts and movies to the occasional dinner theater. With Seppina as their unwitting chaperone, they had perfected the art of surreptitious handholding and quick slips out to the parking lot. Ironically, even as they got more time together, they were getting less time alone together, and the tension of sustaining the pretense was beginning to take its toll.

The lime-green VW with the flower decals pulled into the driveway and Vera stepped out. "Hi, Seppina. Fixing up some new flower baskets, I see."

"Yup, trying to keep the place looking nice so as the neighbors don't complain. Gets harder and harder as the years go by. What brings you here?"

"Didn't Paolo tell you? I'm here to drag you both to the symphony. The Commonwealth Philharmonic is performing an all Bernstein concert. I was down this way anyway, so I thought I'd come early. Maybe I can help you with those flowers."

"Oh, you don't have to do that. You're already doing this concert for us. I think Paolo did tell me about it after all, but I am getting forgetful, you know. Do I have time to clean up and change? I can't go to a concert looking like some hired land-scaper, now can I?"

"Go ahead, there's plenty of time. Where's Paolo? What's he up to?"

"He's out back, in the gazebo. And you can guess what he's up to."

"Writing?"

"Is the pope Catholic? Does Paolo do anything else?"

"I'll go say hi and see if I can get him away from his notes for at least a few minutes."

She found Paolo deep in thought, staring at the screen of his tablet. "And what's my favorite playwright working on now?"

When he looked up to answer her, she kissed him. What was meant as a greeting peck became open-mouthed hunger. "It's been so long. I've been missing you, missing having you in me." She squeezed between him and the wrought-iron table and straddled him as they continued to kiss.

"Me, too," he said, catching his breath. He slipped his hand inside her blouse and she reached for his zipper. "Wait. We can't. What if my grandmother decides she needs a different trowel from the toolshed?" He withdrew his hand and pulled his zipper back up.

Vera exhaled sharply. "Maybe that wouldn't be the end of the world. Maybe it's time we came out in the open. It's not that long before you turn eighteen and you're off on your own."

"Look, the worst that can happen to me is that I get grounded or my allowance is cut. If word got around that you were molesting a student, you would be fired. That would be the end of your career."

"Molesting a student? Is that what this is?" She playfully pushed at his chest.

"Don't get violent with me, woman. Just because you're on top, doesn't mean you can physically abuse me." He gave her another playful kiss, which she interrupted.

"Oh, so now we've gone from molesting to abusing? Do you want to fight about it, mister?" She grabbed his wrists and started wrestling.

"Off, quick!" He pushed her away. "Here comes Nonna."

Vera climbed sideways off his lap and almost tumbled into the screen of the gazebo.

Seppina stepped out from around the corner of the house. "Just wanted to let you two know I'm going in to cleanup and change. I'll meet you downstairs in, say, twenty minutes."

"Okay, Nonna. We'll be there."

"Do you think she saw us?" Vera's whisper was hoarse.

"Maybe. Yeah. Let's hope not."

o o o

Vera pivoted in the passenger seat to face the back as Paolo took the off-ramp. "So what did you think of the concert, Seppina?"

"I liked the medley from 'West Side Story,' especially 'America.' That was good."

"But what about 'Chichester Psalms'? See what I mean about Bernstein as one of the great Twentieth-Century composers?"

"Well, I don't know. Maybe I am too old-fashioned. It was kinda loud. And it reminded me of that Stravinsky stuff: so much bashing and clashing."

"Well, what about the Twenty-Third Psalm movement? Wasn't that sweet. I mean, yes, the boy soprano was a little unsteady at points, but still ..."

"Well, it did start out pretty, but the words ... It wasn't any Twenty-Third Psalm I recognized."

Paolo glanced at her in the rear-view mirror. "That's because it was in Hebrew, Nonna. That was the original, from the Bible."

"Maybe, but I always loved, 'The Lord is my shepherd, I shall not want.' So beautiful."

"*Adonai ro'i, lo echsar.*"

"What?"

"Same thing. The Lord is my shepherd, I shall not want."

"All that in a couple of words?"

"Biblical Hebrew, Literally 'Lord shepherd, no want.' It's a very compact language."

"How do you know all this? Not from studying the catechism."

"From St. X. They require two terms on the Hebrew Bible. Since I didn't get that at Peabody Academy, I had to make it up. Kinda interesting. Actually, I like languages. Spanish class is one of my favorites."

○ ○ ○

By the time they pulled into the drive, Vera had fallen asleep. "Poor thing. She must be exhausted," Seppina said. "Why don't you drive her home? Tomorrow's Saturday. We can work out how to get her car back to her in the morning."

Paolo was uncertain about his grandmother's suggestion, which seemed to come out of the blue. "You sure? It'll take me more than an hour up and back. I mean, is that okay with you?"

"Of course, it's all right."

Vera opened her eyes and gave her head a shake. "What's all right?"

"If Paolo gives you a ride home. You seem really tired, and I don't like the thought of you nodding off or something."

"It's going to be after midnight by the time he gets back. That's really too late."

"Well, maybe you have a couch where he could stretch out, then he could give you a ride back in the morning to pick up your car."

"Well, yeah, I suppose ..." Vera and Paolo looked at each other, unsure of how to respond.

Seppina leaned forward from the back seat and put a hand on Vera's shoulder. "I wouldn't want to put you out. If it's too much trouble ..."

"Oh, it's no trouble. I can give him an extra pillow. As long as he doesn't mind being woken up in the morning by an eager Shar-Pei wanting to be fed and let out, he's welcome to sleep on my couch."

"All right, I suppose." Paolo tried to make it seem like reluctant surrender. "I'll just duck in and grab my toothbrush.

o o o

Paolo struggled to keep his speed down on the way up to Amesbury. As soon as Vera unlocked the front door, he lifted her up and over the threshold. "Can you believe this? We are going to get to spend the whole night. We get to sleep together—I mean *sleep* together, for real."

"I know. Funny, it almost felt like Seppina was setting us up."

"Naw. that's crazy. Well, maybe, I ..." He took her by the hand and started gently tugging her toward the bedroom.

"Where do you think you're going. You get the couch tonight, like I told Seppina. You wouldn't want to turn me into a liar now, would you?"

"The couch? Oh, really?" He pulled her toward him and planted kisses on her neck and ears.

"Yes, really."

"Oh, really?" He slipped his hand up under her skirt. She let out a sigh.

o o o

Mooshu did as expected in the morning and nosed the bedroom door open to climb in bed with them, padding and circling like a cat before wedging himself between them.

"Pushy dog you have, lady."

"Not as pushy as some former students."

"Students? Plural? I see, I'm just the latest of a long line of exploited teens, another in a trail of broken-hearted boys: lured, loved, and abandoned by the ... dramatic flourish ... Proscenium Predator!"

She whipped the pillow from under him, snapping his head back against the headboard with a wooden thud. He put up his arms as a shield while she walloped him with the pillow. As Mooshu ran up and down the bed in excited ellipses, offering her weak yelping version of a bark, Paolo slipped out of bed. "How about I fix us coffee?"

"You know how to do that? The K-cups are in the left-hand cupboard, second shelf. Can you manage?"

"Klutz though I am, I can manage."

He returned with two steaming mugs. "Cream, no sugar for you, and double of both for me."

"You know, you're a real wuss, Paolo. Two sugars, two creams? Yuk."

"Not a wuss, I just never liked coffee. Chocolate is my drug of choice."

"Like I said, you're a wuss." She blew a kiss at him. "But a cute wuss."

"Hey, what's this?" He picked up a magazine from the nightstand.

"The new issue of *Up-Stage*. It's a journal about new plays for high-school drama groups. I haven't read this one yet, but the feature is about a play based on letters from some kid who was separated from his parents during World War Two."

"Oh, yeah." He scanned the cover. "Arturo Dermott. Seems like everywhere you turn these days there's something about him." He flipped to the main story. "Hmmm. 'Return Flight: a play in two acts for young performers'." He started reading. "Oh, yeah, you're right. Says here the guy was sent from Italy during the war to live with his grandparents here in the States—in North Boston, in fact. Let's see: the play is based on letters he wrote to his parents back in Italy over several years. Seems the letters were found after the war, then misplaced, and recently rediscovered and authenticated as being from Dermott to his parents. It says here that the title of the play is taken from the fact that his parents told him the trip by steamship to America in 1938 was his 'return flight' taking him home. Then when he flies back to Italy after the war, he thinks of that as his real return flight."

He flipped the page. "And here's a picture of him at my age, and ..." Paolo froze.

"What is it? What's wrong?"

"Nothing, I guess. Just a weird feeling." He closed the magazine and put it back on the nightstand. He sat down on the edge of the bed, staring at the floor and thinking about trust funds and doctors who were always on call. Mooshu climbed onto the bed and into his lap. He scratched her behind the ears. "Sometimes I wonder who I am, Vera."

Chapter 29

Danny worked the mouse pointer in lazy circles. Something was nagging at him, something that didn't add up. If the Franzetti kid was Arturo Dermott's son, why was he living in a modest home in a Boston suburb? Why was the heir to the Dermott fortune *in cognito*? What was there to hide?

Danny pulled up the word document with the JPEG of the scrap of foolscap along with his quickly typed notes of Bernat's translation:

> *The highway is too long. We must detour through underbrush and learn from bananas. Dr. Fonseca y Morales is the tour guide. He will agree because he is our ace in the hole. He can sink the hole-in-one on the ninth green. The Koreans have good relations with Afghans, but the Chinese have better labs. We will be planting olive trees whose fruit I will not see. I prefer pit bulls, but beagles are better with fine print. Clear title, nothing less. The answer is cross, thorn, zed zed zed. I should have tried this earlier. It works.*

What if it was drug-induced word salad, free association about something that puzzled Dermott at the time? A puzzle. Treat it as a puzzle, not so much a code but the symbolic language of a disciplined mind suddenly given free-reign to muse in metaphor.

Danny reached for his ever-handy legal pad and started making notes, connecting words and ideas with lines in his own rough approximation to mind-mapping. He stared at the sheet, looking for unlikely patterns. There were dog breeds: pit-bulls and beagles. What kind of beagles were good with fine print? Yes, of course, legal beagles, lawyers who could secure clear title. Clear title to what? Cross, thorn, zed zed zed. Three zeds, what is that? He wrote ZZZ on his pad. Sleep, snoring. And cross and thorn. Hang on a minute. What's a cross? He drew an X. And thorn? Wasn't that a runic letter in the old English alphabet? What is it now? Oh, yes, as in Ye Olde Tavern. So: XY and then ZZZ.

Now what? Back to the dogs. I missed this, Afghans and Labs are also dog breeds. He looked back at the original text, where he found the Catalan word *laboratoris*, clearly laboratories not Labrador retrievers. But what is this about Koreans good with Afghans? Afghan hounds? Korea? He remembered something about that, but it eluded him. He Googled "afghan hound Korea" and there it was, near the top of the first results page: "South Koreans Clone First Canine." Suddenly the sketch he had made became a clear picture with nearly every piece of the puzzle in place. What is special about bananas? Until the New Agron Revolution with genetically edited varieties, nearly all the commercial bananas grown in the world were genetically identical. And where did Fonseca y Morales fit in? He was a doctor specializing in fertility, in vitro fertilization, implanted embryos, mitochondrial transfer. The mind-bent metaphors made sense: hole-in-one, ninth hole, all of it fit together.

Danny was thinking about what his next move would be when his phone rang with the Italian rock ringtone: Francesca.

"I'm here in Boston. I just landed; we're still taxiing. Can you pick me up at the airport? I don't have any luggage, so I should get through the visa checks pretty quickly if my papers are as good as I think they are."

"How did you get here? You never said anything."

"You said to cover my tracks. I had some help. I can't wait to see you; I'll tell you then."

"Which airline? Where do I pick you up?"

"I came in on Lufthansa, of course. You'll find me. I'll be the gypsy girl with the big smile."

○ ○ ○

Francesca had been right. Danny spotted her outside Terminal E on his first pass around Logan. It took what seemed like many minutes to crawl forward in the heavy traffic and finally find a gap that allowed him to pull over to the curb. He slipped out and stood by the car, waving. "Francesca, over here."

She ran through the crowd, grinning. At the car, she embraced him and kissed him repeatedly. "Save it," he said. "There will be time later. Get in."

As he waited for a break in the traffic to pull out again, he reached over and patted her thigh. "How did you pull it off?"

"It was quick but complicated. Luca helped me."

"Luca? I thought he …"

"He is, but he left me something before he died. I found a packet in the apartment when I stopped by to change. You were right. It was a trick to get me back to Italy. They let him die to lure me to Rome. He could see it coming. He left me a doctored passport and directions, I guess by way of somebody he trusted."

"But you were …"

"Maybe you underestimate gypsy girls. Before I left Frankfurt, I got a refund on the full-fare ticket you bought me. That wasn't easy, but they gave me a travel voucher. In Rome, after I got Luca's message, I left the apartment within minutes and drove straight up all the way to Austria, where I booked to Boston. Simple. And here I am, Anya Tedeschi, from Milano. I don't know how Luca did it, but the passport was flawless. Even my picture was good. How's that for covering my tracks?"

"Damned good, if I say so, but we'll see. I have a lot to share with you. I think I figured out that note in Catalan and what is going on. Let's go to my hotel, then we'll get you some new clothes. Well, maybe we'll see to some other things, first."

Chapter 30

The message from security was ominously brief. We are taking care of the reporter, it said. I had visions of accidents that were not accidents and disappearances that baffled local police. Helen, always the realist to my alarmist tendencies, reassured me. Corporate security was not like the CIA with its extrajudicial special rendition; the Foundation and its kin were not part of some network out of a new James Bond film, she said. I was not fully convinced. The fact that we got the heads-up from security was itself a sign that the reporter was becoming a problem, yet the Financial Tribune article had been non-threatening.

Helen told me not to worry, that the Foundation had vast resources and access to many creative minds. I asked her to be more specific, but she offered nothing concrete, either because she didn't know what was possible—or because she did.

The silver-gray Mercedes pulled out of the hotel garage right behind Danny as he left to drive out to see Orlando Rossi again. The driver kept his distance but never allowed more than one car to get between him and Danny's Ford rental. It wasn't until the turn onto Orchard Street in Chelsea that Danny became aware that the same car was still behind. Was it actually following him? A chill ran through him. Luca Volpone had been killed because he was digging into the Dermott affairs, and Luca was a cop. Danny was just a reporter, now working a beat for which he was singularly unqualified.

Danny tensed as the car pulled up alongside, then drove on past and turned the corner. It was driven by a big wrestler-type with a woman in the passenger seat, but Danny did not get a good look at either of them.

○ ○ ○

Orlando was not particularly happy to see Danny but offered a beer anyway. "Sure." Danny shrugged. "How about a Miller's?"

"All out. Bud Light or Bud Light, name your poison."

"A Bud is fine, thanks."

Orlando returned from the kitchen with the beers and handed one to Danny. "What brings you back? I thought we covered it all last time. I really don't like chewing over this stuff more'n I hafta."

"I really just have one question."

"Ya coulda phoned."

"I know, but I thought in person might be better."

"Whatever. Shoot."

"Well, I was wondering, ah, whether Carla Franzetti might have been pregnant when she became a subject in that medical research."

"No, no way. See, they tested the girls. They couldn't use any girl who was pregnant. I suppose because of whatever drugs they was testing or whatever. Why?"

"Because Carla was pregnant when she returned to Boston. That was the same year that you said you came back."

"Now that's damn weird. How in hell could she get pregnant in the hospital?"

"You did say you broke in and visited her."

"Broke in is not the word for it. I walked in the front door with a bunch of other people, some kinda tour or something—Asian doctors, Chinese maybe—then I split off down this corridor: for authorized personnel only. And I was only with

Carla for a few minutes before this nurse pokes in and then dashes off. Next thing I know, I got guys with guns chasing me."

"So, there's no way Carla could have been carrying your baby?"

"No way."

"Okay, I guess that's all I need to know. Thanks." He set the unopened can of beer down on the glass-top coffee table.

"That all? Don't you want to finish your beer?"

"No, I need to get back and do some more work. I really appreciate your help. Give my regards to your wife."

o o o

The traffic light was changing as Danny approached, but the car behind him squealed its tires as it swung out and around him, then cut back in to stop suddenly in front of him. Danny slammed on the brakes, but too late. He plowed into the car's right rear, scattering red shards from the taillight lens. It looked like the same silver-gray Mercedes that had been tailing him earlier. The passenger, a woman, remained in the car as the driver got out and, without inspecting the damage, rapped on Danny's window and twirled his finger. Danny nervously rolled down the window and looked up into the fat face of an overgrown bulldog. "We're sorry. Meet in the coffee shop at the hotel in an hour." He lumbered away, got back into the car, and sped off, running the red light amidst a chorus of honking horns.

o o o

The coffee shop of the hotel was nearly empty, so it was easy for Danny to spot the woman in the pinstripe pantsuit. She stood as Danny approached. "Hi. You must be Danbury Bradman. I'm Penelope Robertson."

"Call me Danny, please. How the hell do you know my name."

"And call me Penny. I'm so glad you're here."

"Did I have a choice? Where is the muscleman?"

"Oh, Fred? He's hitting the men's room. He'll be back in a jiffy."

"In a jiffy, huh? Okay, what is this all about? You two have been following me, and then you make me rear-end you, and then you leave the scene of an accident? How am I supposed to deal with the car rental people now? Like, tell them I was 'front-ended' by a hit-and-run driver?"

"Don't worry about the little fender-bender. We'll pay for the damage. Fred gets impulsive, and he's not the best driver, but he's good at what he does and gets what he's after."

"What exactly does he do? And what is he after?"

"You?"

Danny glanced around nervously. "He's after me, you say."

"Well, he's after what you know, anyway." She looked up. "Oh, here he is."

Crossing the room, the man looked like a sumo wrestler in a business suit. He shook Danny's hand with a crushing grip. "I'm Fred Quincy. You have something we want." He sat down and leaned his head close to Danny's "And we want it very badly."

The color drained from Danny's face as he tried to remain calm. "Really? What do you think I have?"

"I thought you were an investigative reporter. I'm surprised you haven't figured this all out already. Here's my card."

Danny read it and frowned. "Acquisitions Editor? Dihedral Publishing Group?"

"Yeah, and this is my colleague from our legal department, Penelope Robertson. She's very effective, very."

"Dare I ask at what she is so effective?"

"Getting her way, getting what she wants."

"She said the same thing of you."

"Did she, now. A regular mutual admiration society, aren't we, Penny?"

"Look,"—Danny inched his chair away from the table and mentally measured the distance to the side entrance—"I still don't know what you want."

"You're working on a story. We want the exclusive rights."

"Say what?"

"The Dermott story, the untold story: we want it."

"How do you know ..."

"Really, Mr. Bradman, how hard do you think it is to track what you've been doing? We talked with your editor. It was obvious your colleague Maxi Hauptmann was not the investigator; it had to be you. From there one thing led to another, and now we have you, right where we want you."

"I ..."

"Show him the contract, Penny." She reached beside her and retrieved a sheaf of legal-size paper held with two acorn clips at the top. She handed it to Fred who righted it and passed it on to Danny. "Go ahead, read it."

Danny scanned the first page, then flipped through successive pages. Suddenly he stopped and pointed. "The advance."

"Negotiable."

"High six figures? Are you serious?"

"I said, it's negotiable. Also the sliding scale royalties."

"I don't know what to say. I mean, I thought you ... Well, let's just say a book deal was not what I had in mind."

"It's more than just a book deal. We're asking for world serial rights, reprint, film and television, translation: the works."

"I don't know. I'd at least like to get a feature article in *Harper's* or *The Atlantic*."

"Done. We planned to do excerpts in advance of publication anyway as part of building buzz. We just want to orchestrate the whole business to maximum effect. And maximum payoff, too, of course."

Danny kept skim-reading through to the end. "There's a non-disclosure clause."

"Of course. We don't want to risk any leaks or to cue the competition. Besides, if word gets out that we paid this much, from now on everyone else will squeeze us for a similar deal."

"I don't know."

"Okay, a million flat, then: a quarter on signing, a quarter on delivery of the manuscript, and the rest on publication. And we'll give you all the time you need. We want your best work."

"Wow. I really don't know what to say."

"Say yes. I can even change the payment and you can sign right now. I'm authorized to do that, aren't I, Penny?" She nodded. "So, let's do it."

"I need some time to think. Can I take this and read it more carefully?"

"Of course. We're in town for a couple more days. Remember, though, you're not the only journalist on the planet. Somebody else is sure to come along eventually and start dogging your footsteps. If you miss this chance, they won't." He stood. With a subtle nod of his unsubtle head, he signaled his lawyer companion to rise, too. They both shook Danny's hand and left him standing with a folded document in his hand.

He was busy thinking about joining the wealthy circles of his former readers. The ominous bulge under Fred's coat went unnoticed as a chubby arm held the door for his lawyer partner.

Chapter 31

Francesca was not in the room when he arrived. He ordered champagne from room service and was stretched out waiting for delivery when the door lock whirred and clicked. Francesca's smile lit up the room as she entered. "Have I got some news for you," she said.

"Wonderful! And I have some incredible news for you. I've ordered champagne; should be here any minute."

"Terrific. So, you go first. What's your news?"

"No, ladies first."

"Okay, silly. Guess where I've been?"

"No idea."

"I've been digging through dusty archives at the Boston Public Library, scrolling through microfilm at the Christian Science archives, and pawing through files at the board of medical registry or whatever it was called." She danced her way over to him and stood with her hands behind her back. "I have a name, a doctor's name."

"What doctor?"

"The doctor who has been taking care of our mysterious boy, a doctor with ties to Dermott."

"How?" He sat up.

"Okay, it starts with a newsletter piece that mentioned the doctor in connection with the Franzetti birth, which was a bit of a local medical story because the mother was clinically dead when the boy was delivered by cesarean. Then, when the doctor renewed his medical license some years later, he was affiliated with a private hospital. The address turns out to be a converted residential building owned by Fabiano Properties and leased to a Fenix Foundation. Fenix Foundation supposedly does medical research in collaboration with a partner organization in Italy, an organization with a very unlikely name."

"Not *Volo di Ritorno*?"

"No, not *Fondazione Volo di Ritorno*. This is *Centro di Romolo e Remo* which, in turn, partially funds Return-Flight. Voila!"

"*Eccellente! Romolo e Remo*: I assume that's the legendary twins Romulus and Remus. Fits."

"But wait, my over-eager *giornaliste*. Guess who Fabiano Properties is? That was Dermott's maternal grandparents, the ones who raised him. The Fenix Foundation that leases the building is only a couple of miles from the address where you said the boy is living. And now you have a name: Dr. Leonard Royal Cahners. I have hard copies of all these connections. So, what about your news?"

Danny filled her in on the strange encounter and showed her the contract. She read it slowly. "I am no lawyer, and I don't know about publishing over here or in England, but in Italy, this would be rather unusual. You would be signing away all your rights to the story in all forms forever, and you can't talk about the deal until publication, after which all public appearances or statements have to be approved, 'in advance, in writing' it says."

She punched the air with her index finger. "They would own you *and* the story. If they wanted to, they could delay publication and keep you from saying anything—indefinitely."

"Yeah, I guess it seems extreme, but, it's also an extreme amount of money."

"I don't know, I think you should talk with someone first before you sign up for this?"

"Who can I talk with?"

"A lawyer. Or how about Mr. Sour Grapes. Certainly he would know about this kind of thing."

"Trauben hates me."

"No he doesn't. He spoke very highly of you. I just think sour is his style. Why don't you give it a try. Look, it's early. He might still be at his office in Germany."

Trauben answered on the first ring. "What is this about, Danny? Why do you keep calling me? You don't work for me anymore."

"I know, but since you're my favorite editor of all time and you used to work in book publishing, I thought I'd ask you about Dihedral Publishing Group."

"Never heard of them."

"Well they heard of you, said they talked with you last week about me."

"Last week? No. There was a man and a woman from the tax office asking about you, but—"

"Guy built like a blimp and blonde woman built like a sprinter on steroids?"

"Yeah, that's them. You know, by the way, they were carrying. To get through the metal detectors at building security, they had to check their guns. Both of them."

Danny thanked Trauben for the information. After hanging up, he passed on what Trauben had told him.

"What are we going to do, Danny?"

"Stall."

Chapter 32

Medicine is about doing things in order. Whether it's internal medicine, which is my specialty, or surgery, there is a defined sequence in which you conduct an exam, order tests, or make incisions. It can lull the unwary into a sense that life, too, is ordered and orderly. The detective work of diagnosis, when it pays off, rewards the physician with a rush of realization, an illusion that sense can be made of all of life and living things. Sense can, indeed, be made of human beings, but only by underestimating them. Understanding is the consequence of simplification, deep insight the result of oversimplification. So I was taught in med school by a brilliant but eccentric professor of psychiatry. I didn't accept his oversimplification at the time.

Word reached us at the Foundation that security had solved the problem of the reporter. Even cement-nerved Helen admitted she had grown anxious as the invisible intruder circled closer to our encampment. But our people had come through, our people had protected us. We could go back to routine and the play-acting of everyday life. Simple.

Roy answered the direct line in his office. "Cahners here."

"It's Paolo, Dr. Cahners. I need to meet with you. Can you come over to the house this afternoon? It's important."

"I'm not sure. I'll have to check my schedule."

"Check it, doc. I am almost certain that you'll find that you're meeting with me this afternoon at 1:30."

"Aren't you supposed to be in school then?"

"I have a late lunch and a free period for the rest of the day. I'm done by 1:15."

"Okay, I guess. Can you tell me what this is about?"

"Me. It's about me. Der."

"Well, yes, of course. Are you coming down with something? Is there some problem at school? Something with your grand-mother?"

"I'll see you then." Paolo hung up.

○ ○ ○

When Dr. Cahners entered the front hall, Paolo was standing before the small oval mirror that hung at the foot of the stairs. "What's up, Paolo?"

"Who do I remind you of?"

"You're picking up bad habits from me, answering a question with a question."

"Whatever. But who do I look like? Who do I remind you of?"

"*Whom* do you remind me of? Is that the question?"

"Okay, whom, if you gotta be picky."

"If you're going to be a writer, these little things matter."

"Not anymore, except to you. And Seppina. She is always on my case about grammar and usage. GrammarGuido on the Web says that 'who' as the object form is now generally regarded as acceptable. Also, I am not going to be a writer. I am a writer."

"Fair enough. So how is school going? Finals are coming up, right?"

"You're doing it again, doc. You owe me an answer before you can deflect with more questions. This is not amateur night; we keep score here. Try to keep up."

"Okay, but then afterwards I get to deflect, right?" He winked.

"Screw it. Just tell me *whom* I remind you of."

"You remind me of myself at your age."

Paolo imitated the sound of a raucous buzzer. "Wrong. Unacceptable answer. Who do I look like?"

"You look like you."

"Jesus, doc, you are impossible. Literally. Look at me. Do I look anything like Toni or Seppina? Do I look like my mother? Do I look like any of my family whose pictures decorate the mantel over there? Who the hell am I, and where do I come from?"

"Didn't we go this round once or twice before?"

"Yes, and we feinted and pulled our punches to a draw."

"Nice metaphor."

"Nice dodge. Look at me. Take a good look at me." He could see the tension increasing in the doctors face. "Could you pick me out in a lineup?"

"Sure, of course. I could do that. Easily."

"All right. Now we are getting someplace. Come on up to my office, doc. I have something to show you."

"Could you tell me what this is about?"

"I could. But I won't. You'll figure it out soon enough." He led the way toward the pantry and the back stairs to the attic. When they reached the top, Paolo pushed ahead and held the door for Dr. Cahners. On the far wall, just below the hexagon window, which was now covered over with construction paper, a folded bedsheet was tacked. Paolo had rigged a pocket LED projector on a stack of boxes in front of it.

"Here's the lineup." He walked over and flicked the switch on the little projector; a row of five face-forward headshots appeared on the improvised screen. "Do you recognize any of these faces?"

The doctor was sweating. "Well, I ..."

"Take your time, study the faces. Any of these look familiar?"

"Is this a trick question or something?"

"You said just now downstairs that you could pick me out of a lineup. Which one, doc?"

"Well, the second from the right, well, obviously it's ..." He stopped. The hair was wrong. There was a faint diagonal scar just above the left eyebrow. "Did you Photoshop this? I mean, it's good, but ..."

"Who is it, doc? It's truth time."

Cahners upended a suitcase near the wall and perched on it, knees splayed. He stared up at the face that was Paolo and was not.

"I know who it is, doc. I just want to hear you say it."

"That ... that's a picture of Arturo Dermott, I believe. Arturo Fabian Dermott. How did you ..."

"Image search. I took a self-portrait with a webcam and asked Google to match it. You know, those algorithms have gotten really good over the years." He looked down at the floor, shaking his head. "My father, my father was the billionaire inventor, richest man on the planet at one point. But why didn't you tell me? I read that he had no children."

The doctor bit down on his lower lip and stared in silence into the distance as Paolo, eyes widened, continued. "No, wait a minute. Now I get it. I was wrong. I didn't take it to its logical conclusion. I researched the man, went over summaries of the patents he received. And I still didn't quite see it. Now I do. With enough time and money, especially money, whatever you want is possible. He wanted something more than a son; he wanted one better." Paolo looked from the tension in the face of his doctor and back to the projected image saved from an online article. The young inventor in the photo seemed to be looking out at them, intelligent eyes curious as to what might come next. "Get out, Doctor Cahners. Get the fuck out of here. Now!"

Chapter 33

Quincy and Robertson kept calling, pushing for a meeting. The thought of meeting them in person sent Danny's heart into overdrive. "I know you two are eager to get this book deal settled, but I don't think we're going to get there any faster by meeting for dinner or drinks."

"Mr. Bradman, talking face-to-face always speeds things up. Hell, there's even research on it. Deals get done when parties are in the same room. Social science has proved that, you know. Just sit down with us, at least have coffee, talk. We'll work this out."

"I'd love to, Mr. Quincy, but—"

"Call me Fred."

"My attorneys are still going over the contract, Fred. As soon as I hear back from them, I'll give you a call. Believe me, I'm as eager to be finished with this as you are to reach an agreement."

"I keep telling you, we can negotiate. If an even mil won't do it for you, tell me what will. I'm ready to go to the mat for you with my boss. May I be completely honest with you?"

"I wish you would."

"Yeah. Okay, so the truth is I get a percentage on this contract. The better you do, the better I do. In the end, we're on the same side here."

Danny held his tongue.

"You still there, Mr. Bradman?"

"Yes, Fred. Look, let me put in another call to my lawyers and try to hurry them up a bit. I'll keep you posted. Just hang in there. A few more days." He hung up before the man could badger him any further.

Francesca stepped out of the bathroom. "How did it go?"

"Still keeping the hangman at bay. I don't know how much longer we can play it this way. I didn't study counter-espionage tactics at Columbia."

"We'll think of something. The more time we buy, the more chance we have, right?"

"Maybe. If I could get independent confirmation for enough of the pieces, maybe I could get the story out before these goons can kill it—or kill us. The way things are going, I think I can hold them off for at least another week, maybe two. Eventually, though, they are going to lose patience and decide there are other means to obtain our silence—messier, more efficient, and most likely a lot more painful."

"What if you agree and sign the contract. Do you think they would actually pay?"

"They might, you know. After all, Dermott's evil empire certainly has the funds. In 2007 when *FT* did the numbers, they were sitting on an estimated €12 billion in cash reserves. What's a million or two here or there? On the other hand, why should they pay me and trust me if they don't have to?"

"Maybe for the same reason as we're keeping them at bay: buying time. A million or two could buy them a year or two extra, as long as they believe that we believe they are actually going to publish a book in the end."

"You're right, which means for now we have to keep them believing we believe."

o o o

Paolo held the pie in one hand while he kept the screen door open with his hip and jiggled the key with his free hand. His copy of Vera's key had never worked very well. As he was coaxing the lock, her VW pulled into the driveway behind his Chevy Bolt. She got out and started unloading the boot in front. "What a surprise. What brings you here? I thought we weren't meeting until Sunday?"

"I am the bearer of berries. My Nonna insisted I hand deliver one of her blackberry pies. I swear she's pulling our strings."

"Maybe she is. Good for her. Good for us." She looked down at the pie. "Mmm, that looks and smells so good. Still, I hate to think you had to drive all the way up here just to be a delivery boy."

"I hope I'm more than that, but I really don't know what I am anymore."

She saw his face quiver as his eyes closed. "Oh, what is it? Come in, let's talk. Here, let me get the door. My key works better."

o o o

The cramped kitchen had just room enough for the usual complement of appliances and a drop-leaf table with two chairs. Vera reached across with the corner of her paper napkin. "You have blackberry lipstick and even a blackberry goatee."

He made a swirling swipe at his mouth with his napkin. "Is that better?" It was said with resignation, without energy.

"No, it's not better. I mean, you got the pie filling all right, but something is really wrong. Talk to me. Let's go in the living room and sit."

"Can we go in the bedroom instead?"

"You just got here; we have all evening, maybe all night."

"No, not that. I just want to hold you, to be held."

They cleared the dishes, stowed the other half of the pie in the refrigerator, and wound their way into the bedroom. The latest issue of *Up-Stage* was still on her nightstand. "Remember this article?" He held it up.

"I remember you being suddenly upset. I remember you wouldn't talk with me about it. What is this about now? That article?"

"Look at this." He flipped to the last page of the article and folded the magazine to expose the picture of Arturo Dermott at the age of seventeen. He held the picture up beside his face. "What do you think? What do you see?"

"Wow, yeah. He does look a little like you. Must be the Italian genes. Or some distant connection, umpteenth cousins or something."

"Not distant."

"You mean you might be close cousins with the Italian Edison?"

"Closer than that."

"Closer? Like nephew?"

"Closer."

"Not son, he didn't have children, at least that's what I read."

"Closer."

"What's closer than father and son? You couldn't be his brother, could you? No."

"Closer."

"I don't get it."

"Look at the picture. Really look at it." He handed it to her. "Look at the eyes. The left one is ever so slightly smaller. The half-smile is crooked. And the Dumbo ears. Look closely at the pattern of ridges and swirls there. Look at the hairline, the shape of his widow's peak." He pulled his own hair back from his forehead.

"What are you saying?" Her voice dropped to a whisper. "You're scaring me, Paolo."

"Who am I, Vera?"

"You're Paolo, and I love you. Paolo Carl Franzetti."

"Labels, Vera, handles by which we can drag people from place to mental place. Who am I?" He leaned across the bed until his face was inches from hers.

"I love you, you're my Paolo."

"No!" It was a quiet vocal punch that made her blink. "I am Dermott: Arturo Fabian Dermott."

"Paolo, please, you're scaring me. This is crazy. Or ..."

"Or? Or what?"

"I don't believe in ghosts. I don't believe in reincarnation."

"Do you believe in yourself?"

"Well, yes, I guess."

"Do you know who you are?"

"Yeah, pretty much. I think by now I know who I am. As much as anyone, I suppose."

"I don't. I don't believe in myself, and I don't know who I am. I don't believe in myself *because* I don't know who I am. I lied when I said I was Arturo Dermott, just as I lied every time I have ever said I was Paolo Franzetti. I am not Dermott. And I am. Both. Neither. Nobody." He started to cry, a jittery, shaky cry that slowly grew into violent heaves.

She held him for the many minutes it took for his sobs to subside. "Whoever you are, whatever you believe," she said, "I love you. And I want to know what you know."

Chapter 34

The next weeks were tough on all of us. Paolo nose-dived into a swamp of self-pity, anger, and confusion. He virtually locked himself in his attic office again. For the first time in his life, he skipped school, claiming to be too sick to attend. He was also skipping meals, then sneaking down at night to raid the refrigerator. Seppina was calling me every day, and I tried to reassure her that it was an adolescent crisis and nothing to be too alarmed about. I couldn't tell her what it was actually about, and I had my fingers crossed that Paolo wouldn't spring his story on her. If I had thought about it, I probably would have concluded that he was too close to her, too tuned into how she did her life, not to spare her of his own accord.

During my residency, when I did my rotation in the ER, I learned that medical emergencies tend to come in clusters; they are not spread evenly over the weekdays and the weeks. Periods of relative calm are interrupted by insanely intense combinations of crises. There were those on staff who held to essentially a superstitious view of the phenomenon, but there is a simple statistical principle involved. Apart from exceptional outliers, like the immediate aftermath of the Boston Marathon bombing, the clusters are the consequence of the laws of chance.

Whatever explanation you might choose—statistical or mystical—you can count on the odds of sooner or later facing shit from multiple fans at once.

Paolo unfolded his hands and looked down at his palms. "I'm a freak, Dr. Cahners, not even a freak of nature. I was born this way, but there was nothing natural about it. I suppose not even my fingerprints are mine."

Cahners kept his own hands folded in front of him on his desk. "I wouldn't call you a freak. Medically, in fact, you are unremarkably normal."

"Except for *la cabeza*." He tapped his temple.

"No, even there you are far from unique. True, your measured IQ is extremely high, but there are literally millions worldwide who are as smart or smarter."

"Maybe, but none of them are someone else, and none of them have the brain of Arturo Dermott."

"It's not all genetics and wiring, and nobody knows that better than we do. I've talked about this before. What you do with your brain, how you go through life, everything you think and do—it all shapes your brain. The neural connections—"

Paolo slapped his hands on the desk. "Fuck neural connections. Every other person starts life dealt their own personal hand of cards. I got dealt somebody else's cards. It was a conjurer's trick, prestidigitation with a doctored deck. Ever since I figured it out, I've been thinking, trying to wrap my head around it. Why did he do it? I'm him, and I still can't fathom why he would do this to me."

"He didn't do it to you or for you. He did it for himself."

"But why?"

"Ego. Because he could. Because there was nothing in his way or no one to stop him. It's one of the problems when wealth becomes so vast and so concentrated. The man had no family and no real friends. He could never make relationships stick, save for those bound by contract. He didn't want to die without an heir."

"I hate him for it." Paolo shook with a mixture of laughter and anguish. "I'm him, so I guess that means I hate myself. God, what a fucked up mess. I am the only person on earth who truly has neither a father nor a mother. The woman who gave birth to me was a surrogate, and no sperm fertilized the egg from which I developed. And I know next to nothing about the man who supplied the genetic material. He died before I was born, and it's not like I grew up with family stories. But I am him. So ..."

"No, you are not him. If anything I would say you are a more complicated, principled person than he was."

"Did you know him?"

"No. Helen Bentley, head of the clinic here, met him once. There are Board Members who knew him, but nobody knew him well. I am told he never socialized, never talked about himself, and never did much other than work. He was putting in eighty-hour weeks right to the end. In fact, he was in one of the research labs working on some project when he collapsed."

"You—I mean this clinic, the Foundation, the Board or whatever—must have files, information that's not generally available."

"We do. And there's an entire vault full of material that will be turned over to you when you turn twenty-one. Before that, I'm afraid that what I can tell you is limited to basic facts and my own best guesses. I don't even know the contents of the vault; I'm told that not even the Board members know.

"As you yourself have said before, once you turn eighteen, you can take legal action to try and get records unsealed, but it's not at all clear whether Dermott's will or your interests would prevail. And it could be expensive and complicated, with battles over jurisdiction, what country's laws apply, where actions would proceed. All that would be expensive, and until you reach twenty-one, your allowance is fixed. You may think of it as generous compared to some of your peers, but it wouldn't even get you in the door of a really good law firm."

"Contingency fee."

"That's unlikely. What decent lawyer would jump into such a mess? A better call would be to just wait. All things come to ... Anyway, it's all spelled out in the will and the charter of the Foundation."

"Would you at least tell me what you know. I mean, now. I don't want to wait years to find out who I am."

Cahners let out a throaty laugh. "Why should you be any different from the rest of us? We all wait years to find out who we are. Hell, even now I'm still unsure about some of it myself. No kid of seventeen knows who they are, especially those who are sure they already have it figured out."

Paolo sighed, a deep, drawn-out exhalation. "You got me, checkmate, I resign."

"Good for you. Resignation is an important step toward enlightenment."

"So now you're the Zen master, too." He grinned at his doctor.

"I'm versatile. And I will tell you everything I can, I promise."

"Carefully worded promise, oh Master. And what of those things known to you but not among those of which you can speak." He bowed in his seat.

"Well, Grasshopper, of those I cannot speak." He bowed in return. "Let us, then speak of those things we can."

○ ○ ○

Paolo and Dr. Cahners embraced when they finally finished the long session. Just after Paolo left, Helen Bentley came into Roy's office. "There's someone asking to see you. I can turn him away, but maybe that would not be the best way to handle things."

"Who? What things?"

"Dan Bradman, the reporter who's been tunneling into the cellars of our private estate."

Cahners shook his head. "We can't talk with him. You know the rules. We don't talk with the press. Only headquarters can do that, and they never do."

"He has a rather impressive portfolio with him. I think he may have already nailed us."

"Then there is nothing to be served by meeting with him except to confirm whatever he has. He's not likely to accept denials. This is a matter for security. I thought they had this under control."

"I thought so, too."

"Well, my call on this would be to show him the door. Tell him no comment. I'll call the hotline."

Helen turned left out of Roy's office. She threw back her shoulders and marched toward the waiting room. As she made the turn at the end of the hall she could see through the glass door that she was already too late. Leaning forward in the chair across from the reporter was Paolo, gesturing in clearly animated conversation.

Chapter 35

Roy was dialing the security hotline when Helen stepped back into his office. "We have a problem, Roy. Our visitor ran into Paolo, and now they're talking in the waiting room."

"Hold on, the hotline is ringing. Oops, now it's being transferred. And ..."

"Quincy. Security." The voice was abrupt, all business.

"Yes, this is Dr. Cahners at the Fenix Foundation Clinic in—"

"I know. What's the situation?"

"The reporter from the *Financial Tribune* is in our waiting room wanting an interview. Paolo Franzetti is with him."

"Okay. We can't afford a scene at the clinic, and we don't want to compound problems with the boy. You'll have to finesse."

"What exactly do you expect me to finesse, Mr. Quincy?"

"First priority is to extract the boy. Debrief him if you can, then get him on his way home. Play along with the reporter. Be forthcoming but give him only the bare minimum necessary to keep him satisfied. We'll ping you when we arrive in the neighborhood. Wrap up the interview then, and we'll intercept him after he leaves and is clear of the facility."

Roy did not like the sound of the word *intercept*. "What's going to happen with him."

"My worry, not yours. We'll find a way to persuade him to drop the story and not go public."

◦ ◦ ◦

Roy opened the door into the waiting room with a calculated look of mild surprise on his face. "You still here, Paolo?"

"Mr. Bradman and I have been talking about soccer and science."

"Great. I have to meet with Mr. Bradman right now, but I want to catch you about something before you head home. Could you hang out here for another few minutes while I show Mr. Bradman to my office?"

"Sure."

After ushering the reporter down the hall, Roy hurried back to the waiting room. "Did you say anything to him? I mean ..."

"You kidding? I may be going through some rough water, but I'm not suddenly stupid. We made small talk, that's all. If he knows anything about us, he didn't get it from me."

"Okay, good enough. Remember, you can call me anytime. And try not to make your grandmother worry."

Paolo rolled his eyes and rose to leave.

Back again in his office, Roy apologized to the reporter. "I am sorry to keep you waiting, Mr. Bradman, especially since I really can't help you. HIPAA—government confidentiality regulations, you know—I'm just not allowed to give out patient information, and clinic policy prevents me from either confirming or denying any information you might have, whatever its source."

"Call me Danny, please. I'm not here for an interview. I'm here to tell you what I know and to ask for your help in calling off your brute squad."

"Brute squad? Ah, yes, *The Princess Bride*. But I'm afraid that, unlike Prince Humperdinck, I do not have a brute squad."

"Ah, but there you're mistaken, and I believe you are aware of that mistake. I'm referring to the mismatched pair of pseudo publishers that have been hounding me, trying to buy my silence even as they maintain the implied threat of physical force."

"If you're speaking of our security people, I know nothing about them or their activities."

"Except that you called the squad after I arrived."

"How ... ?"

"The surveilled can also surveille. My ... my team texted me when your team began their gallop onto the scene."

"I guess you do know what you're doing, then."

"You're not wrong there. So let me outline what we know about you and your very special charge."

He spent the next fifteen minutes laying out the picture he and Francesca had constructed. "So, that's it. About the only glaring void is the how. How was Dermott able to accomplish such a breakthrough? But we're working on that."

"Well, I must say it makes for an interesting story—a work of fiction, yes, but fascinating."

"Are you denying the story?"

"Neither denying nor confirming, just admiring the screen-writing."

"We have the documentation, the audit trail from Italy to Boston and back." He slid a thick folder onto the desk. "See for yourself. Those are merely copies, of course. And there are duplicate copies in strategic hands."

"I would expect nothing less from you. But, as I said, I can't help you."

"You can help by calling off your dogs."

"They're not my dogs." The intercom buzzed and Roy picked up the handset. He listened for a minute, then hung up. "The dogs are here, Danny. They just pulled into the front parking lot. I'll show you the back way out, then I suggest you and ... and your team pull a vanishing act. I trust you know how to do that effectively." He led the way through the shared bathroom of the two-office suite and out into the hallway farther down.

"Thank you, Dr. Cahners, but I don't know why you're doing this."

"Neither do I. Follow this corridor around to the right and out through the door at the end. Cut through the backyard; the gate's unlocked. Be careful. I'll try to stall the brute squad. Now hurry before they storm the castle."

The rotund Mr. Quincy was shouting at Helen when Roy arrived at the front desk. "I suggest you keep it down, Mr. Quincy. This is a medical facility, and I would not want to be party to you losing your job."

"Just tell me were the little Jew runt is."

Roy stiffened. "If you mean the reporter, he's in the bathroom, blissfully unaware of your arrival. Unaware, that is, unless your yelling has announced your presence."

"Look, you ..."

"You look. All it will take is a phone call from Helen and you will be escorted from the premises by the local police. On the occasion of your release, you will likely find yourself among the unemployed. Is that clear. If so, say 'HUA' and then follow me into my office to sit quietly until our overseas guest finishes his bathroom business and reappears."

After Quincy was ensconced in the office, Helen caught up with Roy in the hallway. "You are enjoying this, aren't you, Roy."

"I am, Helen. I never liked bullies, even if they are our bullies. Tell me, can you turn in a bad report on our overweight security man?"

"I can do better than that. I can have him recalled to Rome. He'd be gone on the next flight. But keep in mind, his replacement might be worse."

"Or might be better."

"For better or worse, you better attend to the man in your office."

"I will. We'll give our earnest investigator another ten minutes. When he fails to show up from the men's room, the bully and I will go check to see if he fell into the toilet or something. There we'll find the window with the faulty latch has been left ajar. My, how terrible, the man must have snuck out to the side alley. Pity, that."

Chapter 36

The call from Bradman the next day was unexpected. The call from Paolo was even more unexpected. Yes, medical emergencies come in clusters, but that does not mean we doctors are actually prepared for the crap life throws at us. It is even possible that this time we contributed to the chaos. With our attention monopolized by Paolo and the threat of exposure, we had lost sight of some of our other responsibilities.

Would it have made a difference? Perhaps not, but the examined life is paved with what-ifs and if-only. "The moving finger writes and having writ moves on." And we read the writing on the wall in the vain hope of learning enough to guess from the graffiti what the next chapter brings. In truth, we can seldom even guess the next sentence—or phone call.

The late departure from the clinic meant plowing through the peak of the rush-hour commute. Roy pretended to be indifferent to the traffic, but each lane-hopping jerk who could not be bothered to signal and each tail-gating idiot who jammed on the brakes at the last split-second took its toll. It was, he knew, the price of being a control freak. He had turned down the foundation's offer to provide him with one of the latest self-driving vehicles, but Greater Boston's ever worsening congestion had been pushing him to reconsider.

The hands-free phone link on the center console flashed a caller ID that he didn't recognize. He considered rejecting the call—he had enough to deal with trying to negotiate the approaching on-ramp—but it might be important. He thumbed the button on the steering-wheel. "Cahners here."

"Bradman here. This'll be quick. Francesca and I left the country but are still pursuing the story. I want to make a deal."

"Spell it out."

"We won't break the story until after the boy turns eighteen if you won't send another brute squad after us."

"He turns eighteen in less than a year. At least let the kid live out the rest of this chapter of his life; wait until he turns twenty-one."

"That's a long time to sit on a story."

"You won't be sitting on it, you'll be filling in the blanks, finalizing, amassing all the documents and data, turning first drafts into final copy. Besides, you get an exclusive out of it. No one here will give out anything to anyone else."

"I know what you're trying to pull, doc, but I'll take it anyway. I want your word that your security people won't go after us."

"I can't promise that, but I can promise that Helen and I will do our best to keep them off your back. That's the best I can do."

"And the best I can do is to say we won't publish before the kid's twenty-first birthday unless we get wind that the squad is after us again."

"Done and done."

"Cheers, doc. You're all right."

The call disconnected and the phone chimed again almost immediately. This time Roy recognized the caller ID; it was Paolo's mobile number. "What's up Paolo?"

"It's Nonna Seppina. Something's wrong."

"What's wrong?"

"Well, she hasn't been eating too well lately, but I didn't know that because ... I guess I should have been watching her more closely, but ... Anyway, I got home and found her lying on the couch, moaning. Her stomach is all bulging, and she says it really hurts. You know her, she never complains. I think something might be really wrong. Oh yeah, I think she may be a little jaundiced, but I'm not sure. She says it's just her summer tan, from gardening."

"Okay, I'll be there. Twenty minutes. Try to make her comfortable, but don't give her any medication."

o o o

Paolo was wiping her forehead with a dampened washcloth when Roy arrived. Roy set down his bag beside the couch and took out his stethoscope. "Does she have a fever?"

"I don't know. I'm sorry. I should've thought to check. I just thought this might be soothing."

Seppina reached up and patted his arm. "Oh, it is, Paolo, it is. You're a good boy."

Roy checked her temperature. "It's normal. Could it be something you ate? What did you have to eat today."

"Nothing really. Some cereal this morning, but I wasn't really hungry, and then I felt full after just half the bowl."

"Okay, lie back down, I'm going to check your abdomen. Paolo, be a good boy and wait in the kitchen for a few minutes. I'll call you when we're done here."

Roy finished his ad hoc examination and called to Paolo. "You can come back now."

"So, what do you think, doc?"

"I think you did the right thing to call me. We should take a closer look. I'm going to admit you to the hospital, Seppina, for some tests and a scan. It could be nothing or it could be something we need to take care of." He held her hand and stroked it to reassure her. "Don't worry. I'll tell you if and when it's time for you to start worrying."

"You're still the kidder, doctor, always were. But I know I'm in good hands."

"You are, Seppina, you are. Look, I'm going to call for transport to the hospital. Paolo, do you want to grab my bag and bring it out to the car for me."

Paolo took the hint and trailed Cahners out to his car. "You palpated a mass, didn't you."

"I keep forgetting how well-read you are on medicine. Yeah, I palpated a mass. We won't know just what we're dealing with until we get lab results and see the scans."

"Sounds like cancer, right? Liver? Gall bladder? Pancreas?"

"You're getting ahead of yourself by leaps and bounds, boy. We wait and see."

"But it doesn't look good, does it?"

"Don't borrow trouble. Whatever it is, maybe we caught it early enough. Besides, the progress in cancer treatment over the last decade has been amazing. Whatever we're dealing with, there will be lots of options."

"That's the standard speech, doc. I'm not your standard family member."

"True, but I really mean it when I say we'll know better in a few days. Patience, Grasshopper."

Chapter 37

Seppina fumbled for the button that would tilt up the back of her hospital bed. She looked more than ever like she had been using artificial tanning cream. "So, Dr. Cahners, are you ever going to tell me what is going on? I've endured two nights of trying to sleep with all these lights on and three days of being poked, prodded, and pestered for blood ... and everything else. What's the verdict?"

"Well, I wanted to wait for a consult with Mark Anschluss, an oncologist up at Dana-Farber. We met this morning; I'm ready to fill you in."

"I suppose I'm ready to be filled in, although I feel rather full already."

"Glad to see you haven't lost your sense of humor, Seppina. Good attitude is part of the battle."

"So, it's gonna be a battle, huh?"

"I'm afraid so."

"It's the big C, right?"

"You have cancer, yes."

She stiffened and held her breath. "You're gonna cut it out, right? Operations terrify me, you know, ever since Carla. I had a cesarean with her—doctors said my pelvis was too small—and then it was Carla with Paolo. She died on the table, you know. Yes, of course you know; you were there. I really thought she was going to recover. I wanted to believe she would come out of that coma. I prayed for a miracle, but ..."

"Don't worry, Seppina, we're not going to operate: no surgery, at least not now."

"That's good news."

"Not exactly. Surgery is not an option because the cancer has spread. You have pancreatic cancer, what is termed an invasive adenocarcinoma, just our fancy way of saying the cancer has gotten loose and is rioting around your insides, so to speak."

"What do you do? How do you cure it."

Roy bit down on his lower lip and sucked air through his teeth. "We may not be able to cure it, but that doesn't mean there's nothing we can do."

"I'm going to die."

"We're all going to die, Seppina."

"Some of us sooner than others. How long do I have?"

"That depends on a lot of things. You could have some good years, still. I'm afraid you will have to put up with a couple more nights with the lights on because I'm going to order one more test that will give us a clearer picture of what we're up against. It's a new technique called SUBRS, for Selective Uptake Bound Resonance Scan. Basically, we inject you with a medicine that spreads through your body. It's engineered to look for and grab onto any cancer cells it finds. When we put you back into that big scanner machine, the medicine makes the cancer spots light up like they were carrying lanterns. Where it is and how far it's spread helps decide what we do next."

"Does Paolo know?"

"Not until you tell him. Unless you want me to tell him."

"You tell him. He'll want to know all the medical stuff, and I don't know if I can get it all right. I'm not as good at remembering all the little things these days."

"I know exactly what you're talking about. That's why I keep this notepad with me wherever I go."

"Just like Paolo. Look, why don't you let him be with me when you deliver the sentencing."

"Don't make it sound like criminal court, Seppina. We're doctors, and I'm going to see you get the very best that modern medicine can offer." He gave her arm a squeeze.

She watched him leave and waited until his footsteps faded before she started praying through her tears. After the *pater noster*, she whispered, "Please, Lord, let me keep taking care of Paolo, at least until he's grown up."

○ ○ ○

"Okay, you two, here's the update. We got the SUBRS results, and there are little bright dots all over."

Paolo nodded. "Stage 4, right doc?"

"Yeah, Paolo, what we call stage 4. If you were a little younger, Seppina, and in better shape, we might start one of the really aggressive combination therapies like FOLFIRINOX or even one of the more recent enhanced versions, but they are all highly toxic cocktails, and Dr. Anschluss concurs that you are not likely to be able to tolerate those treatments."

"You're saying her performance status isn't high enough."

"Have you started med school when I wasn't looking, Paolo?"

"No, just reading up on pancreatic cancer. Sorry, please go on. I assume you'll start her on chemo. Which regimen?"

Roy grinned as he bent over Seppina. "Would you believe this kid?" He gestured with his thumb. "Next thing you know he'll be taking over my job at the clinic." He straightened up. "We're going to start you on chemotherapy, a more or less standard well-proven treatment, which is ... ?" He turned to Paolo. "That's your cue, young Doctor Franzetti."

"Ah, er, gemcitabine with nab-paclitaxel. Right?"

"Wrong. Thank you for playing. You must have been reading old medical journals—or Wikipedia. That would have been standard practice ten years ago, but now we have glinabitine folinate in combination with efrovimab. I do wonder who the heck comes up with these names. Anyway, this pair is at least ten percent more effective than gemcitabine combination therapies with fewer side effects.

He turned back to Seppina. "Which is good news for you."

"Since when is chemo good news?"

"Since it could buy you a big chunk of good time."

"Is that what it comes down to now: chunks of time."

"I can't promise you more, but you might just be that exception to the rule. Right now, I need to write the orders for the chemotherapy and some medication to make it easier to handle the side effects."

"What about the pain? It really hurts all through here."

"I'll up the dose of painkiller, too." He patted her shoulder. "Get some rest while you can." He started for the door with Paolo in his footsteps.

"I'll be back in a few minutes, Nonna. I want to talk with Dr. Cahners."

In the corridor he faced Roy. "How long? How long does she have?"

"Barring some unforeseeable medical crisis, odds are very good she'll see you graduate from high school. On the other hand, it's not too likely she'll be at your college graduation. Five year survival rates for patients with her cancer at her age is down around ten percent. With new therapies, short term prognosis has gotten markedly better over the last decade, but long term is another story: virtually unchanged in twenty years. Pancreatic cancer is, to put it bluntly, incurable. Still."

Chapter 38

Not surprisingly, developments of that year brought out my philosophical side. The surprise was the theological thread running through more and more of my thinking. God had not entered my thoughts in decades, but now I was thinking He gives and He takes away. Every cloud is lined with silver—or platinum in the case of pancreatic cancer—an oncology insider reference that Paolo would have understood. My antipathy toward organized religion and the dulling delusion of higher powers was weakening as Seppina demonstrated the very real comfort that some people could draw from their faith.

On the recommendation of his guidance counselor, Paolo had applied to the customary even-dozen colleges. Shortly after Seppina was diagnosed, Paolo started receiving acceptance letters. He got twelve of them. He was accepted outright at eleven and wait-listed on one—including all the usual top suspects. The top picks— Stanford, Cal Tech, and MIT— all offered big merit-based scholarships as an extra incentive. We expected him to choose one of them—or maybe it was more what we had always planned for him. We were not prepared for his choice. Boston University, an apparent backup pick, had been at the bottom of our ranking, but we were not factoring in their fine arts programs in writing and theater arts that made it his top choice. And, of course, there was another reason: it would keep him in the area.

The kicker came when Paolo opted for deferred admission, taking a gap year to help care for Seppina. Both Chaim and Helen were very unhappy with this turn of events, but I was secretly pleased. I would not have acknowledged it at the time, but part of me still had fantasies that Paolo might go into medicine instead of following his heart or the path the Foundation had mapped out. And time spent with Seppina might teach him a lot, especially coupled with his deep dive into oncology that continued into the summer.

Paolo took Vera's hand as he led her into the dining room. "Don't peek, now. Keep your eyes closed. Both of you." He steered Vera to the right spot and then stepped away. "Okay, you can open your eyes."

Vera found herself standing beside a newly installed hospital bed with Seppina looking up at her with a smile of surprise. "Hello, Seppina. It's good to see you out of the hospital. How are you feeling?"

"Not so good. But I'm feeling better right now seeing your smiling face again." She reached out a hand and took Vera's. "I'm glad you're Paolo's friend." She nodded as a way of emphasizing the thought.

"I'm your friend, too. In fact, I'm hoping we can spend time together this summer: maybe take in a concert, do a little gardening. I'd love it if you could teach me the secret of your blackberry pie."

"Tapioca. You have to thicken the filling. Flour doesn't work and leaves a funny taste. Cornstarch just doesn't feel right."

"You'll have to show me just how to do it the way you do." She looked around the room. "So, you're sleeping here, downstairs, now."

"Yeah, I can't do the stairs anymore. Paolo fixed this up to be my new bedroom. Pretty nice, huh? He hung the big-screen TV on the wall over there because there wasn't room for the credenza in here. I have the remote and the phone right where I can reach them. I mean, I can get around a little with my walker, at least on good days. Not today, though. It's like the flu, only worse. My head hurts and I ache all over. And this itchy rash: it's like the chicken pox I had as a kid."

"So the medication isn't helping?"

"This *is* the medication, Dr. Cahners says. He's trying different stuff for the side effects. It's a lot of pills. And when the painkiller wears off, ooh boy. You don't want to be around for that. Tell her, Paolo. You know, dear, the boy puts up with a lot of gripin' from his grandmother."

"It's not so bad, Nonna. I can deal."

"Maybe you can, but what about me? I'm the one with the cramps that tie me in figure-eight knots." She reached for a straw-equipped glass of ice water and took a sip. "See, even when I can't get up, I can mostly take care of myself. So, you two should go do something together. With all the stuff happening around here, you haven't had much time for each other." She smiled and looked from Vera to Paolo and back. "Yeah, that's good. He's finally taller than you. Good. And you two really should go. I'm a little tired from all this talking. I think I'll try to get an afternoon nap. So, run along and let an old woman rest." She turned her face to the wall, then turned back. "Oh, there was a call, somebody trying to reach you. I think it was that reporter fellow." She turned her head away again.

o o o

In the living room, Paolo sat on the couch and pulled Vera down beside him. She hooked one leg over his. "So, she thinks it's good that you're taller than I am. Have you said anything to her? I mean, she acts like she knows what's going on."

"She probably does. She's no dummy. But I haven't said a word to her; she wouldn't want it that way. She's more comfortable with leaving the big stuff unspoken. In her own way, she has been letting us know that she accepts us as a couple, and we have to accept that."

He fumbled in the pocket of his shorts. "Let me check on this phone call before we get too comfortable." He waited as his mobile synched with the house network. "It's from that reporter. I don't want to talk with him." He thumbed the phone off.

"Aren't you going to at least listen to his message?"

"I suppose." He turned the phone back on to play the message.

"Hello, Paolo. This is Danny Bradman calling from Valencia. Francesca and I have been making progress, closing in on important details. Our source here has agreed to tell us more, then next we hope to be off to China where we have located a couple of scientists involved in the project. Call me back tomorrow before six, your time, and I'll bring you up-to-date on what we've learned. Cheers."

"Are you going to call him back?"

"I don't know. Maybe."

Chapter 39

A warm salt-laden breeze off the Mediterranean tousled Francesca's hair as she and Danny approached the table. Bernat stood and offered his hand. "Our friend the singer is running late, but he says he's ready to sing for you."

"Good." Danny surveyed the setting. "Is this place any good?"

"Not bad, but it has a pathetic wine list. The house red is drinkable, but there is nothing else worth the money."

"And you say Fernando picked this place?"

"He did. He has given up alcohol, found religion with some cult-like ten-step program."

"Do you mean twelve-step?"

"Whatever. Ten, twelve, twenty: it means nothing to me. I'd never do that. It's pseudo-religious mumbo jumbo, as far as I'm concerned."

"It works for some people. What changed for our wine-drenched guitarist friend?"

"His liver started screaming for mercy. Oh, look, here he comes."

The man striding down the avenue looked like he had just come from the barbershop after picking up a new outfit at *Uomomania* or some other trendy men's clothing store. Without Bernat's announcement, Danny might not have recognized him. Danny stood in welcome. "Fernando, you are looking good. Please, have a seat. You know Bernat, of course, and my colleague, Francesca Zingari."

Fernando bowed and kissed her hand. "Such a pleasure to see you again, Francesca of the gypsies."

"Oh, *parli italiano?*"

"No, I don't speak Italian—except with lovely gypsy ladies." He pulled out the remaining chair at the table and moved it to sit down next to her.

Danny leaned across in front of her. "Bernat said you are ready to tell us more about Project Cameo. Did I get the code name right?"

Fernando chuckled. "Code name? You reporters always want to spice things up, turn even the simplest story into an espionage caper."

"This is hardly a simple story. So, what was it called, then?"

"Just 'the project'."

"But I've uncovered multiple references to Project Cameo."

"Perhaps, but we never called it that. However, shouldn't we order first, before we get mired in archaic trivia?"

Fernando dominated the conversation throughout dinner but said nothing more about the project. He waited for coffee to be served before getting to the promised topic. "Yes, so, we begin. I do not know everything—I was only a lab technician—but my father was at the center of things, one of the first to be brought in by Señor Dermott. My father, perhaps you recall, was a physician who helped women with fertility problems. He would often talk with me about his work, especially after we moved to Italy. I think he felt isolated there. No one was allowed to talk about their work outside the research complex or the hospital. But we both worked for Dermott, father and son, so we felt we could talk with each other.

"From the beginning it was exciting to my father, even though what we were doing was illegal—or maybe because it was. At least I think that was the case for some of the team.

Dermott, though, was never excited about anything, not even when we would make some big breakthrough."

Danny flipped open his reporter's notebook. "Why do you think he did it, then? What was it really about for him?"

"My father said that Dermott had always wanted a son, but neither of his marriages lasted. In any case, he refused to accept that his own genetics would be diluted—cut in half—regardless of who his mate might be. He thought about seeking out the perfect mate through genetic screening and then paying for donated eggs, but none of the candidates seemed to rise to his criteria. What he actually wanted was a son who was a duplicate, who he knew would be just like him, therefore perfect in every way: just as brilliant, just as creative, just as driven. He could get along with no one, but he reasoned he could get along with himself.

"On that last point, I am a skeptic. My father, who worked more closely with Dermott than I did, once said that the man seemed to have more than his fair ration of self-loathing. That may be a big part of what drove him away from others and so into invention. Machines and mechanisms he understood; humans, even he himself, baffled him. At the level of cells and fluids and chemistry and genomes he understood the human race. Those elements he could master and bring under his control—with the help of others, of course. That was his only use for others. He could not do all the work himself, so he had to recruit collaborators, assistants. This he could do because he had more money than anyone in the world.

"Frankly, I think ego is the ultimate engine of human endeavor. That and fear of the void. What drives people to pay to have themselves frozen after they die? The vain hope that, unlike the rest of humanity, they might survive and cheat death. Pathetic egotism. And then there are the billionaires who squander wealth on the misguided hope of uploading their personalities onto immortal computers. Dermott was just a wealthier member of the same sad club chasing his own flawed version of immortality through genetics."

Danny looked up from his notes. "Do you know anything of the technical details, how the cloning was accomplished?"

"Details? Only in some areas, the ones in which I and my father worked. But I know the outline of how it was done. The rest, the other details, you can get from the Chinese."

"Do you know any of them? The Chinese?"

"No, but I know where they worked. I can tell you that. But let me finish what I was saying." He stopped to sip his coffee, freezing the moment.

"It was a grand undertaking that Dermott saw as made up of a series of separate smaller problems to be solved. Some of these had been somewhat solved, although imperfectly; some were lines of research already underway; and some required fresh approaches. The first challenge was to be able to take cells from adult tissue and deprogram them to revert to stem cells, cells with the potential to become anything. Some years earlier, lots of people were claiming to have worked that one out, but some of those people were frauds and the others had devised only incomplete or unreliable solutions. We nailed that one, and it only took about twenty million euros.

"We also needed an egg that could accept the genetic material from Dermott with absolute fidelity and fertility, both the mitochondrial genetic material, which comes from the maternal line alone, and the DNA from the nucleus, which comes from both parents. Dermott would not accept any genetic differences. We needed to stimulate the egg to begin dividing and become an embryo just as if it had been fertilized by a sperm. Finally we needed to enable the embryo to be implanted in the uterus of a surrogate mother, and we needed it to develop normally into a viable fetus and be carried to term.

"These were all well recognized problems with partial solutions. Dermott was merely pulling them together and engineering improvements. He expected to see final results in two to three years. He launched independent projects and built separate research facilities to work on each distinct line of inquiry. The results would then be brought together to successfully create Dermott's clone. One laboratory in Korea was doing basic science with non-human embryos to understand why some embryos failed to develop properly and why defects marred many of those carried to term. The new lab in China was working on taking the animal findings from Korea and elsewhere and applying them to human embryos. The research they were doing was prohibited nearly everywhere in the world, but it went ahead anyway using thousands of human embryos."

Francesca looked surprised. "Thousands? Really?"

"That may even be low. We are talking about nearly a decade of intensive research. And the groups tried everything, even making artificial eggs. Dermott developed his trait-specific gene editing technique to enable highly selective genetic manipulation, to be able to repair genes, turn them on and off, basically play with and fine tune the human genome. For him, money was no limitation. They didn't just sequence his entire genome, they sequenced the genome as recovered from different cell lines in his body. A separate, very ambitious line of research reconstructed what he called his root genome, his genetics before mutations began to accumulate differentially over his lifetime. His gene editing system was then used to recreate this original genome in his induced stem-cell line.

"Dermott was constantly inventing things to facilitate the work. He developed a new line of autonomous computer-driven micro-manipulators to automate extraction and insertion of genetic material to and from human cells. Someday, someone will trace how many people were involved and how many hundreds of millions of euros went into the various research projects. Anyway, once we built the basic science and proved out the techniques, it was time for the Dolly phase."

"The Dolly phase?"

"Dolly the sheep, the first successful mammalian clone back in 1996. Out of 277 clones delivered by surrogate sheep, that lamb was the only one to survive to adulthood. In effect, we needed human sheep to carry embryonic Dermotts. We recruited young, healthy women, women adrift or with severed ties, to become surrogate mothers. We provided food and housing and paid them well. We followed each pregnancy extremely closely. We continuously monitored blood samples from the mother and took periodic samples of amniotic fluid using a technique devised by Dermott to reduce to near zero the risk of miscarriage or fetal damage. We used expensive, extremely high-resolution non-invasive imaging to closely track fetal development. Still, of the first ten volunteers, only one carried to term, although the baby died within hours from a cause that was something we were not monitoring. Half of the other fetuses aborted spontaneously; we terminated the rest for one reason or another.

"Then we went back, tweaked our procedures, and refined our measurements. The second cohort included twenty volunteers. Four carried to term, but none of the babies were considered acceptable. With each wave, we increased the sample size until we understood precisely how to achieve the results we were after. Finally, after many failures, we succeeded."

Chapter 40

I am sure that many will find this to be self-serving—perhaps it is—but none of us at the Boston clinic, all of whom were late-comers to the Cameo Project, had thought through the implications, certainly not the full implications, of what the research entailed. Yes, we knew there had to have been failures along the way. Failure in this context was a scientific construct, a statistical concept, not a reality about actual human beings.

We discussed these things, of course, part of the local biomedical salon that we had created, our private forum for the free flow of ideas with only the most tenuous tethers to everyday life. What happens when an experiment goes awry? What is done with the discarded samples when the research subject is human fetal development?

It was all intellectual discourse at a distance, a method for walling off thoughts from the unthinkable, conversation that enabled us to avoid dealing with the painful immediacy of what had been done, if not by us, then in our names.

Francesca stared open-mouthed at Fernando. "Are you saying the babies were ..."

"Euthanized, then autopsied. Those, at least, are the scientific, the medical terms for what we did. We had little choice. We had to learn from our mistakes. That's what Dermott drilled into everyone. He was the patron calling the tune."

Danny leaned forward. "Can any of this be documented? I

mean, there must be lab notes, something. You can't conduct scientific research without records."

"Oh, I'm sure much of it is someplace, encrypted, locked in vaults, under guard, but there are public records, too."

"What? You must be joking."

"No, the surrogate mothers obviously knew they were pregnant and the ones who gave birth knew they had given birth. There had to be a story and a trail of records to explain that a baby had died. There are death certificates—all doctored, of course—but they are on file, all from the same precinct, all within the same short time period and in successive waves. A good reporter should be able to dig those out."

Francesca had her hands over her face. Danny reached over and touched her shoulder. "This is tough, I know. That's why we have to get the story out."

Francesca looked at him with reddened eyes. "Yes, you're right, but I think I've heard all I want to hear tonight."

"I have one more question." Danny turned back to Fernando. "The boy, Dermott's clone, was born almost two years after Dermott died. Why did the work continue?"

"I left after that first group of four babies. I assume they kept going because they were still being paid. They had a mandate to produce a result. It's about money again. When the patron is rich enough, whatever tune is picked, the pipers play—and play on."

o o o

In the taxi back to the hotel, Francesca was silent. As they waited for the elevator in the hotel lobby, she turned to Danny. "We have to go back to Italy. Fernando said there should be records, public records. We can ferret them out, build a case against Dermott, against the people who continued his agenda."

"And we can put our heads into the hangman's noose."

217

"Danny, this is my world. I'm an archivist. I know how Italian civil registration works. I can retrieve the vital records we need to make the case."

"You're right. We have to see this one through wherever it leads us. Let's hope the deal with Cahners holds, even when we start digging in their own backyards."

"Or in their graveyards."

Chapter 41

Helen intercepted Roy on his way out of the clinic. "How is Giuseppina doing?"

"Not too bad, not too good. She's not tolerating the chemo as well as we had hoped. We're switching her to another regimen. There has been some shrinkage of the primary tumor, but not as much improvement at other sites. Anschluss thinks the cell line mutated as it spread, so we are, in effect, dealing with a number of different cancers. We're looking into that. It's really too bad that we caught this so late, but that's often the story with pancreatic cancer. The symptoms are just too subtle or too indistinct until it's too late. How about your end of things?"

"Well, our legal team is helping her put her affairs in order so she can avoid probate. Paolo is taken care of by the provisions already in place in Dermott's will and the trust fund, our charter. All that stuff is just paper shuffling, complicated but routine. The Italian connection—not so routine."

"What's that about?"

"Don't you read my memos?"

"Not really, Helen. I've been busy being a doctor lately."

"I understand, but at least open the ones marked 'Alert' in the subject line. Our reporter and his Italian girlfriend have been digging into vital records back in Dermott's home town. Are you sure they'll keep their promise?"

"No, not for certain, but I would still lay odds on it as long as our security people stay clear."

"Security is in surveillance mode for now, keeping careful track of those two from a remove but poised to act quickly if they make a wrong move."

"We have another few years. They promised to sit on the story until Paolo turns twenty-one."

"You know, I'm really not so worried about Paolo. The dossier they're building is more than just the basis for a financial exposé. It could become the core of a criminal case against the whole enterprise. Security wants to make another attempt to buy them out. Exactly when the story breaks is not what worries security. They want to make sure it never breaks. They believe they just have to raise the stakes high enough. Everyone has a price, Roy."

"Maybe. Just because the lot of us struck a deal, doesn't mean everyone else can be bought."

"No, but let's hope those two can be. If not ..."

Roy studied the carpet for a few thoughtful seconds. "I have to get out to the house, Helen. Keep me posted. And I will read your memos, I promise."

o o o

With three cars in the driveway, Roy had to park on the street, risking being ticketed for not having a residence sticker. In addition to Toni's old Chevy, now Paolo's wheels, and Vera's VW, there was a white van with wheelchair access blocking them in.

Roy called out as he pushed open the unlocked front door. "Hello. It's Dr. Cahners. Where is everybody?"

"In here, in the bedroom."

Roy rounded the corner to find a grinning Seppina being helped into bed by Vera and Paolo. "What's with the van in the driveway?"

Vera pulled the sheet up and adjusted the bed. "We rented it to make it easier for Seppina to get out and about."

"We went to the symphony." Seppina fairly beamed. "Do you know, if you call ahead, they take out seats so you can get in with a wheelchair. And the ushers were all so nice. We were toward the back, on the aisle, but the sound in Symphony Hall is just so amazing."

"That's great, Seppina, but nobody told me."

Paolo finished folding the wheelchair. "I didn't know we had to tell you."

"She's my patient, and she's very sick."

"She is also my grandmother, and today she was feeling very good."

The five-second staring match broke with Roy offering a raised-eyebrows smile. "Then I guess it probably was good to take advantage of an opening. What did you hear, Seppina?"

"Schubert's Ninth. Oh, how I do love those opening bars. And also something modern that I didn't like as much, a concerto grosso by some cowboy from Texas."

Vera plumped Seppina's pillow. "Concerto Grosso, No. 1, 'Panhandle', by J. Dean Gilchrist."

Cahners squinted. "I don't know that one, Vera."

"Neither did we, doc, but it was exciting, a world premier commissioned by the BSO."

"Is he really a cowboy?"

"I don't think so, but his students at the University of Texas call him Cowboy Dean, apparently because of his classroom antics. At least that's what we were told in the pre-concert talk."

"Sounds fun, but I do wish you kids would clear any future expeditions with me first. At least keep me in the loop."

Vera narrowed her eyes at him. "We *kids* will do our best to keep you informed of our plans, but this was only decided yesterday, and we were ready to cancel if Seppina didn't feel up to it."

Seppina reached out and patted Vera's hand. "Don't be hard on her, Dr. Cahners. She's so good, like a daughter to me. Aren't you, dear?"

"How wonderful for you both. But right now I'm going to ask her and your grandson to wait somewhere else while I check you out. I brought some new portable equipment with me so we can check your blood and get nearly instantaneous lab results without having to take away samples and wait for some lab technician to get to your blood work. Oh, yes, and Monday, your new nurse shows up."

"I already have two wonderful nurses, right here.'

"Indeed you do, but this nurse is medically trained. We're starting you on some different chemotherapy and want to keep an extra close eye on you. The alternative would be to admit you again to the hospital. Would you prefer that?"

"Heck no."

"Good. Okay, let's take a look at you and get some numbers."

○ ○ ○

The exam and tests took the better part of an hour. Roy found Vera and Paolo in the living room watching streamed reruns of the classic Netflix Sci-Fi series "Blue Star, Red Star." He waited for them to look up. "Well, I'm done in there. I gave her a sedative. She's resting after all the excitement of the last couple of days. She said you went out for a picnic yesterday."

Paolo tapped his phone to pause the episode. "To the gazebo out back, that's all. She liked it so much that we got inspired to try something more ambitious."

"That's all well and fine, but you need to know something about Seppina. She's going to have her good days and her not-so-good days, but just because she's in better spirits doesn't mean she's actually any better. In fact, she's very weak now and not likely to get stronger. Her immune system is a wreck, and her numbers are getting worse. I'm even inclined to attribute her bright mood to neurological effects of the chemotherapy.

"The bottom line is I really don't want you to do anything like this again. With her compromised immune system, she's susceptible to picking up all sorts of opportunistic infections from being out in public. We don't want to make things worse than they are."

"She's dying, doc. How much worse can it get?"

"A lot worse."

"I want whatever time she has left to be as full and happy as it can be."

"So do I, Paolo. That's why careful management of her treatment is so important."

"What about her life, doc? What about her managing her life? She happened to want to go with us."

"That may be true, but that doesn't mean it was a good idea."

"You don't get it, doc. I thought modern medicine was finally starting to understand about quality of life and end-of-life issues. It's not about how long my grandmother lives, but how well she lives. That's my bottom line. I really don't want you telling me or her what we can or cannot do with her last days."

"I see." That was all he said before rolling the portable lab out the front door to load it in the trunk of his car.

Chapter 42

Early summer passed like a ride on one of those fairground kiddie rollercoasters that roll leisurely along an undulating track. It was up and down for Seppina, never into deep crisis but never showing marked improvement. The second course of drugs was as bad as the first and no more effective.

I wanted to go for broke with the still enormously expensive customized immunotherapy approach, but Paolo started lobbying for treating her with an oncolytic virus, an infectious agent specially engineered to seek out and destroy scattered colonies of cancer cells. Thanks to recent advances in gene editing, many of them benefiting from Dermott's inventions, the microbes were getting better and better at telling the difference between normal and cancerous tissue and were able to kill ever higher proportions of the target cells with fewer adverse effects than many other therapies.

Dr. Anschluss managed to get Seppina accepted for compassionate use of a promising experimental therapy that combined an oncolytic virus with a platin, a platinum-based chemical payload functioning as a kind of suicide vest to improve the kill ratio. We readmitted her to administer the enhanced viral therapy and kept her long enough to verify that the virus was multiplying and invading the cancer sites, then we sent her home, back into the care of Paolo and Vera.

Paolo opened the front door. "Hey, doc, you're late. That's a first. Come on in. She's been expecting you."

"I am sorry. I had to fill out a whole stack of extra paperwork because of the treatment we have Seppina on. The bureaucratic burden keeps getting worse and worse. And everything is tracked by these advanced computer systems, with neural nets and deep learning and all that techie stuff you read about. I don't know how it works except that it pesters and threatens me if I don't fill out certain forms just right and submit them in plenty of time."

"Well, go on in. She's waiting."

Seppina was sitting in her wheelchair when Roy entered the room. "Well, look who's up and out of bed. How's my favorite patient?"

Seppina tossed her head back. "I wouldn't know about her, but I'm feeling pretty good, doctor."

"You must be feeling chipper to treat your old family doctor with such flippant repartee. Let's have a look at you and see how you are doing."

"Are you going to poke me?"

"Just to get some blood for my ever thirsty portable vampire machine. And I'm going to use the hi-res ultrasound band to image your abdomen. So, tell me, are you really feeling better or are you faking it to get rid of me quickly?"

"Faking it so I can get rid of you. Vera and Paolo are taking me to the park for some fresh air."

Roy turned to Paolo and narrowed his eyes in mild disapproval.

"Just across the street, doc. Don't worry. The fresh air will do her good. I thought, you know, while she's on the upswing."

○ ○ ○

Roy completed his examination, and Paolo watched as he repacked equipment in the living room. "So, what's the word, doc?"

"Well, I do have to admit it appears your suggestion of oncolytic therapy is looking like a good call. The primary tumor is substantially smaller already, her bloodwork looks good, and she says her appetite is back."

"It is, she has actually been eating—not a lot, but a lot more than she was a few weeks ago. The change in her has been amazing. I didn't think this sort of thing, remission, was possible with Stage 4 pancreatic cancer."

"Well, we'll see. Remission is probably too strong a word, but miracles can happen."

"I didn't think you believed in miracles."

"I told you I don't believe in God. Miracles are another matter. A miracle is simply what we call an unexpected positive outcome that we don't understand. Miracles are well documented; the evidence for God is, shall we say, equivocal at best. Keep in mind, we're still in the early weeks with the new therapy, too early to attach a name to what's happening, but so far so good. I'll see you both next week."

○ ○ ○

As if in response to Roy's cautionary note, Seppina started to decline almost as fast as she had improved. Paolo cornered the doctor on the way out after another checkup. "What is happening, doc. She was doing so well there for a few of weeks. Now she's in such pain."

"Right. She was doing better, but now it's beginning to look like a replay of the Vietnam War. Did you study that in school? The history books don't spend a lot of time on Vietnam anymore, maybe because it was the first war ever that America lost. Anyway, what is happening with Seppina reminds me of a much quoted quip from a Vietnam War-era commander who said that, in order to save some village, they had to destroy it. The treatment put the cancer into temporary retreat, but the slash-and-burn tactics of all the combo therapies have also done nerve damage, leaving Seppina in chronic pain. So, I'm going to switch her pain medication to nasyntrophine."

"Nasyntrophine?"

"Yeah, a potent new synthetic opioid, latest in a long line of drugs designed to be more effective and less addictive, although we don't worry much about that in cases like this. I don't see Seppina becoming a drug addict in her last days. Even if she did, so what?" He held up a prescription bottle. "On the street, nasyntrophine is known as Nasty or Sin, which are apt names for a little blue pill with the power to wreck lives. And, it's relatively easy to overdose on. You know, Paolo, it amazes me that pharmacologists keep on underestimating the human capacity for chemical abuse."

"Maybe that's because big pharma benefits regardless of whether their pills are sold through the pharmacy or on the street corner."

"True. And my headaches keep getting worse."

"Headaches?"

"Nanny-state paperwork headaches. After the 'opioid crisis' back around the time you were starting kindergarten, a stack of new regulations was introduced limiting and closely monitoring prescription painkillers. The regulations didn't do a lot to mitigate the crisis, but they certainly complicated the practice of medicine. In addition to the red tape necessary to prescribe an adequate supply of nasyntrophine for my dying patient, I will have to complete a fresh set of forms whenever I might need to up the dose. Plus, I can't give her more than a ten-day supply at a time, even through our in-house pharmacy."

Chapter 43

September approached on a chariot of fire, with more record highs and uncomfortably high humidity. The newly installed window air conditioner in the dining room was straining away when Paolo entered carrying a wicker basket. "We're having a picnic, Nonna. The nurse is going to get you ready."

"I don't know, Paolo. I don't think I can manage going out today."

He ignored her pained expression. "You're not going out. Out is coming to you. We're having a picnic right here. Vera is getting the blanket from the car, we'll spread it on the floor. You get to stay up there stretched out on your regal adjustable divan, overseeing the whole affair. I've made sandwiches—easy-eating fare: peanut butter with your favorite jelly, seedless blackberry. We have a bottle of pink champagne on ice. I checked with Dr. Cahners and he says you can have a sip. It might even be good for you."

"What has gotten into you, Paolo?"

"Life, love, and another month with my beloved Nonna." He bent and kissed her forehead.

She smiled weakly, then grimaced. "Could you get me my pills?"

"Sure, but that means you have to go easy on the champagne. You can't mix drugs and alcohol."

"I don't think there's much danger of me overindulging. I think I'll pass on it today. I can barely swallow some days. Dr.

Cahners is talking about putting a tube in me, but I don't know. It's all getting so hard, and it all hurts so much. I just don't know anymore."

"It'll be all right. I'll take care of you, that's a promise. Now, let me get this picnic all set up."

○ ○ ○

Paolo stood by the bed in Seppina's temporary bedroom, listening to her breathing in the dark, each shaky intake followed by a whining exhale, a quiet high-pitched moan. He could not tell if she was asleep, but her cries had awakened him and brought him from the living room where he and Vera now slept on the sofa-bed.

"Are you awake?" he whispered almost inaudibly.

"Yes," came the reply between pained breaths.

"Can I get you anything, Nonna?"

"A sledgehammer might help. I can't sleep, the pain is too much."

"You took your sleeping pill, right? When did you last take your pain medicine?"

"Midnight."

"Well, we're supposed to wait at least another hour before you get any more."

"I know. I'm sorry I woke you up. I try to be quiet."

"I know you do, Nonna. I think we can cheat a little on the meds. I've read the indications sheet and looked up nasyntrophine on WebMed. I'll give you two. That should help get you through the night. In the morning I'll call Dr. Cahners and see if there might be something more he can do."

"You're such a good boy." She reached for the water glass and took the pills from him, swallowing them with another moan. "It hurts sometimes to swallow."

"I know. Try to sleep now."

He tiptoed out and left the door ajar. The sofa-bed creaked as he climbed back in. Vera rolled over and laid her arm across his chest. "Is she okay?"

"No, she's in a lot of pain, and it doesn't seem to stop. I wish we could do more. It hurts to see her suffering so. And for what? She doesn't want to go into hospice care, and she doesn't want tubes in her arm, and ... She's a stubborn old lady. And I love her so much. She's all I got."

"You have me."

"I meant, like, family."

"We can do something about that. Seppina already treats me like her daughter-in-law."

"Are you proposing to me on a squeaky sofa-bed in the dark of a hot night?"

"Well?"

"We have to wait ... until I'm eighteen. And we can't tell anyone, even Seppina. I think she's happy with you as long as she doesn't have it spelled out for her."

"Paolo, wake up. We're sleeping together in the room next to her. How more spelled out could it be?"

"I don't know how to explain it, but I just know her. We shouldn't shove her face in it. She's old fashioned ... and fragile. We shouldn't do anything to upset her or give her more pain than she already has." He lifted Vera's hand from his chest and kissed it. "But my answer is yes. I do. Sometime soon, after my birthday."

○ ○ ○

Vera slipped her makeup kit into the overnight bag and closed it. Labor Day weekend had passed with the heatwave unabated, and she was reluctantly preparing for a teachers' start-of-school workshop. "I hate to be leaving you like this. It'll be the first night we've been apart since we ..."

"I know. But don't worry, I'll be fine. We'll be fine. And this weekend workshop is important. I think it's good for you to be back teaching. It's been a tough summer."

"Do you think she enjoyed today?"

"I think so. She was a little out of it by midafternoon. The extra meds and the champagne ... It was fun that she decided to try it this time but a little surprising when she kept asking for another sip. I was watching her closely, but she seemed all right. And the day nurse checked her vitals before leaving."

He walked Vera to the door. She set down the bag and hugged him. "I don't want to go. I don't know why. I guess I'm in a clingy mood. I really love you so. I feel so lucky, so blessed."

"Me, too. Drive safely. I love you."

"Call if anything comes up, okay?"

"Okay."

○ ○ ○

Roy pawed around for his smartphone on the night stand and swiped his sign-in swoosh on the screen. "Cahners here."

"You better come."

"Paolo?"

"Just come."

231

Chapter 44

However well prepared we are, regardless of how much time in ex-
tra innings life grants us to get used to it, the loss of a loved one can
still hit like a disallowed judo-kick below the belt. A prolonged ill-
ness with a disease from which there is no reprieve does not make
the blow any less painful. Doctors and nurses are trained to deal
with losing patients. The best of them learn to distance themselves
just enough from the human suffering to be able to cope but not so
much as to lose their humanity, their ability to empathize that is so
essential to being a good practitioner as well as a good person.

All the lights were on when Roy arrived at the house. He found
Paolo standing beside Seppina's bed, silently staring down at
her pale face. On the stand beside the bed, an amber prescription bottle lay open on its side, a single blue oval resting just
outside its mouth. Roy casually picked up the pillow at Paolo's
feet where it had fallen from the bed. "I am so sorry." He righted
the pill bottle; it was empty. "Oh, boy. It doesn't take a lot with
nasyntrophine at this strength. I never saw this coming, but I
suppose I should have. I don't understand it, though. She was
Catholic. I would never have expected she would ever take her
own life."

Paolo said nothing.

"Did you call an ambulance?"

Paolo shook his head.

"I'll do it. Did you call a priest?"

"I suppose I should."

"I can do that, too."

"No, I'll call St. Theresa's."

"I'll take care of it. I'll be right back."

Paolo was still standing, staring, when Roy returned. "They'll be here in fifteen minutes." He put his arm around Paolo's shoulder. "This has gotta be hard, I know, but she was in a lot of pain and she was already dying. At least she's not in pain anymore."

Paolo turned and rested his head for a moment on Roy's chest. "I know." He pulled away and faced the bed, starting a quiet recitation, a low-pitched, almost monotone chant, an erratic dirge in double time.

> The dead feel no pain,
>> Neither know they any joy.
>
> The unborn without aim,
>> adrift through nameless void,
>> speak nothing in their silent cries.
>
> Nothing is not,
>> and nothing's but a name
>> that darkness sighs within the night.
>
> The nighttime leaves with a soaring shout,
>> splitting the dream with a glancing beam
>> of rising light,
>
> only to return once again in doubt
>> to whisper still of unspoken fright.
>
> The night, and night again—
>> endless, invincible, indifferent to the brief lived day
>> between,
>> endless, invincible, indifferent to the brief lived day
>> between.

"What's that?"

"A song, goth-rock poetry. It was one of Sosamma's favorites, from Graphene Promises: 'Infinite Black,' I think, by Jolene Maples, who fronts the band. It just,"—he looked down at his shoes—"just came to mind. I'll be all right. I just need to be alone for a while."

Roy left Paolo standing there, staring, saying nothing. The priest and the ambulance arrived at nearly the same time. Roy told the ambulance people to wait while Father Donovan finished the last rites. Then Roy himself pronounced Giuseppina dead and told the paramedics he would take care of notifying the Office of the Chief Medical Examiner and providing the paperwork. "She had cancer, pancreatic adenocarcinoma, terminal—obviously the cause of death." The mild misdirection was intended as his small gift to her friends and her church community.

○ ○ ○

Helen took the call from the coroner the next day. As soon as she got off the phone she called Roy into her office. "They're doing an autopsy. Why do they have to do an autopsy? She had terminal cancer."

"It's required in some cases, such as any case of suspected suicide. But I talked with the ME last night. I thought this was settled, that she died of natural causes, terminal cancer. It should all be routine. If there's any exposure for us or Paolo, it should be minimal. And the results might even be informative. We might learn something about the cancer. We'll know when they release the findings."

"Well, they said they would release the body to the funeral parlor after the autopsy so that the funeral can go ahead as planned, but they also said it could be awhile before they deliver a final death certificate."

"I still don't get it. What are they after? What good will it do if they rule her death a suicide, except to bring shame to her memory?"

"I know, we certainly don't need this. I'm going to see what I can find out and try to get this thing derailed. I'll file an objection on Paolo's behalf as next of kin."

"Clear it with Paolo, first."

"Why? Publicity and legal scrutiny are things we should always avoid as much as possible."

"He's a legal adult now, we have to accept that."

○ ○ ○

The body was finally released to the mortuary two days before the funeral, still without a final finding issued. Roy attended the funeral but avoided the viewing at the funeral home beforehand, a custom that he understood but for which he could never shake a deep distaste. It was to him a Christian thing, this painting and arranging of the body for a final on-stage appearance at the front of a chapel or for a parade of mourners at a funeral parlor.

In church for the funeral service, Roy found himself feeling like an outsider, a secular Jew standing apart from the committed Catholic community that surrounded him. It was a sense that he had not felt so strongly in decades.

For the second time in two years, Paolo sat silent in the front-row pew for a service that seemed to stretch into the very eternity of which the priest spoke. Beside him, Vera strained to achieve a similar stoicism that still eluded her. Paolo comforted her as she sobbed openly, quietly, all the while his eyes fixed on the crucifix above the altar.

After the graveside ceremony, Vera and Paolo announced that they were headed north for a few days of retreat. "You deserve some time to yourselves," Roy told them, taking a hand from each of them in his.

"You've been so good to us, Dr. Cahners." Vera kissed him on the cheek.

"You can call me Roy, Vera. You both can. I hope you can consider me a friend." He looked Paolo in the eye. "There are going to be an awful lot of details to take care of and bits of business to straighten out when you get back, but you'll have our help and support. I know it may not look that way at the moment, but things are going to work out."

"Oh, I know that, doc." He shook Roy's hand and nodded gravely. "We'll be back."

Chapter 45

Helen finished the morning briefing, then hung back as the conference room cleared. "Paolo took it hard, didn't he, Roy, even though he knew it was coming."

"I think a part of him wanted to hold out for a miraculous remission that wasn't going to happen. It's never easy to see someone you love suffer and die."

"You're right, of course. I lost my mother to emphysema after years of watching her suffer. In the end, it was a blessing, but that didn't make it any easier when I held her hand as she took her last breath. I still miss her, and she died nearly ten years ago. At least I had my brother and sister; now I have Edgar. Who does Paolo have?"

"Vera Prentiss."

"I'm a little surprised that's still going. I'm impressed. Do you think it will last?"

"I think so. I think they may already have tied the knot without telling anybody."

"Our boy is full of surprises. We were all prepared to be raising another Arturo Dermott, and look what we got. Instead of a glossy print, we get a color negative—almost unrecognizable."

"I'm not so sure. The last chapters of this story have yet to be written."

○ ○ ○

Paolo and Vera were still away when the autopsy results were finally released. Roy took the call, nodding and making notes as

Helen watched and waited patiently. When he hung up, he stared down at his notes, mouth open, making clicking sounds with his tongue.

"What is it, Roy?"

"You want a summary?"

"No, I want a full written report. Don't be silly, Roy. Just give me the lowdown."

"The lowdown. Right. Okay, the cancer had spread to the liver, stomach, and lungs, with patches throughout the body cavity. We knew that already. The oncolytic treatment must have worked for a while, but the cancer was somehow coming back with a vengeance. Nevertheless, the cancer was not what killed her, although it would have before much longer.

"My guess about the pills was on target. She had residue from several nasyntrophine tablets in her stomach and fatal levels of metabolites in her blood stream, but that was not the cause of death."

"Get to the point, Roy. What did they find?"

"The coroner's report concludes that the cause of death was asphyxia: she was suffocated and was alive but unconscious when her air supply was cut off, most likely, considering the absence of evidence of trauma, by a soft mass, such as a pillow, over the nose and mouth."

○ ○ ○

For Paolo and Vera, the lakeside cabin in New Hampshire, with neither television nor Wi-Fi, had become their honeymoon suite and a respite from drama. They spent their days sleeping late, hiking the adjacent network of trails, then driving to a country store a few miles up the road to pick up supplies for a simple supper and the next morning's breakfast. On the third day, they reluctantly dropped off the key and headed back so Vera could restart her teaching.

Southbound traffic on Interstate 93 returning to Massachusetts was moderate but moving. Just over the state line and passing the Methuen exit, Paolo noticed the strobing blue lights in his rearview mirror. Vera stirred in her sleep as he pulled off into the breakdown lane with the highway patrol on his tail. A blinding-white spotlight blazed through the rear window, turning the gray dusk into bright day and awakening Vera. "What's happening," she said, her voice thick with sleep.

"We've been pulled over for some reason. I wasn't speeding or anything. I—"

He was interrupted by a voice on a bullhorn. "Stay in the car, both of you. Keep your hands where we can see them, and do not make any sudden moves."

Two state troopers exited the patrol car and approached the VW, one on each side, with hands poised near their holstered handguns. "Can we see your license and registration, please."

"Sure, officer." As he reached to unhook his seatbelt, the officer jerked and reached toward his handgun.

"Slowly. I said no sudden moves."

"I'm just going for my wallet with my license. The registration is in the glove compartment. This is her car."

The patrolman bent down to be able to see into the car. "Can I see your identification, too, ma'am?"

They handed over their licenses and the car registration. The officer holstered his weapon and returned to the patrol car. He was back in a minute. "It's them," he said to his partner on the other side of the car. "I need you both to step slowly out of the vehicle, please. Keep your hands where we can see them."

Paolo got out with his hands out in front of him. "What is this all about?"

"I have a warrant for your arrest, Mr. Franzetti. Ms. Prentiss is wanted for questioning."

o o o

Roy had his cellphone in his hand when he entered Helen's office. "Paolo just called. He's been arrested, and they brought Vera in for questioning."

"Oh, Jesus." She stood up and started pacing. "We are going to have to move fast. I'll get legal on this as quick as they can and have an attorney sent over to them. We'll put in play contingency plans to create some distance for the rest of the operation, if that's even possible at this point. I'll see what Ramona in Public Relations might be able to do to muzzle the media. I'll ... look, can you get a copy of the coroner's report over to legal? And send your notes right now. I'll talk with Chaim about Paolo's mental status, and—"

"All that is very sensible, Helen, but it's already probably too late. Paolo's under arrest. Most likely, we're all going to be subpoenaed at some point. This is it. We need to worry not only about Paolo but also how to keep the rest of us out of jail."

"Worry all you want, Roy, as you have always been wont to do, but we ourselves have done nothing wrong and broken no laws. The worse they can pin on you is supplying the wrong diagnosis to the ME, and you can fend that off easily enough. It was your assessment at the time and an understandable mistake given the circumstances. No, it's Paolo and the enterprise that are at risk."

o o o

When Roy showed up at the clinic the following morning, Helen was already at her desk. "I assume you've seen or heard the morning headlines," he said. She closed her eyes and nodded. "It doesn't take long for bad news to spread, does it? I thought Ramona was going to try to fend off the vultures."

Helen shrugged. "She tried, but we are talking about what the vultures are calling a monstrous crime, the murder of a helpless, seriously ill elderly woman by her grandson. Because Paolo is already eighteen, Ramona couldn't even keep his name out of the news."

"I know, and then there's Vera Prentiss. The local news said she was picked up for questioning and there were hints that she may be involved. Some enterprising reporter checked public records and discovered that they were married. The speculation mill that has replaced what used to be journalism is already constructing elaborate scenarios hinting at manipulation of an impressionable young boy by a predatory teacher."

"Can we really rule that out, Roy?"

"What are you talking about? We most certainly can. I know those two. I've seen this relationship develop from the beginning, and it sure looked to me like Paolo was the one taking the lead. If anyone is immune to manipulation it would be our Paolo, and I'm quite confident Chaim would back me up on that. Our 'boy' is a young man and anything but impressionable. I expect our people to be as aggressive in coming to the aid of Vera as to Paolo. Is that understood?"

"Okay, Roy, no need to get testy. But the local NPR outlet said she was taken into custody as a possible accessory to murder."

"I don't think it will take very long to rule that out, especially as being away at that conference gives her an ironclad alibi. Besides, I don't think there was any murder to be an accessory to, whether before or after the fact. We do need to get another autopsy done, stat. We better get legal on that if they haven't already made the move."

"Already in progress." The intercom line buzzed and Helen picked up the handset. "Okay, thanks. Show them to conference room B and have them wait."

"Who's that?"

"Our enterprising financial journalist and his sidekick, back from Europe and ready to feed the frenzy in the making. They want to talk with us before going public."

Chapter 46

Vera was baffled by the turn of events, along with the rest of us. With an unassailable alibi and no evidence against her, she was released. Paolo, on the other hand, was charged and denied bail because he was considered a flight risk on the basis of nothing more than that he had "fled" to New Hampshire.

Paolo was kept in isolation, supposedly for his own protection, an argument we reluctantly accepted as having some validity. In truth, Paolo had no problem with solitary confinement. He explained to us on one visit that he already had years of practice in the self-imposed isolation of his attic retreat. Vera visited him as often as was permitted, but Paolo resolutely refused to talk about the case or the upcoming trial.

The urge to touch him overwhelmed Vera. She wanted to reach through the Plexiglas that separated them and stroke Paolo's unshaven cheek. "What happened? You can tell me. You can tell me anything. Just talk to me."

"I really don't want to talk." His voice was thin through the old fashioned telephone handsets that each of them held. "There is really nothing to talk about. Not now anyway." He glanced up and down the row of prisoners on his side of the barrier. "How's Mooshu?"

"Mooshu is fine. I think she misses you."

"Sure she does. School?"

"Meh. The arts department is in a funk again. Budget battles.

You know. They want me to direct the next school play on my own time."

"That's bullshit. Don't do it. Once you start giving it away, they'll never stop asking."

"I said I'd think about it."

"Don't."

"I don't want to lose my job, not now. Besides, I need to keep busy. And I need to keep paying the mortgage."

"Talk to Doc Cahners. Roy can probably help."

She studied the chipped Formica that surfaced the long counter between them. "I can handle this. I've been on my own since college. I don't like asking for help."

"Hey, we're married now. They, like, the Foundation, may even be legally bound to take care of you. Talk to him."

"I ... Roy is a sweet man, but ... I just want you with me."

Paolo took his handset away from his ear and looked at it as if it might guide him in what to say next. He slowly lifted it back. "I know. Me too."

There was silence as they locked eyes. "Oh, those reporters are back," she said, at last.

"Bradman and Zingari?"

"Yeah. There've been leaks to the media, extracts from an up-coming special report to the *New York Times*. Roy said he heard they got a seven-figure advance on a book deal. He seemed pleased by that, even though they let the cat out of the bag about, well, about the ... the cloning thing. He said he had to admire them, finishing the story and saving their own skins—and their integrity as journalists. Plus, they pocketed the big bucks."

"Bully for them. We'll see what they write. I worry about you and ..."

"They told Roy that they were not about to join the flock of media vultures swooping down on us. Those two are really more interested in the bigger story of Dermott and his off-label research. That's what Roy called it." There was another empty pause, this time interrupted by a loud buzzer. "That's it, my sweet Paolo. I have to leave."

He nodded, returned the handset to its cradle, and mouthed the words *I love you.*

"I love you too."

○ ○ ○

Roy pantomimed heaving his laptop against the wall as Helen entered the office. "Venting, Roy, so early in the morning? Please don't take it out on the computers."

"It's the media, especially the digital tabloids and the podcasts, well, and certain of the cable news networks—no need to name names. All they do is sensationalize and hyperbolize to play on public paranoia and prejudice."

"Is that a word: hyperbolize?"

"If not, it should be. Now they're trumpeting about the—get this—'inexorable consequences of playing God' and about 'toying with Nature's genetic code'. They are making Paolo out to be a murdering monster, a clone who kills in cold blood, who mindlessly murders the frail elderly woman who raised him. Dermott and those who were responsible were 'power-mad pseudo-scientists' who unleashed on the world the Franzetti Frankenstein. Franzetti Frankenstein? Spare me. It doesn't matter to these self-styled journalists that there is not one whit of evidence or any scientific basis for the linkage being touted. But, the public will believe what they will believe."

"Are you done with the morning rant?"

"No, but I'll press pause. What's up?"

"The District Attorney—fired up, no doubt, by career-cranking media attention—has decided to go for murder one and appointed Deborah Oschinsky to lead the prosecution. She's a seasoned trial lawyer with a solid conviction record, not flashy but formidable. Our boys in legal have responded by recruiting none other than Jackson Billington to head the defense team."

"Are you talking about 'Bad Boy' Billington?"

"The one and only. He wants to talk with us this afternoon and then start meeting with Paolo about his defense strategy."

Chapter 47

Billington, a colorful and controversial orator with a disputed pedigree tracing back to the Mayflower, had famously won acquittal for the Wellner brothers in what everyone else regarded as an open-and-shut case. His skills at skating at the very edge of contempt of court and in inciting juries to acquit in cases of clear guilt was legendary, earning him the sobriquet of the Jack of Jury-Nullification, an alliterative recognition of his ability to persuade ordinary citizens to flout the law in the privileged space of jury deliberation.

The moment he joined the Foundation team, Billington shifted into high gear. Starting with motions to dismiss, then for demands, rejected in every case, that reasonable bail be set for Paolo, and moving on to motions for a change in venue and for in limine rulings to exclude certain arguments and testimony. Relentlessly, he kept both teams and the judge in the case busy. Modern American jurisprudence is an edifice of complexity and sophistication, at its intricate best when it comes to a murder trial and bordering on baroque high drama when compounded by pretrial publicity, of which there was no shortage in this high-profile case.

Jackson Billington was an imposing and elegant intrusion in his trademark three-piece gray window-pane worsted suit and blue bowtie. A big man in every dimension and every sense of the word, he marched into the conference room, tapped his walking stick on the conference table, and began talking without even waiting for an introduction.

"The prosecution is clutching its collective crotch. How do we know that, you ask? By their overreach. Murder one? My left buttock. They already signaled they're not interested in pleading out. Arrogance, they're playing to the press and the public, so cocksure of conviction. My father always said, you go for broke and you can end up broke." He paused to inhale loudly through his nose.

Helen took advantage of the moment to interrupt. "But the evidence—"

"Evidence?" He snorted. "Look, your own medical people here can tell you, just ask. Forensic evidence in these cases is as mushy as a saltmarsh. Homicidal smothering can be difficult to detect and the findings are ambiguous at best, especially in the very young and the elderly. The second autopsy, the one your team requested—smart move—it produced, shall we say, somewhat different findings. No surprise. I intend to make the most of those differences. If the prosecutor has any brains, she'll let us plead down, and your boy will be out in five to seven. This crap case should never go to trial."

"Is that your strategy, to work out a plea bargain?" Helen asked.

"My strategy is to beat the crap out of this Oschinsky clown. We'll paper the damn court with pretrial motions, push their hot buttons, move for a change of venue. We'll play so many cards so fast that they won't even know whether the game is Texas Hold 'em or Pinochle."

Roy's narrowed eyes signaled his cynicism. "Sounds like legal legerdemain. Should be a good way for all the lawyers to accumulate billable hours."

"Damn straight." His eyes telegraphed amusement mixed with disapproval. "That's how you keep the kid from spending the rest of his days behind bars. Put a price on that, doctor."

○ ○ ○

The man, who exploited his height and bulk in the courtroom and in dealing with opposing attorneys, tried to make himself small in the locked interrogation room at the jail. Paolo sat across from him at the metal table, dwarfed by comparison. The room, painted in bland institutional green, could have been almost anywhere in the vast borderless edifice of the criminal justice empire. It was, instead, where Paolo was meeting with his attorney, the flamboyant Jackson Billington.

"The DA is acting aggressive, son, but you should know that the actual evidence is weak. Right now, our overtures to plead down to a lesser charge are being rebuffed, but we will keep trying. In the meantime, we are keeping the other side dancing to our tune with plenty of pretrial motions.

"So, here is the bottom line, Paolo. They actually have a pretty pathetic case. The only evidence against you is circumstantial and equivocal. They have an autopsy report and a lab report on the pillow, fingerprints from the pill bottle, that's it. The autopsy was a rush to judgement, and the pillow proves nothing. Our own autopsy, from one of the top forensic medicine teams in the country, pretty much trashes theirs. So, there you are. They're left with motive and opportunity but diddly actual evidence."

"Motive?"

"The burden of caring for your grandmother."

"That was no burden. I chose that. I even put off starting college. I loved taking care of her."

"Of course, you did. But that isn't even going to be an issue. It'll never even come up."

"But I want it to come up. I'll tell them."

"No you won't. No way are we going to put you on the stand. You just sit there, looking small and young and vulnerable, and the jury will build the testimony in their own imaginations.

Frankly, the case is so weak that I'm surprised they decided to prosecute. Well, no. I'm not surprised, considering. No offense to the judiciary, son, but I think some who now occupy the bench and prowl the halls of the district attorney's office are even more into publicity than me. Win or lose, those types get to strut their stuff in the limelight. With a lower profile case, this would never go to trial."

"You're saying they might lose ... I mean, we might win?"

"No one ever knows for sure what a jury will do, but if it goes to trial, I am cautiously confident that you could walk out of that courtroom a free man."

Paolo's gaze flicked over the stainless steel surface between them. "I don't know, then."

"Look, there's no reason to be glum. You've got a great legal team on your side with me as point man. I've come through in far worse cases."

"But ..."

"Just keep thinking positively, my boy. You're in good hands."

o o o

Vera intercepted Billington in the parking lot. "What do you think?"

"What do I think about what?"

"About Paolo? How is he? Is he going to be all right? What was your take?"

"My take? I'm not a psychiatrist, miss, but I am pretty damn good at reading people. I'd say he's depressed. Hardly surprising, given his living conditions, wouldn't you say? But, there's also ..."

"Yes? What?"

"I don't know, resignation maybe, almost as if he had already given up. I tried to give him a pep talk, I mean, not false hope, but a realistic appraisal of the odds, which I think are good. It didn't seem to make a difference. Anyway, as long as he keeps it together, we'll keep doing what we do." He placed a hammy hand on her shoulder. "I wouldn't worry too much."

"How much is too much?"

Billington looked at her, for once at a loss for words.

Chapter 48

The long seven months leading up to the trial passed in a blur that felt like both a suspension from reality and an assault by it. The five-part Bradman-Zingari piece in The Times *was followed by their devastating exposé in* The Atlantic. *The impact was immediate and global. New laws were introduced and under deliberation by legislatures, assets were seized, laboratories were closed, and in China, erstwhile researchers, once darlings of the regime, simply vanished. The clinic and the Fenix Foundation survived, not only because we were small and clean, but because we had been carefully walled off throughout our history. We did have to relocate, and all of us learned to keep even lower profiles than we were accustomed to, but we got through it.*

If anything, my friendship with Paolo and Vera deepened, mostly through Vera. Rising to the challenges, the sometimes flighty young woman had settled into a stoic solidity. If Paolo had once been her sea anchor, she was now the emotional breakwater that kept him from being inundated by the tide of events. Through her, I learned that he was writing again, chipping away at some major work that, true to form, he would not talk about, even with her.

As the trial approached, he drew on her for energy, and she leaned on me for support.

Vera Prentiss entered the courtroom escorted by Roy Cahners. As soon as the press noted her stylish maternity outfit, the cameras started clicking and the video pool camera panned to follow them up the aisle. Acting as her mobile shield, Roy kept repositioning his body to block the worst of the optical assault until they reached their seats. From across the aisle, Danny Bradman and Francesca Zingari gave them a discreet wave.

Between reporters from print and online media and the video pool from the cable outlets and podcasts, there was limited room for spectators. After a key ruling five years earlier, cameras were permitted in court unless specifically ordered to be excluded—with cause—by the presiding judge. Adam Tarniak, an ambitious young judge with aspirations of higher office, had no objections to media presence. The trial of the decade was his moment to shine regardless of which side prevailed.

Roy leaned his head close to Vera's. "Did you ever wonder why it is that digital cameras with fully electronic shutters are programmed to make loud clicking noises? I just figured it out. The cricket storm of shutter sounds gives the impression that the photographers are actually doing work. It becomes the audio hallmark of press conferences. The President approaches the podium and the stutter of shutters is like electric applause."

She gave him an upward-angled look. "Trying to distract me, are you?"

"Relax. I'm the one who is going to have to take the stand. They can't call you because you're the spouse. Everything is going to be fine."

"Easy for you to say. You're not facing the prospect of raising a son as a single parent while your partner sweats in solitary."

"I really don't see that happening. Billington says, and I quote, their case is as limp as overdone spaghetti."

A sudden rise in decibels of the background susurration signaled the arrival of the defendant. Paolo's attention was fixed straight ahead as he was brought into the packed courtroom and escorted to the defense table at the front. He nodded briefly toward Vera, who smiled bravely back. Roy took her hand and gave it a bonus squeeze for reassurance.

The bailiff did his "all rise" routine as the judge entered. Tarniak, panning the packed courtroom with his flat Slavic face, gaveled the court into session, the charges were read, and he queried the attorneys. "Is the Commonwealth ready?"

"We are, Your Honor."

"Is defense counsel ready?"

Billington rose as rapidly as his bulk permitted. "Yes, I do believe we are, Your Honor."

"A simple affirmative will do, counsel. Court is not interested in what you believe."

"Of course, Your Honor. I ..."

There was a quiet explosion of whispers at the defense table as Paolo and Billington leaned into each other. Billington jabbed a finger at Paolo's chest as Paolo shook his head.

"Is the defense ready, Mr. Billington?"

"Your Honor, I need a moment with my client."

The judge's narrowed eyes twitched as if he were contemplating further action. "You have had seven months with your client. Are you ready for trial?"

"Begging the court's indulgence. I just need a moment." He turned to Paolo and whispered, "No drama, boy, no last minute change of plans or new plays for the quarterback. If you want to pull me from the game, you can do so after you see how the kickoff plays out. Now shut up and let me do my job." He turned and rose again to face the bench. "My apologies to the court; the defense is ready."

The rest of the first day was taken up with opening statements. Deborah Oschinsky spoke with a resonant voice salted with the slightest hint of an accent, a much diluted legacy from the Yiddish-speaking grandparents who had raised her.

"This is, whatever else it involves, a simple case of murder in cold blood. The Commonwealth will show how the accused not only administered to the victim a fatal dose of a powerful narcotic but, growing impatient with the slow onset of the effects, hastened her death by smothering the woman with her own pillow." She proceeded to lay out her case slowly and systematically, a saga that she not only spelled out by the evidence to be presented but grounded it in the long story of Paolo's origins, making it seem as if the tragic end was the all-but-inevitable outcome of a sad and unnatural beginning. She was taking advantage of the latitude so often allowed in opening arguments to build the link in the jury's minds between the case before them and the case of Arturo Dermott, a case already tried and decided in the court of public opinion.

Billington, aware that he could have objected, let it pass, choosing not to risk appearing to be rude or intrusive at the outset of the trial. He also did not want to detract from his coming grand entrance into the ring.

After the lunchtime break, Jackson Billington slowly raised his bulk from the defense table to take over the trial, his voice booming out as he crossed toward the jury and gestured toward the spectators. "We should be surprised, not by the case outlined by the prosecution but by the fact that the courtroom did not burst into applause after such a stunning first act. The storyline is so persuasive, the scenario so perfect, surely it ought to be turned into a made-for-internet movie, nay, an entire season-long streaming series." He raised his hand as if warding off an objection that he trusted would not come. "In all seriousness, let me begin again. We will show you, the jury, that the case as outlined by my esteemed opponent for the prosecution is a complete fiction without basis in fact. You, the jury, will ultimately decide whether to believe the drama or to believe the dreary facts." In his peripheral vision he could see the prosecution team edging forward in their seats, weighing whether to object to his overdrawn language.

"We will show that the so-called evidence to be paraded by the prosecution is not evidence of any crime, much less of anything criminal on the part of the accused. My client, the defendant, is, in fact, a devoted and loving grandson who gave up college and put his entire future on hold to care for his dying grandmother, a generous soul who suffered with her in her suffering as she succumbed, inevitably and inexorably, to the scourge of incurable cancer. We will show this young man seated here to be a gentle poet, incapable of bringing harm to any living soul.

"Most importantly, we will show the true facts of Giuseppina Franzetti's death and the actual circumstances that led her loving grandson to be at her bedside on that fateful night. We will show you how the medical examiner reached, in haste—"

"Objection! Impugning a witness who has not even testified."

"Sustained."

Billington smiled at his success in luring his opponents into making the first objection while still in opening arguments. He drew out the pause with his gaze down on his folded hands, as if in patient tolerance for a rude interruption. "We will, I should say, show how the autopsy by the medical examiner led to erroneous conclusions about the cause of death. Furthermore, we will show the true facts of Giuseppina Franzetti's death—not the convenient or concocted fiction, but the truth, however painful it might be to face."

While the prosecution waivered over whether to object again, Billington plunged ahead. "Enough. I will not at this point take more of your time and attention, ladies and gentlemen of the jury. There is little need to lay out in advance every single one of the many flaws in the case as already outlined for you by the prosecution. I am confident that one exposure will be more than enough to be convincing. Thank you." He returned to his chair, nodding in a truncated bow toward the judge and then the prosecution table before seating himself.

○ ○ ○

Over the following days, as the prosecution laid out its case, Billington skewered witness after witness, beginning with the underpaid pathologist who had conducted the original autopsy.

"Your report,"—Billington held up the copy entered into evidence, rolled into a tube and wielded like a pointer—"it took you days to reach a conclusion and release it, am I right, Dr. Mehta?"

"Yes, we had other cases."

"Would you say your department is adequately staffed?"

"Objection, irrelevant." Oschinsky half rose.

"It goes to the credibility of the findings."

Judge Tarniak responded almost immediately. "I'll allow it, but get to the point, counsel."

"I'll withdraw the question. Tell me, Dr. Mehta, were you working at this facility in 2024?"

"Objection, irrelevant."

"The question goes to professional experience of the witness."

"Sustained." Tarniak looked over the top of his glasses. "Defense has already stipulated to the witness's qualification as an expert."

"Well, then, Dr. Mehta, were any of your autopsy results among those thrown out in the scandal over shoddy and falsified findings—"

"Objection!"

"—from your department in 2024?"

"Objection! Badgering the witness and irrelevant to the matter at hand."

"It goes"—Billington interjected quickly—"to credibility of the findings in the matter at hand."

"Sustained. Counsel will confine himself to the current case."

"Then, Dr. Mehta, would you say that your conclusions are the only possible ones regarding the cause of death of Mrs. Franzetti?"

"Well, forensic medicine is not an exact science, it—"

"Just answer the question, please, doctor. Are your conclusions the only possible findings in this instance?"

"Well, no ... but ..."

"That is all. No further questions."

At the break, one of the Foundation lawyers asked Billington why he didn't finish with the witness by taking apart his findings one at a time. "I didn't need to. This way, I am keeping the prosecution off balance. Now they are wondering what I might have up my sleeve, but I already played my hole card by raising the 2024 mess and planting the seeds of doubt in the jury's minds. These will germinate and sprout when we call our own experts, who are better credentialed, not overworked and underqualified, and far more polished on the stand. Act one sets up act two. What will stick with the jury is the contrast and the story our guys will tell."

○ ○ ○

After calling the autopsy into question, Billington took on the fingerprint expert in a protracted cross-examination that revealed how a potpourri of prints had been found on the empty nasyntrophine bottle and none could be recovered from the pillowcase. The nurse called next by Oschinsky testified that Paolo had frequently administered medication, including nasyntrophine, to his grandmother. Billington transformed her into a witness for the defense by drawing out testimony to the loving way in which Paolo had helped care for Giuseppina.

The moment Roy had dreaded finally arrived when he was called to the stand as a witness for the prosecution. Oschinsky started at the beginning.

"You have been the private physician for the accused since he was born, is that correct?"

"Yes, that is correct."

"Could you tell the court how it is that you came to be involved in his birth?"

"Objection, your honor. Counsel is violating your order barring discussion of this matter."

Oschinsky's voice rose. "This is a hostile witness and it goes to the relationship between the witness and the accused."

There was a pause as Judge Tarniak looked down and to the side. "Counsel, approach the bench." He waited while Billington and Oschinsky walked to the front. Leaning forward and in a lowered voice, he addressed Oschinsky. "This matter has been ruled on; my order *in limine* stands. If you persist in skating toward the circumstances surrounding the origins of the accused, I shall be forced to find you in contempt of court. Is that clear, counsel?"

"Yes, perfectly, you honor."

When she resumed, Oschinsky's questions were all carefully worded and narrowly focused. She finished with a line of inquiry about the exact nature of Giuseppina's illness and the prognosis.

"What was her condition on your last examination, two days before her death?"

"She was in pain, great pain, that was only partially ameliorated by the nasyntrophine I had prescribed. She was dying."

"Are you an expert in cancer? Are you an oncologist?"

"No, I'm a primary care physician, internal medicine, but I was working with Dr. Mark Anschluss, an oncologist with the Dana-Farber Cancer Center. He—"

"Thank you, doctor. Your witness."

Billington sauntered up to the witness stand. "Based on your own medical experience and expertise, Dr. Cahners, what were the prospects for Giuseppina Franzetti?"

"Well, as I said, she had pancreatic cancer that had metastasized, spread throughout much of her body, and all treatments had failed. Her prospects were grim."

"Grim. What exactly does that mean? Was there any chance of a cure?"

"Not really. Virtually no patients her age and with her condition survive for long."

"How long did you think she might survive?"

"Objection, your honor, calling for a conclusion."

Billington responded. "The witness is a medical doctor with intimate knowledge of the patient's condition."

"The witness is not here being called to testify as an expert," she countered.

Tarniak took a breath. "I'll allow it. Objection overruled."

"Based on your knowledge of her as a patient and your experience as a medical practitioner, how long did you think Mrs. Franzetti had to live?"

"Days, maybe weeks. She was dying."

"No further questions, you honor."

Oschinsky stood up. "Redirect, your honor."

"Proceed."

"Dr. Cahners, again, based on what you know, would you say there was no chance, none at all, absolutely no possibility of some spontaneous recovery?"

"None, none at all."

It was not the answer Oschinsky was expecting. For a moment it looked like she was considering continuing, but then she stepped back. "No further questions, your honor."

○ ○ ○

Billington's theatrics continued until the prosecution rested their case. With the start of the defense the following day, he transformed himself into a gentle giant elevating his own witnesses and amplifying their statements in direct questioning, then gently protecting them with targeted objections during cross examination. He called, in succession, the chief pathologist who had completed the second autopsy, followed by Dr. Anschluss to corroborate what Roy had told the jury, and finished with calling to the stand a forensic scientist who tore holes in the last piece of evidence entered by the prosecution, the presence of the victim's saliva on the pillow. After two days of testimony, Billington rested his case.

Roy turned to him in the hallway on the way out of the courthouse. "Why so soon, with only three witnesses?"

"Because overkill can kill your case. I have already decimated the case against Paolo. And I will chop it into tiny bits with my summation. Did you look at that jury today? Reasonable doubt, that's all it takes to acquit, and doubt was all over their faces. The burden of proof is on the prosecution. They failed to prove their case, and I will make sure the jury hears that loud and clear."

○ ○ ○

Oschinsky's closing arguments were a by-the-book replay of her opening statement, a clear and concise summation of the prosecution's interpretation of the evidence against Paolo. It was flawless, persuasive, and devoid of passion. "On the basis of the unambiguous evidence presented," she said, punctuating with a hand-chop, "there is no choice but to conclude that the accused,

Paolo Carl Franzetti, did willfully murder his grandmother in cold blood."

Billington leaned close to Paolo. "That's it. It's over."

"What do you mean?"

"Look at the jury. I can read them like an e-book. They don't buy it. Some part of them may want to, given who you are, but the sale didn't go through. And I'm about to clinch it with my closing statement. Just watch this."

"You mean ..."

"I mean you are in good hands, son. Trust me."

"They might let me go?"

"Not guilty. I can see it written like a banner across their foreheads."

Tarniak gaveled the court back in session. "Is the defense ready with a closing statement?"

Billington started to rise but Paolo tugged at his sleeve. There was a quick whispered exchange, with Billington shaking his head. "No way," he hissed.

The courtroom started buzzing with mumbles and whispers; Tarniak rapped his gavel twice. "Order! There will be order or I'll have the courtroom cleared."

Billington half rose. "With the court's indulgence, your honor, I need a moment with my client."

"Haven't we been through this once already, counsel? Okay, another moment, that's all."

"Yes, your honor." He turned to Paolo and spoke quietly. "You can't be serious, not now. Do you know what this means?"

"I'm serious. I can't take the chance. I need to know for sure." Paolo spoke just above a whisper. "I know what this means. If you won't do it, Mr. Billington, I'll dismiss you and do it myself."

"Firing me will accomplish nothing."

"Then do it."

Billington was shaking his head as he stood to face the judge. "Your Honor, if it please the court, my client wishes, against the advice of counsel, to change his plea."

The rushing intake of breath throughout the courtroom was audible.

"Now, at the end of trial?" Tarniak's mouth was agape in disbelief.

"Yes, Your Honor."

Tarniak looked lost for a moment before reaching for his gavel. "Court will take a short recess. Counsel, I will see you in my chambers."

○ ○ ○

The courtroom quieted in an ebbing wave when Judge Tarniak reappeared.

"Counsel, how does the defendant now plead?"

"The defendant pleads guilty, Your Honor."

The courtroom virtually exploded. The trial of the decade was suddenly over with none of the drama of a Jackson Billington summation, none of the suspense of jury deliberation, none of the tension of waiting for a verdict. Judge Tarniak gaveled the court back into order and told Paolo to rise. "Is this correct? You want to change your plea to guilty?"

"Yes, your honor, I do."

"And you are fully aware of the consequences if you change your plea?"

"Yes, I am, your honor."

"Has anyone tried to persuade you or coerce you into changing your plea?"

"No, no one."

Tarniak, mindful of the many eyes on him and not wanting to risk a misstep, was being meticulous. "And this is your intention, you are acting of your own free will?"

"Yes, your honor, this is my intention, mine alone. I plead guilty. It is my choice."

Having verified the plea with Paolo, Tarniak set a date for sentencing and adjourned.

As they waited while Paolo was handcuffed and escorted under guard from the courtroom, Roy closed his eyes. "Did you know anything about this, Vera?"

"No, he never said a word to me. We never talked about it: not the trial, not Seppina's death, nothing. All he ever said was that things would work out, he was certain of that. One way or another, things will work out, he said." As Paolo reached the exit, she bowed her head. "Paolo," she whispered, "my Paolo."

Chapter 49

The sentencing hearing was anticlimactic, nowhere near as well attended as the truncated trial. Vera and I sat in the front row again. The hearing was a brief formality and the sentence was mandatory. Paolo, an adult tried as an adult, had pleaded guilty to first degree murder. Massachusetts has no death penalty. The sentence, therefore, was no surprise to anyone: life in prison without possibility of parole. Because he had pled guilty, there would not even be an appeal as would have been mandatory had a jury convicted him.

With the sentence read, Paolo was led past the front row. He looked down at Roy with a gentle, knowing smile fixed on his face, a smile that Roy recognized.

"You engineered this whole thing, all of it, didn't you, Paolo?"

The smile held steady as he leaned toward them. "Design, Roy. A life, too, has a design, and not only in terms of genetics or biochemistry." For some reason, the guards escorting him stood by, waiting as he spoke. "You know, a life may already have been perfectly planned, programmed even, yet still be redesigned at any time." He spoke slowly, as if mentally laying out each word in the block hand in which he always wrote. "Arturo Dermott made something new by using an old design. He made me, the first of a kind. And now, with my own new design, I have made of me the last. This way there will never be another. New laws still being debated will be passed.

"I am Dermott, don't forget that: Arturo Dermott, the world's greatest engineer. And you say I engineered this. You have a way with words and a flair for irony, Roy. You could have been a writer."

He reached out his manacled hands toward Vera, who tried to touch him as the guards intervened and pushed him on. "I love you, Vera," he said over his shoulder. "Forever. I'm sorry, but it had to be this way."

The courtroom slowly cleared, but Roy and Vera didn't move. "What happened, Roy?"

"He wanted to make sure that this never happened again, to make an example of himself. We just misunderstood him, as we did from the beginning. We expected him to be Arturo Dermott reincarnated, to carry on unfinished work, as if the twin would speak his brother's words rather than merely with his brother's voice. It seems that Paolo always was the engineering genius that Arturo Dermott had been, but he led a different life and turned his genius to different ends."

"Did he really do it, I mean, the pillow and all? Or did he just say he did?"

"Personally, I am pretty sure his confession was legitimate, but this was not about the terrible cold-blooded murder painted by the prosecution. She was dying anyway, and she was in great pain. She was too deeply religious to even consider taking her own life. Paolo ended her suffering, an act of compassion, some might say. And, like the playwright of his own drama, he set up the climactic final act, leaving nothing ambiguous. In its own way, it's the sort of scripting that springs from the mind of a too-bright adolescent—without regard for consequences and calculated at the same time."

"Still, Roy, how could he do this? He's walking away from me, from our life. I can't get my head around that."

"I'm not so sure I completely understand either. There was

always that part of him that stood apart, watching, figuring us out, these strange beings around him.'"

"You're right. Even with me, he had a way of always holding something back, as if he were alone even when we were together, a piece of his mind cranking away as though he were solving some problem. Even when he was creative, writing plays, composing poems, it was methodical."

"Well put. In the end, Paolo bested Arturo by figuring us out, grasping how people work, systems far more complicated than anything that ever held Dermott's attention. He could do what he did because he saw himself as somehow separate, different, as if he were another species."

She looked down at her lap. "What is going to happen to him?"

"I know this will be hard to take, to accept, but I really believe he'll be all right. What he always wanted to do with his life was write. He'll certainly have the time for that. He always said he needed little. Paper and something to write with were enough. I don't think the world has heard the last from Paolo Franzetti."

"And what about me?"

"Well,"—he glanced down at her belly—"pretty soon you are going to have a lot to keep you busy. And then? Well, we'll just have to see what the next chapter brings."

Epilogue

Paolo died in prison. That was not unexpected, of course, but none of us expected it so soon. His body was found in the shower room with the letters 'GMO' cut into his chest. The technical error of the label did not prevent the message from being clear: he was a freak, an unnatural, engineered freak. The autopsy concluded that he was still alive when the inaccurate acronym was carved. The proximal cause of death was blunt trauma to the head: they bashed in his brains, hammering his head against the tile wall. There were no signs of struggle.

From the start, he had been kept in isolation for his own safety, and there should not have been anyone in the shower room with him. No one seemed to know just how the lapse in security had happened, and, as is common in such cases of prison violence, the perpetrators were not identified.

Though he did not live to see this story published, a few weeks before he was killed he got the news from Vera. Karl Paul Prentiss weighed in at a healthy eight pounds two ounces. Mother and baby were doing fine at an undisclosed location. Our team was not elated, but we were definitely buoyed by the news. We had a mission, a purpose again, all spelled out with foresight in the Foundation's charter. We were not the only ones with cause for optimism. An entire generation of lawyers in Italy and America would make a good living off the coming decades of spurious claims and counterclaims, legal actions and legislative interventions, but we had faith in the trustees of the Dermott estate to prevail in the end.

Like Paolo before him, Karl would not know his father, but he and Vera would be fine. We were a seasoned team and could learn from our slips in the past. Helen, always the stickler for technical accuracy, pointed out that, genetically speaking, Arturo Dermott, who died childless, now had a son. I left our strategy meeting at that point and retreated to the examining room at the clinic, one of the few places I could be confident that no one would disturb me.

My mind kept going back to the confluence of events, the unlikely timing, the collision of birth and death that brought to mind the coincidences of Paulo's arrival into the world. I couldn't shake the feeling that all of this, too, had been somehow engineered, designed, planned.

Chaim had reminded me that we had long known Paolo to have a messianic streak running through his psyche. The boy wanted to save the world through words, even as had the misanthropic Dermott labored to save the world through his inventions. Neither succeeded, though both, in their own ways, were successes.

I opened the padded envelope that had been delivered just the day before and had been waiting on my desk when I arrived. There was no return address, and the postmark was no help: some town in New Hampshire that I didn't recognize. Inside was a lumpy business envelope marked "Roy" along with nearly a ream of paper bound by rubber bands: a manuscript. I tore open the small envelope. Inside was an index card with an intaglio ring taped to it. "Save this for Karl Paul when he's older." I recognized the distinctive ring as one that Toni had worn for many years and bequeathed to Paolo. With the light at an angle, the indented profile seemed to pop out from the red-orange carnelian to become real, to project itself out into the real world of space and dimension.

I read the title page of the manuscript: *Efficient Cause*, a novel by Paolo Carl Dermott Franzetti. Below, the dedication: To Leonard Royal, friend and physician.

I started reading. And I started crying.

The novel, a tale of decision and discovery set within a single day, explores those intricate and unseen forces that lead to a turning point: one of those rare moments when commitment is reified in action and alters for all time the lives of those it touches. It was not about Paolo and the close of his life, except as metaphor, but it rendered unambiguous the choices he made late in his short life. From a position of other, of separateness, the narrative appraises us, the readers, capturing us in the unforgiving prose of dispassionate detachment, an unframed mirror in which we see ourselves reflected.

I see myself in his writing and know who I am. I am Leonard Royal Cahners, MD, PhD, Chief Medical Officer of the Fenix Foundation, friend and physician to a young genius who died much, much too young, the first and the last of his kind.

With only sparse Sunday morning traffic, Roy's mind drifted as he drove out Route 128 toward Cape Ann. Prayer, he thought, is such an odd invention. For many of the people he had known, prayer was a private channel to an unseen god, a medium for personal supplication or thanksgiving, but there were also the prayers of duty, prescribed by custom or religious convention for certain contexts, like the prayers for the dying of the Catholic church or the Jewish tradition of saying the Mourner's Kaddish for departed family.

After leaving the highway at the next-to-last traffic circle, Roy kept checking the street map displayed on the center console. He so hated the insipid intrusion of the synthetic voice calling out turn-by-turn instructions that he had long ago permanently muted it. Now, with the cut in funds, it was probably too late to get the Foundation to supply him with a new self-driving car. The maze of one-way streets in Gloucester were a

challenge, requiring him to approach his destination by nego-
tiating narrow lanes made narrower by cars parked on both
sides. After the final turn onto Middle Street, the synagogue,
Temple Ahavat Achim, was there on the left. He pulled into the
driveway and through to the tiny parking lot in back where he
slipped into the empty space next to one marked as reserved for
the Rabbi.

It had been decades since Roy had last been to temple. He
felt awkward and uncertain whether or not to enter through the
back. He decided to walk around to the front. The setback entrance of the modern brick-and-wide-board building was approached through massive wooden doors set in a freestanding
masonry wall. He had read about the temple on the Web. The
doors had been saved from the fire that had destroyed the original building, and the entryway paving was inset with salvaged
stonework.

Inside, Roy could hear voices. He followed the sound of them
through two sets of doors into a chair-filled, book-lined room
with a faded mustard-yellow carpet. Next to the podium at the
front, the Rabbi was putting on his *teffilin* in preparation for
leading the services. A woman with a massive mane of nearly
white hair topped by a rainbow yarmulke walked over to Roy
and greeted him with a warm smile. "Hello. Welcome to TAA.
I'm Trish." She held out her hand.

"Hi, I'm Roy, Roy Cahners."

"Good to meet you, Roy. Are you visiting, here for the summer, or what?"

"It's the 'or what.' I was looking for someplace on the North
Shore that still held morning prayer services. Your webpage said
you had a Sunday morning minyan."

"Well, we don't always make minyan—it can be hard in the
summer to get ten Jews to give up a Sunday morning, what with

so many people off and away—but it looks good so far. With you, we're eight. Two to go and we have our minyan. What brings you here? Are you shopping shuls?"

"No, not really. I'm here to pray"—he swallowed hard—"to say Kaddish for my son, for Paolo."

o o o
o o o

Also by Lior Samson

The Rosen Singularity | *The Millicent Factor*

The Four-Color Puzzle

The Homeland Connection Novels:

Bashert | *The Dome* | *Web Games*
Chipset | *Gasline* | *Flight Track*

Appendix

From Wikipedia 3.0

Arturo Fabian Dermott (b. October 12, 1926; d. January 23, 2008, age 81, cause of death: <u>myocardial infarction</u>), an <u>Italian-American</u> <u>engineer</u>, <u>inventor</u>, <u>entrepreneur</u>, and <u>scientist</u>. Dermott is regarded as one of the greatest inventors of all time, but is arguably most known for having achieved the first, and so far only, successful human <u>clone</u> (see <u>Paolo Dermott-Franzetti</u>). The world's wealthiest man at his death, his estate funded cloning and other <u>biomedical research</u> until after the <u>Franzetti Affair</u> (see).

Early Life. Born in <u>Florence, Italy</u>, Dermott was the only child of Raquel (née Fabiano), an Italian nurse, and Sandford "Sandy" Dermott, an American civil engineer. His mother was <u>Jewish</u> and his father <u>Episcopalian</u>, but Arturo spent his early years without religious instruction.^(citation needed) After the <u>Italian Fascist</u> government under <u>Benito Mussolini</u> began curtailing the rights of Jews and banned Jewish children from public schools, Arturo was sent by steamship in the summer of 1938, at the age of 11, to live with his maternal grandparents, Ruben and Miriam Fabiano, who, several years earlier, had emigrated to Boston, where they owned property.

During the war, Arturo regularly wrote letters to his parents, who remained in Italy. The letters were lost during the war but eventually rediscovered. They became the basis for the two-act play *Return Flight* (2026) which was later made into an <u>art film</u> of the same name by indie director <u>Vera Prentiss</u>. After the <u>Nazi</u> invasion of Italy in 1943, Raquel Dermott was deported to <u>Auschwitz</u> in November, along with other Jews of Florence. She died of typhus the following year. It is believed that her husband was killed in an abortive attempt to rescue her from the station before the train departed.^(citation needed)

Arturo Dermott was a good student but was socially isolated. ^(citation needed) After graduating from the prestigious <u>Boston Latin High School</u>, he was accepted to the <u>Massachusetts Institute of Technology</u>, which he attended for three semesters before dropping out in his sophomore year to launch the first of his many research and consulting companies. He returned to Italy in 1948 and made Rome his home base for most of his life and the center of the vast corporate empire he ultimately established.

Inventions. Dermott filed his first U.S. <u>patent application</u>, for a new form of <u>noise-cancelling</u> <u>close-talk microphone</u>, in 1943 at the age of 17. Because the invention was considered strategic, with applications to aircraft and other high-noise environments, the patent was not awarded until 1947. In all, Dermott is credited with 2,181 patents, the most of any American inventor in history and more than twice as many as <u>Thomas Edison</u>.

Dermott constructed fanciful names for all of his inventions, among them the <u>altistavox</u>, an echo-free stage microphone, the <u>telethermocine</u>, an <u>infrared</u> motion picture camera, and <u>electropentatabulon</u>, a handheld electronic musical instrument. Perhaps his best known invention is the miniature zoom lens (technically the <u>Dermott Flexipanfocal Zoom</u> but widely called simply a Dermott lens) used in most of today's smartphones and many pocket cameras, but his inventions range widely, with applications in construction, aerospace, communications, optics, and even, late in his life, biotechnology.

Working independently, Dermott and his colleagues developed a computer-controlled gene-editing technique (see main article under Dermott Genetic Editor) that anticipated but improved upon the widely used CRISPR-Cas9 approach. Later refinements enabled rapid re-engineering of organisms by trait selection, which has been widely employed by agronomists for developing new commercial crop varieties (see New Agron Revolution). His final patent, awarded not long before his death in 2008, was for a method of creating synthetic human ova from cellular components assembled in vitro.

Cloning Controversy. (See main article at Franzetti Affair.) Sometime in early 2001, Dermott launched an ambitious multi-pronged secret research and development program to create the first human clone. Research facilities in Rome, Italy, São Paolo, Brazil, Macau, China, and Seoul, South Korea, were established to carry out various phases of the research. Affidavits supplied after exposure in the Franzetti Affair confirmed that his intention from the beginning was to clone himself to create an heir who could continue his work as an inventor and oversee his network of corporations and foundations. In one deposition, the former head of *Fondazione Volo di Ritorno* said of the project:

> We [of the medical team] realized at the time that Dermott's plan was not about some far future of speculative fiction but grounded in the present. What we did was simply about unrealized potential, waiting opportunity. Why did we do it? As with so many advances that prove to be mistakes or of dubious value, the answer is simple: because we could. How did we do it? All the ingredients were there, waiting, scattered. All that was needed was to assemble and mix them with wealth, the nearly unlimited resources that a handful of individuals on earth can command. Throw enough money at a problem, and, if it is solvable, it will be solved.

Once the basic research was complete and the techniques for cloning were made sufficiently reliable, Dermott's clinic on the outskirts of Rome began recruiting young women, mostly poor single immigrants, to serve as surrogate birth mothers. Records from the period obtained only after the research was exposed, show that, of the first cohort of ten implanted embryos, four miscarried, five had to be aborted, and the last was stillborn. In the second cohort, of the twenty implanted, none was carried to term; all either spontaneously aborted or the pregnancies were terminated for one reason or another, although these numbers were disputed by Bradman and Zingari in their first book on Dermott.

The original research design to keep expanding each successive cohort was abandoned after the sample sizes became unwieldy. The research continued, but with each cohort limited to twenty. On the fourth attempt, five babies were carried to term, although all had serious but previously undetected birth defects. Following the death of Dermott in 2008, the techniques continued to be refined until, on the sixth round, confidence had risen to the level that only five surrogates were employed. One of them, an American woman stranded in Italy, carried to term a fetus that was considered perfect by the researchers on the basis of extensive in utero prenatal testing. She was sent to Boston to give birth, but was seriously injured in a car accident shortly after arrival and ended up in a chronic vegetative state. The baby boy, Paolo Carl Franzetti, Dermott's clone, was delivered by cesarean at a hospital in Boston (which?) where the mother died during surgery.

Legacy. Apart from the myriad useful inventions, it is arguable that Dermott's most enduring legacy was through his clone, whose actions made it all but certain that no further attempts at human cloning could be possible for the foreseeable future. In addition to the seizure and dismantling of those laboratories still in use, new legislation and a renewed commitment to greater vigilance were the immediate consequence of the Franzetti Affair. The recently ratified UN Convention on Genetic Replication and Cloning (UNCOGRAC) codifies into international law a permanent ban on human cloning and research directed toward that end.

Literary References and Sources. Dermott has been the subject of numerous fiction and non-fiction books and films, including:

The Italian Edison: An Unauthorized Biography of Arturo Fabian Dermott, Ruben Abelman (InScient Books, 2010)

"Dermott: The Legend and Legacy" (PBS four-part special, 2026)

"Return Flight," Misty Flaherty (stage play, 2026)

"An Italian Inventor: Arturo Fabian Dermott" (documentary film, 2027, directed by Bianca Toscana)

Singular Sensation, Deirdre DeNapoli (fiction based on Dermott as a young adult, Hyperdiem, 2027)

"The Dermott Domain and the Perversion of Privilege" Five-part series, Dan Bradman and Francesca Zingari (*New York Times*, 2027)

"The Deadly Domain," Dan Bradman and Francesca Zingari (*The Atlantic*, 2028)

Dermott Dominion: The Buried Enterprise, Dan Bradman and Francesca Zingari (Freiheit Press, 2028)

The Franzetti Affair, Adam Tarniak with Philip Resnik (MacGilliam, 2029)

Efficient Cause, Paolo Carl Dermott Franzetti, foreword by L. Royal Cahners (Hyperdiem, 2030)

Half the World: Power, Politics, and the Super-Rich, Clement Harbing (MacGilliam, 2030; chapter 14 is on Arturo Dermott)

I am Dermott, I am Me: The Short Story of a Clone, Bianca
Toscana (biography, Harbinger and Locke, 2031)
Wielding Wealth: Arturo Dermott and the Cloning Agenda, Dan
and Francesca Bradman (Freiheit Press, 2032)
"McMonster" (animé semi-fiction, 2032)
"Return Flight" (b/w film, 2033, Vera Prentiss, director)

Author's Note

I could not have finished this work without the help of the readers and writers who reviewed earlier versions of the manuscript, who helped fill in the holes of my ignorance, and who extended my vision beyond my own blind spots. I am particularly grateful to Gemma Grau, my friend and expert source on Catalan and Catalunya, who gave me early and encouraging input as well as an authentic voice for important characters.

Cardiologist Mobeen Sheikh, MD, was a source of critical feedback and pivotal medical ideas. For legal advice, I turned to lawyers Phil Samson (no relation) and Pete Morin, who himself writes first-rate fiction. They were both generous with their time and many sound suggestions.

A meeting of the Cambridge Roundtable, an institution dedicated to dialogue between faith and science, introduced me to Harvard geneticist George Church, one of the pioneers of the CRISPR-Cas9 gene editing technique and a leader in reproductive cloning. After an exchange of views, he generously offered to review on my manuscript. To my delight, he has attested to its technical authenticity.

I hope my regular readers who have gotten this far through previous works will not tire of my litany of appreciation to my editor, Janet Lemnah, whose unflagging dedication to her craft adds the final polish to all my writing. She is a gem and a friend.

In the interest of full disclosure, this is not the first time I have told the story of Paolo Franzetti and Dr. Cahners. In 1992, I finished a short story titled "Foreword to *Efficient Cause*" (reprinted in *Requisite Variety: Collected Short Fiction by Lior Samson*, Gesher Press, 2011). I was going through a period in my evolution as a writer where I was experimenting with form. I wanted to see if I could tell an engaging story entirely indirectly, in this instance through the fictitious foreword to an imaginary novel. The non-existent novel was *Efficient Cause*, by the protagonist, Paolo Franzetti. The author of the foreword, through which the story of Paolo was being told, was the equally fictitious writer L. Roy Cahners, which also just happened to be a pseudonym under which some of my earliest short fiction had been published. All perfectly clear?

From the beginning, I had the sense that the real story was far richer and more complex than what could be shoehorned into the confines of short fiction, but it would be years—and nine novels later—before I was ready to take on the task of retelling the tale as a full-length novel. For this, the original short story served not as an outline or template so much as an inspiration. What remained from my earlier writing experiment, besides the core idea, was the split viewpoint, in which a subtle story is approached from both the inside and the outside, with each perspective illuminating distinct aspects of the unfolding.

I have long been drawn, both as a reader and as a writer, to the challenging intricacies of non-linear narrative, to story-telling that plays with time and locale rather than trudging relentlessly forward from one place and time to the next. To tell Paolo's full story, against the steady unfolding of his unique coming-of-age, I introduced another timeline for the pursuit of historic truth through two additional characters: British financial reporter Danny Bradman and Italian archivist Francesca Zingari. In this interwoven retelling, the past catches up with their pursuit of the past as the intertwined truths finally merge into a single narrative in the closing chapters.

I hope the results do justice to the subjects being examined, raising questions that leave readers pondering issues we are likely to face in the uncomfortably near future.

About the Author

Lior Samson is the pen name of a former university professor who has won awards for both fiction and non-fiction writing as well as for his innovative work in industrial design. He has more than two dozen published books, including ten novels and a collection of short fiction. As a consultant and teacher, he has traveled the world, lived in Australia and Portugal, and served on the faculties of two international universities.

He resides in Massachusetts with his family, where he cooks creative fusion cuisine and composes serious choral music. He describes himself as a full-time novelist, part-time journalist and photographer, and full-time support system for the three students in his life—and readily acknowledges that his time sheet doesn't add up.

The readers who write with questions, kudos, and criticism are vital parts of the dialogue he seeks to spark through his writing. He enjoys hearing from readers and appreciates those who take the time to post reviews on Amazon and elsewhere. He can be reached by email at: lior@liorsamson.com